———————— ★ ————————

"Harmony!" Shanahan called out.

The figure stood. Long brown hair. A pair of gym shorts and running shoes. His T-shirt was tied around his neck.

"Over here, Mr. Shanahan."

"What's up?" Shanahan said curtly. He shook his head, angry with himself or his constant get-to-the-point attitude. But then he hadn't come all this way for a weenie roast. He noticed a video camera, some sound equipment and some other electronic paraphernalia he didn't recognize.

"Thanks for coming," Harmony said. He wasn't the relaxed carefree soul Shanahan remembered. Harmony nodded toward the water, and Shanahan knew why the kid wasn't smiling.

She was pretty, but she wasn't the kind of naked lady you wanted to meet.

———————— ★ ————————

"Tierney's 'Deets' Shanahan series offers characters of depth and sensuality and well-placed swipes of razor-sharp humor..."
—*Publishers Weekly*

"A fine book about Washington politics, international art swindles, murder, mayhem, and a deep dark secret."
—*South Bend Tribune*

THE IRON GLOVE

RONALD TIERNEY

WORLDWIDE.

TORONTO • NEW YORK • LONDON
AMSTERDAM • PARIS • SYDNEY • HAMBURG
STOCKHOLM • ATHENS • TOKYO • MILAN
MADRID • WARSAW • BUDAPEST • AUCKLAND

For
Robbin S. Tierney
Ryan D. Tierney

THE IRON GLOVE

A Worldwide Mystery/December 1996

First published by St. Martin's Press, Incorporated.

ISBN 0-373-26221-3

Printed in U.S.A.

*"Mr. Shanahan," she said,
"I'm so glad you are an older man."*

"I wish I could share your enthusiasm, Mrs. Schmidt."

ONE

THE DIRECTIONS were clear.

"Go to the bridge on Michigan Road just past the Museum of Art. Then go west along the path by the canal. There will be woods on your right. Take the second path into the trees," the kid said.

At 10:00 a.m. Shanahan already felt as if he had his face in a pizza oven. He tried to imagine what it would be like at noon. He hadn't walked more than a hundred feet and already he could feel the sweat. He tugged at his shirt, pulling it away from where it clung to his back.

At sixty-nine, he was too old to go traipsing about the woods in August like a Boy Scout. But the kid had done him a favor a while back. Besides, the youth was engaged to Harry's daughter. And Harry was Shanahan's best friend. That made the kid family.

Casey was family too. A mix of hound and God knows what, the speckled, spotted sixty-pound mongrel lived by his nose and was too interested in declaring each bush along the canal his private property to be bothered by a little heat.

He'd pick up the scent of something wild and run along ahead, and Shanahan would have to call him back before he was halfway to Kentucky.

There it was—an opening in the trees, leading back into the woods. That was the first path. He kept walking. In the distance he could see a figure sitting on the bank of the canal. He held a fishing pole. Shanahan wondered what kind of fish would inhabit the shallow canal. A man would have to be pretty hungry to sit in ninety-degree heat for a fish. The water was brown and quiet. A dozen or so ducks huddled together against the levee.

Shanahan wasn't familiar with this part of Indianapolis, wasn't even aware there were paths, let alone woods, this far down the canal that began, or ended, depending on your point of view, in the little village of Broad Ripple. Shanahan did know that the canal paralleled White River. And the kid said he would wait on the bank of the river, not the canal, so it figured Shanahan, would, at some point, have to go through the trees to get to the river.

The fisherman looked up as Shanahan approached. He nodded. Shanahan nodded back. A few feet farther on was the second opening in the woods. It was wider than the first, but if you weren't looking for it, you wouldn't see it.

The path widened more a few feet in. The temperature dropped a few degrees, just enough to make it comfortable for the mosquitoes. Shanahan walked, slapping at the air and cursing to himself.

There were single, narrow tire tracks in the dry earth. Bicycles, probably. It wasn't much of a woods. The tallest of the trees were maybe thirty feet high. Scrubs, most of them. A little farther in, there was a wider opening in the trees. From there the path went both left and right. Nothing straight ahead except a seventy-foot drop into the river. He looked down. The brown water moved south at a pretty good clip, compared to the canal. He looked to the far side.

Across the river were more woods, with small, empty earthen beaches here and there at river's edge. Spots for fishermen, he thought. No one occupied them at the moment.

The kid had told Shanahan to keep going left. Told him whenever he had a choice to go left. Shanahan took the path to his left, passed by an empty Budweiser carton and a few crumpled cans. The path went on forever. Shanahan had had no idea this would be an expedition. Casey wandered but kept Shanahan in view.

Periodically the path would come close to the river. There were smaller trails that led down to the water. But these were to his right. The river was on his right. He wondered if he'd taken the wrong turn somewhere. If the kid was on the river, then at some point he should take a right, not a left. But the kid had definitely said "left."

Shanahan kept going. Sweat seeped into his eyes, stinging. He rubbed them. He was already tired—and thirsty. He wished he'd brought something to drink. He wished he had found out why in God's name he was doing this, anyway. What was it that was so important?

He started memorizing little landmarks, like the abandoned pair of jockey shorts only partially covered with nature's debris, and a McDonald's cup spiked on a dead branch. They weren't enduring landmarks, but they'd do for a day on the trails.

There were other markings as well. On the dead trees by the river's edge, roots half in and half out of the muddy water, there were strange, almost other-worldly images. Closer, he could see they were simply tatters of white plastic bags on the bare branches. It struck the old detective that they were like foreboding signs in the jungle movies, warnings from some savage, flesh-eating tribe against further trespass.

He saw a patch of light, way up to his left. There was no left or right at this point; the path continued straight ahead. Shanahan walked down carefully, out from under the umbrella of the trees and into the sun again, blazing so white-hot he could barely see. The air was heavy. It was difficult to breathe.

There were a few straggly trees on a beach that was a mottle of earth, sand, and gravel. Between the trees and the water was a path of sorts, so Shanahan again headed left. He heard a splash in the water. He looked. The water was still. Only a ripple a few feet out broke the silver surface.

He was surprised at the size of what had to be an inlet to the river. It was a large circular body of water ringed by trees. From this vantage point Shanahan couldn't see where the river fed it. Dragonflies hovered over the still water close to shore. Other than that, it was dead still. Shanahan could hear his heart beating.

He passed by some charred wood—a small camp fire, perhaps for one person. The beach had some give to it. His feet sank an inch or two with each step. The surface was littered with bait bags, bent beer cans, and spent prophylactics.

Through the spindly branches of the trees, he saw a figure, sitting on a large rock, head down in his hands. He was pretty sure it was the kid. Casey was already racing toward him.

"Harmony!" Shanahan called out.

The figure stood. Long brown hair. A pair of gym shorts and running shoes. His T-shirt was tied around his neck.

"Over here, Mr. Shanahan."

"What's up?" Shanahan said curtly. He could have extended his hand and said something like, "Nice to see you again." He shook his head, angry with himself for his constant get-to-the-point attitude. But then he hadn't come all this way for a wienie roast. He noticed a video camera, some sound equipment, and some other electronic paraphernalia he didn't recognize.

"Thanks for coming," Harmony said. He wasn't the relaxed, carefree soul Shanahan remembered. Harmony nodded toward the water, and Shanahan knew why the kid wasn't smiling.

She was pretty, but she wasn't the kind of naked lady you wanted to meet.

TWO

U.S. SENATOR David Holland was having breakfast, if
you could call it that. Tomato juice, toast, and coffee. He
sat in a lower-level restaurant of the Grand Hyatt Hotel,
across from Washington, D.C.'s convention center, and
a block from what residents called Chinatown, though it
was more a wish than reality. A couple of Chinese restaurants and maybe a laundry.

The forty-two-year-old, second-term senator from Indiana was bleary-eyed, and his usually handsome face
was pale and drawn. He was in no mood to chat with
colleagues or reporters, which is why he chose to put
himself back together here—away from the Capitol Hill
crowd.

He was also in no mood to go to the office either. He
had promised to meet with some folks. Eric would handle the appointments the senator would miss this morning.

"Would he?" Holland asked himself. His young, ambitious aide, who was already late for this little morning
get-together, wasn't all that convinced his world, like the
world at large, was going to hell in a handbasket. After
all, it was an election year and although he was popular
personally, he was afraid he'd go down with the President if things didn't straighten out economically.

Then, of course, there was Sally. Christ, he'd have
never married if it wasn't essential to his career. You
could get by in Massachusetts as a bachelor. Hell, you
could get by without anything there, but not in Indiana.
If Holland had it to do over again, he'd marry money,

not beauty. Beauty fades for sure. Money, on the other hand, just gets better with age.

He took another swig of the juice and thought that maybe his eyes were focusing a little better.

SHANAHAN HAD SEEN dead bodies before. A few while he was an Intelligence sergeant in France during World War II, then again in Korea and, though not frequently, in his current line of work. Harmony hadn't. The kid nodded toward the water, directing Shanahan's gaze, but refused to follow it with his own.

"She's dead," Harmony said.

"You touch the body?" Shanahan asked, approaching the nude body of what appeared to be a relatively young and attractive woman. Her face rested on its side, one cheek down on the sand-and-gravel beach, her back to the sun. The body extended out into the still water.

"Didn't need to. I saw her eyes."

Shanahan saw her eyes too. Glazed. The body was in relatively good shape for a floater. He figured she hadn't been in the water too long. She wasn't bloated, nor had the extreme heat of the sun caused much decomposition, except for a section that ran along the outside of her upper thigh and the right cheek of her buttocks.

"You call the police?"

"No, I called you." Harmony was chilling; his smooth chest was goose-pimpled, despite the August heat.

"Put your shirt on," Shanahan said. "Why did you call me?" Then before Harmony could answer, Shanahan asked, "How did you call me?"

The nearest telephone was a healthy trek back through the woods and then a drive somewhere.

"Mobile phone," Harmony said, reaching down and picking up a plastic phone from the pile of electronic gadgetry. "I got your number from information. I didn't..." His voice trailed off, and Shanahan could hear the boy's teeth chattering like castanets.

"You didn't what?" Shanahan took off his shirt and put it around the boy's shoulders.

"I didn't want to talk with them."

"The police? Why is that?"

Harmony just shook his head. "I could've left. I didn't have to say anything. I just figured somebody ought to know."

Shanahan figured the boy was in shock. "All right, let's get out of here. Is that your blue Karmann Ghia parked by the bridge?"

"Yeah," Harmony said, picking up his gear. "We're not just going to leave her here?"

"She's not going anywhere," Shanahan said. He thought about using the mobile phone to call the police, but Harmony obviously didn't want to talk with the cops, and reporting it now might not give the two of them enough time to get out of the woods. Shanahan helped Harmony gather up the equipment.

"Get away from there," Shanahan told Casey, who was sniffing around the floating body. Casey, who was wary of most men, took to women right away. But not dead ones, Shanahan hoped. He headed back the way he'd come, thinking he'd get the boy home, call the police, show them where the body was, and be done with it.

"C'mon, Case," he called to the dog.

As the three of them retraced their steps, Casey continued to sniff. Some scent had caught him. Strangely, though, he was not nosing the ground. His head was much higher, up in the bushes that lined the path, sometimes craning like a giraffe at the highest leaves his neck would allow.

When they got to the cars, Casey seemed obsessed with the area beneath Harmony's car. Shanahan tried to interest Casey in the bridge. But the dog was uninterested. Whatever Casey sought hadn't gone that way.

LYLE BRODY sipped his coffee and glanced around his new office. He had moved in yesterday after a northside firm put in some expensive, state-of-the-art lighting, a striking contemporary desk, and a matching conference table. Stacks of art books remained to be placed in the rosewood modular shelving that lined the bare brick walls.

For now, he sat on a folding chair. Delivery of the new ones wouldn't be for two weeks. He stood, walked to the window, looked down from his second-story window to Massachusetts Avenue, a street angling away from the downtown high rises, a street that had been slow to fulfill the promise of its renaissance, yet still offering the last best hope of a real arts community.

There were new galleries here. Some theater. A couple of interesting restaurants. There was the Chatterbox bar, a place where Jagger and Dylan hung out when they were in town. This was definitely where he wanted his office to be. The city had lined the sidewalks with trees and street lamps a year ago. There was still promise there, if only the economy would pick up again. This was where it would happen, if it happened.

Lyle Brody, himself, had just brokered a multimillion-dollar art deal, something that set not just the local art folks on their ears, but the entire city. Now he wanted to get as close as he could to the people who should regard Lyle as the giant among them.

His sister Sally, who married a congressman, soon to be senator, wasn't the only one able to rise from poverty to grab the prize. Not only had he done it without her help, but he hadn't had to marry success to get it.

Lyle caught his reflection in the window. He smiled. The Armani jacket and black turtleneck looked good on him. At thirty-five, he was coming into his own. Short and balding, Brody wasn't the best-looking of men— Sally took all the good genes—but his recent success was making him more attractive by the minute.

It was Lyle's long-held belief that women didn't go for looks anyway. Power was what they wanted. And weren't the dinner party invitations starting to come in on a pretty regular basis? He looked down and saw the white van pull up out front.

It was his rug, one that would set off his polished wood floors. He had negotiated the Iranian dealer down by two thousand dollars. Now he could go shopping, pick out the paintings. The money to pay for all this was as good as in the bank. Lyle nudged a tiny nagging doubt out of his mind and moved the conference table aside, making room for his new Persian rug.

"GET IN BED," Shanahan said, putting the equipment in the corner of a space large enough to play full-court basketball. Harmony had the entire second floor of a small, abandoned factory in Fountain Square as his residence and video graphics studio.

"I'm all right," Harmony said. Now the kid was perspiring.

"In bed."

"I'm sorry I got you involved," Harmony said. "I didn't know what else to do."

Shanahan wanted to question him further. What was the kid doing there? Why didn't he want to talk to the police? But the kid was still in shock. In due time, Shanahan thought.

"Don't worry about it, I don't plan to stay involved." For now he'd keep the kid out of it. He went to the phone and dialed home. He'd have Maureen put in the call to the police.

MAUREEN SEEMED to have recovered quickly from her father's recent death, despite the fact that any thoughts she might have had about the passing were never discussed. Though eight months had gone by, she had nevertheless refused to read the letter addressed to her—a letter found among her father's belongings. The otherwise plain envelope remained sealed, placed under a stack of blouses in a bureau drawer.

She had gone to the funeral in southern Indiana. The cool, distant attitude she'd had toward Shanahan during those last feeble days of her father's life disappeared and the two of them were as they were before.

Maureen, at forty-four, had put her father, her violent, Bible-thumping first husband, the tragic death of her only son, and the rest of her past behind her, for the most part. She had decided in favor of the future and of the living.

She had met Shanahan at a massage parlor and, despite the age difference, or perhaps because of it, had fallen in love. She had moved in. Recently she had passed her real estate exams and was selling for a small eastside realtor. Only now, after having lived with the man for nearly a year, did she think about making a few changes in the house.

The only things she had brought with her were clothes and her Krups coffee maker. She was still feeling a little haunted by the presence of the ghost of Shanahan's wife, who, though decades gone, still exerted her influence in the wallpaper, furniture, and bric-a-brac. So Maureen was in the midst of sorting through some paint samples when Shanahan called.

"How do you feel about vanilla?" she asked when she heard his voice.

"I don't know," Shanahan said, a smile breaking through and creeping into his voice. "I haven't given it a helluva lot of thought lately. Would you do me a favor?"

"Me first," she said. "You think I could paint the bedroom?"

"I'm sure you could. Now, would you call the police and tell them I've found a body."

"Shit," Maureen said.

"What?" Shanahan asked.

"I'm sorry. I'm talking about bedrooms...Jesus."

"Call and ask for Lieutenant Swann and..."

"Are you okay?" Maureen interrupted.

"Fine. I don't want the call traced here, that's all."

"Where?"

"Where I am," Shanahan said. "Tell Swann to meet me at the bridge on Michigan Road near the back entrance to the Museum of Art. Tell them they'll need a body bag, the coroner, and a couple of real strong guys. You got that?"

"I got it. Shanahan?"

"What."

"I don't know."

"Though I have no idea what you're talking about, I'm sure vanilla's fine."

"I didn't mean that."

"I know," Shanahan said, turning slightly to see Harmony standing there in his underwear. "Don't you have some pajamas or something? You're going to freeze your ass off."

"Who are you talking to?" Maureen asked.

"A long-haired brunette about twenty-two years old," Shanahan said dryly.

"Don't tell me any more," Maureen said. "No. Go ahead and tell me."

Shanahan thought about asking Maureen to come over and babysit, but he wasn't sure he wanted her nursing a good-looking kid hanging around in his jockeys. Jealousy wasn't new to him; however, he was amused at Maureen's. He imagined her pretty face all screwed up in worry and changed his mind.

"Maureen, after you call Swann, why don't you come on over here and make sure this kid stays in bed? I'm sorry, I'm ordering you around."

"This time it's okay," she said.

"I'll be all right," Harmony said. "I just wanted to tell you I videotaped everything."

"Everything?" For a moment Shanahan wasn't sure what Harmony meant. Videotaped the death? The dumping of the body in the water? What?

"I mean I taped the area. I even taped the body. That's when I started getting sick."

"Shanahan?" came the forgotten voice on the phone.

"I'm sorry. He'll probably be all right."

"He will," she repeated, and Shanahan recognized a little sigh of relief in her voice.

"A little shaken up, that's all."

"I have a pencil," Maureen said. "How do I get there?"

THREE

"YOU GOT ANY IDEA who it is?" Lieutenant Swann asked. Shanahan knew and liked Swann. He was young for a lieutenant. He always wore dark suits, kept his hair as closely cropped as a Marine, and maybe played it too much by the book. But, unlike some of the cops Shanahan knew, Swann seemed more interested in finding all the evidence, not just the kind that insured a conviction.

Shanahan looked around. He was amazed. There were at least twenty cops in uniform meandering about, talking among themselves. A little overdone, he thought. Then again, he remembered seeing three cop cars, lights flashing, blocking four lanes of rush-hour traffic—all for a little old lady in a late-model Buick who probably ran a red light.

"You know her?" Swann repeated in his monotone, emotionless way, referring to the corpse still lying in the shallows.

"No. You?"

"Yeah, I think so," Swann said, then went down to the water's edge and looked over the coroner's shoulder.

The coroner, who weighed maybe three hundred pounds and looked a little bit like a young Broderick Crawford, was ankle-deep in water and chewing on a short cigar. He rolled the body on its side, examining the marks. He shook his head. "Weird. Fucking weird, Swann."

The young lieutenant leaned in for a closer look, then nodded wearily and called out for one of the uniforms. "Get a hold of Rafferty. Tell him he better get out here."

Shanahan decided to leave.

"Mr. Shanahan," Swann said calmly.

"Yeah?"

Swann got up and moved up the beach toward Shanahan, stopped to swat a mosquito. "You don't want to know who it is?"

"No."

"Then I won't tell you. You said you were out walking your dog?"

"That's what I said."

"Well, where's your dog?"

"In the car. He doesn't like policemen."

Swann continued, unfazed. "So you came all the way across town to walk your dog." He got no response. "Is that right?"

"It would seem that way. To get here from there means going across town."

"Dumb question," Swann said. There was a glimmer of a smile in the officer's eyes. "Let me rephrase it. Why would you drive clear across town to walk your dog?"

"He likes to fish." Shanahan shrugged. "There's no fish in our neighborhood."

"You finding her... that's kinda funny, isn't it?"

"I find the Marx brothers funnier."

"I mean you being a P.I. You're not working on a case?"

"Not this one. Just doing my civic duty. Reporting a crime... or an accident."

"One more question, though I suspect I'm not going to get much of an answer. Why did you have your wife... I mean somebody else... whatever... call me?"

"I wasn't near a phone."

"Your... lady friend..."

"Maureen."

"Yeah, her. She was out on this walk with you?"

"No," Shanahan said.

"Why do I feel like we're not getting anywhere?" Swann grinned openly.

"There's really no place to go."

"Okay. So there's some things you're not telling me?"

"Don't read too much into it." Shanahan turned, walked up the earthen embankment.

His landmarks—the jockey shorts, the McDonald's cup, and the Budweiser cans—guided him back through the trees. He realized that this was no small matter. They were calling in Lieutenant Rafferty, the P.R. cop. This meant the naked lady wasn't your average floater.

HARRY STOBART did only three things when he took over Delaney's eastside bar. He installed a new big-screen TV, outlawed frozen drinks, and screwed up Delaney's legendary Irish stew.

"Look, this is Delaney's own friggin' recipe," Harry said to Shanahan, his best friend and best customer.

"I'm not hungry," Shanahan said. It was a day full of little lies.

"I could dish up some to go. For later."

"I'm thinking about becoming a vegetarian, Harry."

"Yeah, and I got me a date with Elizabeth Taylor."

"Besides, it's too early to eat." Shanahan glanced up at the TV screen that hovered dangerously over a corner booth. With the volume down, Oprah Winfrey chatted with a panel of angry-looking women. Shanahan turned when he heard Maureen's "Hi, guys," and saw her auburn hair caught in the sunlight from the doorway.

"Your friend's fine, up playing with his computers," Maureen said, sliding into the booth, across from Shanahan. He liked her like this. No makeup, her lightly freckled skin setting off her green eyes. "Nice-looking guy," she said.

"Say no more, my sweet," Shanahan said, faking a smile and glancing toward Harry. "A bourbon for me and a rum and tonic for Maureen."

"Twist of lemon," Maureen said. "Lemon, not lime, Harry."

"For Christsakes, I know that."

"You're not telling Harry about his son-in-law-to-be?" she asked Shanahan.

"I don't know what I'm not telling anybody yet." He glanced up at the TV screen and saw the words "news bulletin" at the bottom of a picture of an attractive, dark-haired woman. "Turn it up, Harry."

Harry grabbed the remote control. A woman's voice accompanied by a photograph of Senator David Holland.

". . . that foul play has not been ruled out. The senator has boarded a military jet at Andrews Air Force Base and is expected to arrive in Indianapolis within the hour. Police are providing no other details in the unexpected death of Mrs. Holland. However, sources close to the scene indicate she may have been a drowning victim. Stay tuned for more updates and the news at five."

Oprah was back. A woman, near tears, spoke into the camera.

"I was only ten. He told me he would kill my mom if I told anybody. . ."

Maureen got up suddenly, heading toward the bathroom. "Aren't the Cubs on, Harry?" she said, not stopping for the answer.

"Playin' tonight, Maureen. They're in San Francisco," he said, his voice trailing off as she disappeared behind the door. He brought the drinks to the booth.

"Change the channel, will you, Harry?"

"Yeah, sure. What d'ya want?"

"I don't care. MTV," Shanahan said.

"You in your second childhood?" Harry said.

"Third." Harry switched to some cartoons as a way of commenting on Shanahan's joke. Maureen returned, her face fresh from a little cold water, Shanahan suspected. "Are you all right?"

"Something in my eye," she said, not looking at him. "I stopped by O'Malia's, picked up a bottle of wine and two of the finest steaks you've ever laid eyes on."

"The truth comes out," Harry shouted from the bar.

"But you'll have to cook them," Maureen continued to Shanahan. "You're so great at the grill. They also had fresh sweet corn, the kind with the little white kernels."

"I'm to cook those too, right?"

"Right." She smiled.

"Shame about the senator's wife," Harry said later as the couple started for the door. "They say drownin' isn't the worst way to go."

"She was dead before she hit the water," Shanahan said.

EDMUND CAREM stood off-camera while the TV crews set up their equipment and other technicians were jostling around the podium trying to make sense out of the half dozen microphones necessary to feed the state's press corps.

As David Holland's poorly financed and badly trailing rival for the U.S. Senate seat, Edmund Carem had to make this appearance in prime time TV count and count big. Four months of campaigning before election, and there was damned little money left for paid commercials, and the TV stations were already getting nervous about extending any more credit.

He had three pink five-by-eight index cards tucked in the inside breast pocket of his dark suit. Each card contained a different statement. Each was short. Give the TV editors too much information, they get to choose the sound bite. He swept back the slightly graying wings of temple hair and glanced again at the index cards. If he played this right, he'd beat the experts and bury Holland. If he played it wrong, his political career would be as dead as Sally Holland.

EVERYONE WAS IN the kitchen. Einstein, Shanahan's large, racoon-tailed cat, sat on the counter, unblinkingly watching Shanahan carve a thin white stripe of fat from the steaks. Eating aside, Einstein's most passionate interest was looking at people eating or preparing food. Only then came sleep, which he also did well, curling on or near anything warm.

Casey sat on the floor, a kind of sad but loyal symbol of his currently unrequited friendship. Maureen, a glass of red wine in her hand, leaned against the counter next to Shanahan, quietly watching the shiny blade carve all but a quarter inch of the fat from the thick red meat. The only sound was the low rumble of the ancient refrigerator.

"What the hell is this?" Shanahan suddenly blurted, brandishing the knife.

Maureen laughed, but no one budged. "It's just the family all coming together at dinner."

"You, the wounded hound," he said to Casey, "go in the other room." Casey obeyed after one last, sad look. "And you," he said to Maureen, "can slice the tomatoes and shuck the corn."

"What about Einstein?" Maureen asked with a devilish grin. "Are you playing favorites here?"

"In the ten years since his declaration of ownership of this house and everything and everyone in it, Einstein refuses to understand any words in any human language except the invitation to eat, which he would no doubt understand even if it were said in Hungarian."

"I see," she said. "For your information, Mister Shanahan, the tomatoes are sliced, the corn is shucked, and the charcoal is lit."

"Thank you, Mrs. Smith. You may stay." He put the steaks on a plate, carried it through the living room, out the screen door, and into the searing heat of the late afternoon. It would be hours before sunset, before there would be any cooling off.

"I did it while you were talking on the phone," she said, following him. "A very long conversation, I might add."

"Yes, it was." The steaks hissed.

Einstein stared at them through the screen door.

"WHY YOU?" Jennifer Bailey asked the young Hispanic sitting on the other side of her glass-topped desk. She could see his Nikes tapping the carpet nervously.

"I knew her," he said without a trace of an accent.

"Just knew her," she said, taking off her glasses. The thick lenses made her eyes look larger and sometimes threatening. She was aware of that and took advantage of it when it served her purpose. But now she wanted him to relax, to trust her. "Why do you feel you need an attorney if all they were doing was questioning an acquaintance of the victim?"

He shook his head, either saying "no," or that he didn't know, or that he wouldn't answer.

"You have to trust me, Emilio. The law protects an attorney-client relationship. What you tell me is privileged, you understand? But if you don't tell me, I can't help you."

Emilio got up and went to the door and stopped. He seemed to be deliberating. About what, she didn't know. Was he worried that a black woman attorney wasn't up to the task? Despite her successful practice, despite her fine offices, despite her stylish clothes, there was always that doubt. She doubted; why wouldn't he? Perhaps her success was a fluke and it would all come tumbling down tomorrow.

"If you would prefer another attorney, I could refer you to several fine people. Very able."

He turned, lower lip quivering. "How—" was all he managed to get out. "Oh, God," he said.

"THE BATTERED BODY of Senator David Holland's wife was found earlier today in White River. Police finally acknowledge that the death of Mrs. Holland..."

"Does she have a name?" Maureen said to the television set as she put her bowl of popcorn on the bedside table.

"Sally," Shanahan said.

"She died. He didn't," she said sharply. "It's not like his car was stolen. Switch back to the Cubs game, wouldja?"

"In a minute," Shanahan said, watching as the face of Edmund Carem appeared on screen.

"Our hearts are with Senator Holland this evening. It is a time to begin the healing. Everywhere. I have asked my campaign manager to pull all our commercials off the air for the time being. I hope that in some small way it will show that all of us, back home, are willing to come together and offer our support in these difficult times— times that would put immeasurable strain on the best of us."

"THAT SON of a bitch!" David Holland yelled, rocketing off the sofa in his Indianapolis hotel room. Eric shut off the TV. He was pouring the senator a glass of Scotch when the phone rang. "I don't want to talk with anyone," Holland said, taking a gulp.

"Yes," Eric said into the phone. He took off his tortoiseshell glasses, laid them on the table, and wiped his brow. "Yes, just a moment ... You have to take it, David." Eric spoke firmly, extending the receiver toward Holland, who'd slumped back on the sofa. The senator got up with a look of disgust on his face.

"Yeah," Holland said curtly. A woman's voice explained he would have to wait "just a moment." He glared at his young aide.

"Davey?" It was a man's voice, one Holland instantly recognized. Even is he hadn't recognized the voice, he'd recognize the familiarity. No one else called him Davey except his mother.

"This is the President." Holland said nothing, and the President resumed after an awkward pause. "I couldn't get to sleep without talking with you about all this—well, you know, this bad stuff. I just wanted to let you know I'm with you on this thing." Holland motioned for Eric to bring him a cigarette. "Davey, are you there?"

"I'm here," Holland said coldly. He took the cigarette Eric had lit for him, then, holding the phone against his ear with a hunched shoulder, reached for his Scotch.

"The sea is gonna be pretty rough out there in Indiana, but you can grab the ..."

Holland laid the receiver in the cradle.

"What'd he say?" Eric asked.

"He was talking about rough seas in Indiana before I hung up on the bastard."

"You hung up on the President?"

"I did it gently. How did he find me?"

"White House operators could find Judge Carter or Jimmy Hoffa if the President wanted to call them. You hung up on the President? I can't believe you hung up on the President. You plan on switching parties?"

Holland handed the bottle of Scotch to Eric. "What? And do the bastards a favor? I get a little tired of his tinny impression of John Wayne. Now you," he said, glaring at his young aide, "go back to your room or out on one of your secret nocturnal missions."

"You don't want the Scotch?" Eric's face showed disbelief.

"No, if I had wanted the goddamn Scotch, I would have kept the goddamn Scotch. So why don't you and the goddamn Scotch take a hike."

"David."

"Don't whine." At the moment Holland didn't like Eric and wasn't sure he had ever liked him. Barton looked and acted like every senator's aide—Georgetown suspenders, striped shirt, and the way he fiddled with his expensive eyeglasses always struck Holland as intellectual affectations. The senator not only disliked intellectuals, he wasn't fond of any affectations except his own.

"You're not going to do anything stupid, are you?"

"Probably. It's become a calling card, hasn't it?"

FOUR

SHANAHAN HADN'T slept well. Steamy August nights weren't much better than steamy August days. He had wrestled with the sheets, finally tossing them aside at 6:00 a.m. and climbing out of bed. Maureen, on the other hand, slept soundly, her naked body lightly misted by perspiration.

At six fifteen Shanahan fixed a pot of coffee, and at seven he relented to the dog's stubborn insistence that they play ball. Shanahan tossed the smudged green tennis ball high in the air, watching his speckled and spotted mongrel go underneath and wait, snagging it seconds before it hit the ground.

He had a momentary flashback of the bruises on Sally Holland's neck. It wasn't his business, was it? Casey brought the ball back, and Shanahan threw a grounder that went careening off a tree into the irises. The dog missed the angle, but quickly found it by scent. They played until Shanahan heard the sound of the telephone inside.

"Shanahan," he said, a little out of breath.

"This is Jennifer Bailey. Did I wake you?"

"No."

"I understand you discovered the body of Mrs. Holland."

"I was the one who reported it to the police, yes."

"Can we get together? Talk about it?"

"There's not a lot to say. You working in prosecutor's office these days?"

"No. I have the same practice as before. But it's important to know as much as I can about the case," she said, her tone cool, professional, and, to him, having worked with her before, familiar.

"I don't understand."

"I'm representing someone who believes the police may implicate him in the murder."

"Already?"

"Would you come see me? Please." There was a little, unfamiliar quaver in her voice.

"Sure, give me an hour."

He went into the bedroom. Maureen was awake. Shanahan sat on the edge of the bed, brushed a few strands of moist hair away from Maureen's forehead.

"I'll be gone awhile," he said.

"The call last night?"

"And someone else this morning. Got a couple of things to do."

"Bring me back some ice cream?"

EVEN IN THE RUSH HOUR it wouldn't take long for Shanahan to get downtown. His neighborhood, barely kempt bungalows housing elderly people barely making it on Social Security, and younger people struggling to maintain their blue collar jobs in the face of a shrinking economy, was only a couple of miles from the spikes of concrete and steel that made up the downtown.

His green '72 Chevy Malibu moved slowly but steadily west on Washington Street, past empty storefronts, auto-parts stores, used-car lots filled with gas hogs, and bars with names like Mary Alice's Saloon and The Runway. Vern's Sports Bar was boarded up, but Fat Boy's Game Room was open.

This was Shanahan's neighborhood, its decline so slow it was hardly noticed. Prostitution, mostly white women and young boys, and gangs, also white, had gained a tenuous foothold years ago. Some nickle-bag marijuana dealers and home-grown street gangs had progressed in the last few years to some not quite so small-time crack and arms dealing. People like Mrs. Schmidt, who had called him last night, were afraid. Afraid for herself. Afraid for her granddaughter. He was to meet Mrs. Schmidt at ten after finding out what Jennifer Bailey wanted from him.

Though they'd had some uneasy times in the past, Shanahan appreciated Jennifer Bailey's straightforward attitude. She hadn't changed. It was apparent right away that there would be no idle chatter about health and weather.

"You told me over the phone that you were the one who 'reported' the body, Mr. Shanahan, in answer to my question using the term 'discovered.' What am I to make of that?"

"Whoa," Shanahan said. He didn't want to lie, but he didn't particularly want to tell the truth, not now anyway. "You answer a few questions first, then I'll let you know what I saw at the crime scene. How 'bout that?"

"You know," she said, looking up over her glasses, "I can legally require your testimony. That's what I think about that."

"Then I take it you are representing or prosecuting someone who has been formally charged in the death of Sally Holland."

She smiled. "Okay. I keep forgetting you aren't..." She stopped abruptly.

"As senile as I look."

"No, no, no," she said, laughing like someone not used to laughing. The lapse no doubt came out of embarrassment. "I was going to say 'anyone's fool.'" Then her face tightened a bit. "Confidentially, the police have questioned a young man, Emilio Ramirez. The general nature of their questions and, I'm afraid, the specific nature of his answers make a formal charge imminently probable.''

"Wait a minute. She was found around noon yesterday. The police not only examine the crime scene, handle difficult media inquiries, and question a likely suspect, but that suspect finds an attorney to represent him—all in the same afternoon. Maybe I should be impressed. But I don't buy it.'' Shanahan got up. "The wheels of justice are grinding at a blinding speed, Mrs.... errr... Ms. Bailey.''

"That's my point exactly.'' She stood up. "It doesn't take a Rhodes Scholar to understand that the city wants to grind up someone for this crime in the most expedient manner possible. That's why I need to know how you came to 'report' or 'discover' the body.''

"I'll get back to you on that,'' Shanahan said. He looked down at his reflection on the glass-topped desk. He hadn't shaved in two days. Christ, he thought, no wonder Jennifer Bailey's secretary looked frightened.

"You could work for me. Officially. On the payroll.''

He looked back at her, surprised. He knew she preferred one of the more prestigious agencies, the kind that never used the word "detective.'' They were "security consultants.''

"You're serious.''

"Very.''

"I'll get back to you on that too.''

WHEN DAVID HOLLAND walked into the funeral director's office, Lyle Brody didn't bother to stand, shake hands, or even say hello. Holland glanced at his brother-in-law. "Lyle,'' he said, merely acknowledging the man's presence.

Alfred Margoven, the funeral director, took the exchange, or rather the lack of it, as an omen. He didn't bother introducing himself, instead handed each of them a card and got immediately down to business.

"We suggest viewing tomorrow from four in the afternoon until nine in the evening, and services the following day—that is, Friday—at eleven in the morning."

"I don't want this to be a media circus," Lyle erupted.

"I can't agree with you more," Holland said. "In fact," he continued, looking at the business card, "in fact, Mr. Margoven...Alfred...I'd like Lyle here to have the final say on every detail with the exception of security. That is, incidentally, out of my hands as well. The governor has informed my aide that the state police will act as liaison with local and any federal authorities to take care of that part of it."

Brody looked at the senator suspiciously.

The funeral director sighed. "Thank you, Senator. Thank you for your consideration." It was obvious he hoped that the brother-in-law would pick up on the senator's cooperative spirit.

Brody moved uneasily in his wingback chair and mumbled something unintelligible under his breath.

"I assure you, we will be sensitive to your wishes," Alfred Margoven said directly to Brody.

"Yes, yes, yes." Clearly, Brody was pissed. "Have you seen Elizabeth?" he asked Holland.

"No."

"You haven't bothered to see your own daughter?"

"She's in Fort Wayne, with her grandparents, Lyle. She doesn't know yet. I'm going up there this evening."

He explained this with as much warmth as he could muster. He wasn't going to waste one iota of emotion on this two-bit opportunist. And he wasn't going to give Alfred what's-his-name any tidbit for the tabloid TV and newspaper reporters who were no doubt registering at hotels this very minute.

Senator Holland excused himself, went through the large double doors, and into the dark stretch Lincoln Eric had gotten from the governor.

"How are you holding up?" Eric asked as Holland slid in beside him.

"Better than you," he said sternly, noticing the pale, drawn face of his aide.

Eric put on his sunglasses as a state policeman shut the door and rounded the car to take his place at the wheel.

HARMONY, having slept most of yesterday away, still managed to sleep until nine thirty in the morning. He poured himself a glass of orange juice. He went to the heap of electronic gear he and Shanahan had carried up the day before and extracted the video cassette from the recorder. He slid it into one of his VCRs and flipped a switch that put it on the largest of his monitors. He sat back in the adjustable chair built especially for artists, grabbed the remote, then swirled to face the set, clicking on both monitor and VCR.

There were the shots of the canal. Harmony particularly liked the effect of the little iron bridge with the weeping willow just behind it, where Butler University's campus met the water. There was a second of black before the picture picked up the canal a little farther down, where one could easily imagine being miles from civilization. He captured the lone fisherman still farther down. He wasn't sure if he wanted or needed that shot, but it was there for him.

He had gotten the hand-held effect he wanted as he walked into the woods. Running now, the trees whipped by the lens, achieving the sense of chasing or being chased. It reminded him of Bertolucci's film, *The Conformist*.

He smiled. That's what he wanted. A sense of danger. The hunt. The chase. It was a good counterpoint to the serene nature of the canal, which, with a little electronic tampering, would look like one of those romantic French impressionist paintings.

He knew what the next scenes would be, and he wasn't sure he wanted to go on, just yet. He clicked the button and the VCR began to rewind. Perhaps he would just look at the first part again. In slow motion.

SHANAHAN WAS BACK in his neighborhood again. On Linwood Street. Mrs. Schmidt lived between Michigan and New York streets. He passed School 58, Ralph W. Emerson Elementary School, "W" for "Waldo." He'd always wondered why they used only the initial. To save money?

This was where his son, Ty, had gone to school. And, he suddenly remembered, this was the street where he and Elaine almost bought a home a zillion years ago. He could picture the street as it had been then, in the mid-forties. Small trees, immaculate homes. Time hadn't been kind.

He pulled up in front of the Schmidt house. A crumbling concrete walk led through the dead brown grass up to the house. The aluminum siding was dirty but in good condition otherwise. However, the wood trim of the windows hadn't been touched in years. Bare wood showed through, and the bottom strips were rotted.

Shanahan expected to find a woman of thirty-five or forty. Instead, he was greeted by a woman his own age or older.

"Mr. Shanahan," she said, "I'm so glad you are an older man."

"I wish I could share your enthusiasm, Mrs. Schmidt."

"I've made some fresh coffee," she said and, having offered him a seat on a faded purple velour sofa, was already on her way to the kitchen. "I went to the Roselyn Bakery early this morning and brought back some bear claws." Her voice faded as she passed through the small dining room, stopping momentarily to smooth out the lace tablecloth. "I used to bake a great deal, Mr. Shanahan, but Francine would rather have store-bought."

Shanahan hadn't heard "store-bought" in many years.

"So there's really no one to bake for, and I'm afraid I lost my touch," she said, coming back, carrying a tray with two cups of coffee, a sugar bowl and small cream pitcher and a piece of pastry on a plate. All the china matched—slightly yellowed porcelain with little pink roses.

Above a fake fireplace that housed fake logs was a picture of the Madonna. Beside it was a plaster Christ, bleeding on the cross.

Shanahan had never been comfortable with grand-motherly types or bleeding Christs.

"My husband was Lutheran, but I've remained a Catholic," she said, having noticed Shanahan's eyes track the religious imagery. Perhaps she was looking for a reciprocal confession of faith from him. He didn't give it. "My late husband, Mr. Shanahan," she finally added with some emphasis.

"When you called, Mrs. Schmidt, you said that you were having some problems with . . ."

"Francine, my granddaughter. You know, it's so nice to have someone visit. Do you take sugar?"

"Yes, a little," he said, putting a half-teaspoonful in his coffee. "Now, about Francine . . ."

"Cream? It's real cream."

"No, thank you."

"That's true. People our age shouldn't have a lot of dairy products. This very nice doctor on the health channel . . ."

"Mrs. Schmidt, I charge by the hour."

"Oh, my," she said. "I go on, don't I? I have so much time on my hands, I barely notice it passing."

"I take it Francine's not here right now?"

"Since school let out for the summer, she rarely comes home, not even at night. I can't imagine what she could be doing, out all hours like that...."

"I'm going to ask you some questions, Mrs. Schmidt. Please just some simple answers."

"Whatever you say, Mr. Shanahan."

Things went smoothly for about ten minutes, though it was obvious Mrs. Schmidt was terrified, thinking Francine might be involved in something dangerous—drugs, gangs, even devil worship. She'd been hearing about the latter on local newscasts. Shanahan managed to gather some basic facts: Francine is fifteen. Her mother died in a fire when the girl was six. Her dad immediately dumped the kid at his mom's. For a while he sent postcards full of promises. They stopped three years ago.

He also learned: Francine is a freshman at Tech High School. She'd dyed her hair several times and is currently wearing it black and spiked. She's seeing some guy whose name is so strange Mrs. Schmidt couldn't remember it. When Francine is home, she stays in her room. Rarely eats. Sleeps in the afternoon until early evening. Has just gone out and gotten her nose pierced.

FIVE

"IT'S A TWO-HOUR DRIVE," Eric said, "and we have some things to talk about."

He looked up, making sure the glass partition was in place so the state trooper at the wheel of the big Lincoln wouldn't hear them.

Senator David Holland looked out of the smoked-glass window as the car smoothly took the banked curve and straightened out on the interstate, slowly gained speed, gliding effortlessly to seventy. Castleton Shopping Center was off to the left and receding. Ahead was flat farmland. It would be soybeans, corn, and blue skies for two hours until they reached Fort Wayne. He was more than familiar with the route and more than a little bored with it.

A two-term congressman from Fort Wayne, Holland's surprisingly successful first bid for senator took him to and from Indianapolis many, many times. They were good times. He was fresh and eager for political battle. He challenged one of the state's most popular senators and won. Sure, there were some dirty tricks— getting the religious right to set up the incumbent with some questionable accusations. Yes, it was gross, unfair. But he didn't do it. He had nothing to do with it. It was all orchestrated in Washington.

"David, you want me to write your public statement?" Eric asked. "You're going to have to make one, you know."

"Shut up, Eric."

"It's not pleasant. I'm sorry. But you're not an average citizen. Besides, we're in the middle of a campaign. What I thought was, you could call a press conference on the front porch of your parents' place. They would be with you, and Elizabeth would be with you. It's an effective way to counter Edmund Carem. What he said on TV—suggesting that maybe you weren't up for a second six years mentally—was a pretty effective beginning of what could be an entire campaign."

David pressed the window button and it slid down. The air rushed in and the car became an instant Turkish bath.

"David, you have a lot on your mind. I'm sorry. But this is my job. We have to make the best of it. Carem is climbing in the polls. Name recognition is getting better every day. If you make yourself inaccessible, a strong case could be made that this tragedy has had a devastating effect on you and your ability to represent the people. If you do it right, David, you'll be swept into office on waves of sympathy. If you do it wrong..."

"Pull over!" David shouted, pounding on the partition.

"I beg your pardon," the trooper asked as the glass slid down.

"I said pull over."

When the car stopped, David looked at Eric. "Get out," he said.

THE LAST THING Shanahan wanted to do was go snooping around some fifteen-year-old's belongings. Kids have rights too. But here was a seventy-year-old woman trying to protect the last person in her life who meant anything from something she had no ability to understand.

"You suppose I could have a look in her room?" Shanahan asked.

"I'm afraid she keeps it locked."

"I don't think that's a problem, Mrs. Schmidt, if it's all right with you."

"She'll be very upset," she said, a look of horror passing over her face.

"You're frightened of her?" Mrs. Schmidt didn't answer. "She doesn't have to know," Shanahan said more gently. Mrs. Schmidt stood up, started to leave the room, then stopped. She looked lost. "Mrs. Schmidt, I can't very well help unless I know a little bit more about your granddaughter. Sometimes a room, like hers, will explain a lot."

Mrs. Schmidt went to the dining room, to the side table, opened a drawer, and produced one of those old-fashioned keys.

"She doesn't know I have it," Mrs. Schmidt said. "It's the master key to all the rooms."

The room was a mess and, after he assured an embarrassed Mrs. Schmidt that it wasn't at all unusual for a teenager's room, he went browsing, careful not to disturb anything.

The floor was littered with all manner of stuff: books, cassettes, crumpled Burger King bags, clothing, and magazines. The litter under one of the windows had been crushed. The smudges on the lower panes of the same window indicated more than a little activity. He opened the window. His suspicions were confirmed by dirty, gray smudges on the aluminum siding below the window—a pattern from the sole of some sort of athletic shoe too large, he believed, to be the girl's.

More than likely, Francine's boyfriend made informal visits. The bed was a mess. On it he found a few Snickers wrappers and a brown paper bag. It was empty, except for a cash register receipt. He couldn't read the faded, purplish numbers, but with a little help from better eyes than his he might be able to figure out where it came from. He put it in his pocket.

Buried beneath some copies of *Creem* magazine, he found what he assumed to be a school notebook. It was spiral bound. Inside, he found some unintelligible scrawls. Maybe just class notes. What was more telling, however, was the repetition of the word "Moogie." That could be a place or a rock 'n' roll star or God knew what else. But it could be the strange name that Mrs. Schmidt couldn't think of—Francine's guy.

He put the notebook back where he'd found it, then looked for telltale signs of drugs. No pills. No powder. But the room, completely closed off from the rest of the house, had the stale but sweet smell of pot. There were also some aluminum tabs, which could have come as easily from cans of Pepsi as cans of beer. So far, the signs indicated nothing too serious as these things go. No hypodermics anyway.

He looked around a few minutes more, hoping to find a photograph of at least one of them. Mrs. Schmidt's photo offering was a couple of years old and of a girl who had not yet chosen her current lifestyle. No luck.

"YOU HAVE a guest," Maureen said apologetically to Shanahan as he came through the front door. "I put Casey out. Had to."

"You put the wrong one out," Shanahan said. "I knew who it was when I saw the car and the bag of cheese curls on the dashboard."

Police Lieutenant Max Rafferty's large and expensively suited body occupied half the sofa. He had his handkerchief out and was dabbing the perspiration on his forehead.

Shanahan pulled a tiny piece of white paper from his pocket, handed it to Maureen. "Would you see if you can tell where this receipt came from. I can't make it out."

"At your age, that's no surprise," Rafferty said. "It's a wonder the state lets you have a driver's license." It was sometimes hard to tell if Rafferty meant to be mean or thought other guys liked a little tough kidding.

"You have a warrant or something?" Shanahan asked him.

"Just some friendly questions. I was in the neighborhood."

"Is there a smorgasbord near here or something?"

"You know, you ought to air condition this place. It's not a nice place to spend a whole lotta time." He unfolded the perfectly ironed handkerchief and wiped the sweat off his cheek. "But I'm prepared to sit here until I get some answers."

"You overstayed your welcome the moment you showed up. Besides, I've already talked with Swann. If I have anything more to say, I'll say it to him." Shanahan walked to the door, opened it. "It's never a pleasure, good-bye, Rafferty."

"You don't get a choice. Swann reports to me on this one," Rafferty said, not bothering to get up. "The guy—you know what we dumb cops call the perpetrator—is nailed. A spic boxer. Class struggle. Unrequited love. Latino temper. Iron fists. Like I said, nailed. Just don't want any surprises from you."

"I did my duty. Read the report."

"Doing his duty. I know, I know. Don't bother me with that shit. There's a little question about how you came upon the scene. And . . . well . . . Swann's taken a liking to you, I guess, 'cause he don't see the need to press you for an explanation. Me, I like to make sure there's no embarrassing facts poppin' up later. And I'm sure an honest, simple, law-abiding citizen like you don't want to get in any legal hassles for withholding in a murder investigation."

Shanahan went to his desk, rummaged through the yellow pages until he found a listing for Jennifer Bailey. He picked up the phone and dialed.

"Jennifer Bailey and Associates," the voice said.

"Ms. Bailey, please."

"She's in a meeting."

"Tell her it's Shanahan." He heard a click, then some music. "What does it say?" he asked Maureen, who sat at the desk looking at the receipt.

"It says 'Malibu Trash.' What kind of name is that?"

"It's a record shop, on East Washington Street, 5600 block, your basic metal shop with an overtone of satanic rites, you know what I mean?" Rafferty said, getting up and moving toward Shanahan. "See, I can be cooperative."

"Mr. Shanahan?" came the voice on the phone when the music stopped. It was Jennifer Bailey.

"I'll take the case," Shanahan said and hung up. Then to Rafferty. "I'm working for the defense counsel now. Talk with my attorney."

Rafferty laughed. "You don't waste any words, do you? Well, you might think about using a few more with me."

"I've wasted far too many as it is."

Rafferty's smile was gone. "You might think you're walkin' the safe side of a fine line here, but there's no line at all. Ain't even a tightrope. You weren't employed at the time. Right?" He poked Shanahan in the chest. The dog, watching from the screen door, bared his teeth, growling deep and low. "Everybody downtown is nervous, real nervous." Now he smiled, but it wasn't well-intentioned this time. "You're fuckin' with the city, the state, and the feds on this one. And an old fart, penny-ante P.I. like you . . . well, you figure it out."

Rafferty paused, looking at Shanahan for some sort of response. He didn't get one.

"You are one stubborn Irishman, Shanahan. The thing is I can get your license pulled and fix it so you can't get a job as part-time security for K Mart. You understand?''

He stared at Shanahan, who simply went into the kitchen.

Rafferty followed. "What were you doing down there, Shanahan? And don't say you were walking your dog."

"Arrest me or get out. You don't have a warrant."

"The nice lady invited me in," Rafferty said.

"The not-so-nice man is inviting you out."

"I'm goin'." Rafferty smirked. "You know, you and I have this love-hate relationship. All the time, we're in each other's way. I believe in, you know, live and let live. So I'm gonna tell you—and I'm telling you nice like— you got lucky before. With the Stone case and with the kids. But this one ain't in your league. Like I said, the feds don't fuck around. You change your mind about cooperating, you know how to reach me."

"Yeah, follow the trail of cake crumbs."

"Now see how you are?" he said.

"I'm going to feed the dog, Rafferty. He's a little bit like you, so if I were you, I sure wouldn't want to be between him and his dinner."

"I'm goin'. I'm goin'." He went to the door.

"YOU AND RAFFERTY—just like old times," Maureen said as she went to his cluttered desk to answer the phone.

It was for Shanahan. He recognized Jennifer Bailey's voice.

"You're a man of few words, Mr. Shanahan."

"The deal is," Shanahan said, "the police are going after your guy. The only thing I can figure is they're a little soft on motive."

"How did you come to that conclusion?"

"Does what's-his-name . . ."

"Emilio Ramirez."

". . . have an alibi for the night of the killing?"

"No. People are generally sleeping at that hour. They haven't confirmed the hour of her death; however, it was sometime between midnight and four a.m. He was asleep."

"Not everybody sleeps alone."

"He was sleeping alone, Mr. Shanahan."

"No alibi."

"But that's hardly enough," Jennifer Bailey said.

"Right. That's why they haven't arrested him. What they're trying to do is determine the place of death and build a case that Ramirez either wanted more out of the relationship than the senator's wife was willing to give or that she was putting a stop to a relationship Ramirez didn't want to end."

"That's what I thought. Pretty flimsy," Jennifer Bailey said.

"I take it, then, they did have a relationship, Sally Holland and Ramirez?"

"Yes. But Emilio says it was platonic."

Emilio? Shanahan was surprised. Already, Jennifer Bailey was using the first name of the client. That kind of familiarity wasn't at all like her. "I'd like to talk with your Emilio."

"I'll arrange it," she said coldly, obviously catching Shanahan's barb. "Can we meet here at five this afternoon?"

"Yes."

"Mr. Shanahan?"

"What?"

"He's a nice kid."

"Sure," he said.

SIX

THE HOUSE WAS a tri-level, with a red brick facade. It was the choice Holland's parents made when they decided they wanted to be closer to a city. The house was in a suburban housing development in Waynedale on Fort Wayne's southside. They moved just after David graduated from high school in the mid-sixties.

In a drive through the curving streets, it didn't take anyone long to figure out the developer had offered only four styles. The only distinction Holland's tri-level had over the one two doors down was that it was immaculate. The lawn was impeccably green and mowed within an inch of its life.

For David Holland, the house seemed a little smarter than he remembered, and the maple tree in front seemed quite a bit larger. He had never really liked it here, preferring the white frame farm-style house on five acres between Fort Wayne and Huntington where he grew up.

David's father was a modestly wealthy man; made it in the plumbing business. He'd built a twenty-two-employee company around his own skills and now had several lucrative contracts. Like many Midwesterners he never let the money show. The shiny Buick in the driveway was five years old, and David expected his mom's Pacer was in the garage, where it usually sat between grocery runs or church business.

Holland hugged his mom and kissed her on the cheek.

"I made some coffee," she said. She smiled as he pulled away, but her eyes weren't smiling. "Lizzie's upstairs. Nobody has said anything about it. Your dad disconnected the cable on the TV."

He looked at his dad, and there was fleeting eye contact.

"I don't know what to say to her," David said. "I thought about it all the way up here and I still don't know what to say."

"Your dad has an idea," his mom said. "Tell him, honey."

"Henry has a cabin on the lake in Michigan...."

"You remember Henry Watkins, don't you?" Mrs. Holland interjected.

"Yes."

"That's it," his dad said. "I thought we'd take Elizabeth up to the lake for a couple of weeks, maybe longer, get her away from all this."

"Honey, it's been a circus around here, what with cameras and reporters..." his mom said, sitting on the white sofa. It seemed strange, being in this room. No one ever used the living room. It was meant to stay clean and pretty. The carpet was white. Two gold satin matching chairs flanked a mock fireplace and looked as if they'd never held a body. One only passed through the edge of the room on a plastic runner—from the upstairs bedrooms down to the kitchen and then down to the family room.

"I'm sorry," David said.

"It's not your fault," his mom said.

His dad, who stood looking out the front door, suddenly turned and crossed to the kitchen.

"Where are you going, honey?" Mrs. Holland asked.

"To get the driver some coffee," he said, and in moments he was out the front door carrying two cups of coffee.

"He loves Elizabeth," Mrs. Holland said. She sat beside David, put her hand on his knee. "That little girl can twist her granddaddy around her little finger." She patted his knee again and smiled. "If he'd had a daughter instead of a son, he'd have spoiled her rotten."

David got up, went to the door. His father and the state trooper were talking.

"Have you had lunch, Davey?"

She had no idea what kind of life her son had led. Not when he was a kid. Not now. Holland always suspected his dad knew something, had some vague, perhaps intuitive grasp of his child's character. His old man and the state trooper were still talking. His dad was laughing. It was so easy for his dad to talk with strangers.

"I have to talk to her, tell her," David said. "The funeral is day after tomorrow."

"Honey, why don't you let your dad talk to her about it?"

"Why?"

"Well, he's so good with her. He'll know just how to say it."

"You and Dad will drive her down, won't you?"

"Of course, Davey. You go ahead. But before you go, I've got some honey-baked ham and some fresh tomatoes. We'll all have something to eat and we'll feel better."

WITH A COUPLE of hours yet before meeting Emilio Ramirez, Shanahan decided to do a little work for Mrs. Schmidt. Maureen had changed clothes and was unsuccessfully trying to fasten a thin gold chain on her wrist.

"Do this for me?" she asked.

"Here," Shanahan said, taking her hand. "I will if I can see it." After a struggle he finally fastened it. "What's up?"

"I'm showing a house at six."

"You have an hour and a half at least."

"I want to get there and make sure everything's the way it's supposed to be." She looked at him. "All right, I'm nervous. It's the first showing by myself."

"You'll be fine," he said.

"If they want to go F.H.A. I'm sunk. I just learned all the F.H.A. regulations, then they changed them. I don't know any of that shit. Points. It's so damn confusing."

"You'll get back with them on that," Shanahan said.

"What about dinner?"

"I'll get back to you on that."

"No, you won't. There's nothing in the house but brussels sprouts, animal food, a rusted tin of sardines, and fifteen cans of Cuban beans that have been around since before I moved in. What were you doing with fifteen cans of Cuban beans?"

"Before you moved in, dinner was simple. Two choices. One was vermicelli in garlic butter. The other was raw onions, rice, and Cuban beans."

"That was it?"

"Yep."

"What about the frozen brussels sprouts?"

"I hate brussels sprouts."

"Then why did you buy them?"

"I didn't. Elaine did," Shanahan said, starting to feel a little foolish.

"My God! Elaine? As in your wife Elaine?"

Shanahan nodded. "That very Elaine, yes."

"She left thirty years ago, that's what you told me."

"About that. They are very old, very nasty brussels sprouts, Maureen."

"Why didn't you throw them out?"

"I never got around to it."

Shanahan fed the animal while Maureen fussed a few more minutes, trying to make sure she looked "professional."

"Look," she said at the door. "If they make an offer on the house, we'll go out to dinner. Some place nice. Wine. My treat."

"Don't count your commissions before they..."

"Then tonight we'll make love."

He watched her get in her Toyota and drive off. It wasn't the offer of sex that made Shanahan smile. It was nice, yes. But the truth of the matter was that it wasn't the sex, but her sexiness, that quality of being alive—that toss of her auburn hair as she got in the car. That's what made him smile. And that, and nothing else, made life worth living.

Shanahan let Casey back in after his post-dinner backyard romp, tossing the green tennis ball for the canine shortstop a couple of times. He'd cut the length of their afternoon workout, though, because he'd promised Mrs. Schmidt he'd help with Francine. How, he hadn't the foggiest idea.

He'd also managed to screw himself over twice in the same day—telling Mrs. Schmidt he would charge her only fifty bucks a day, when it should have been four times that, and cutting his already paltry day rate in half for Jennifer Bailey, who was, after all, doing the legal work for nothing. Then again, she'd have to pay her usual agency four or five times what she was paying him.

"Malibu Trash" reminded Shanahan of the head shops of the sixties and seventies, minus the drug paraphernalia. They sold albums, new and used. T-shirts. Magazines with names he recognized from Francine's room. And posters with long-haired guys and guitars. The names of the groups were unfamiliar—Slaughter, Megadeth, Def Leppard, Skid Row, Guns N' Roses, Poison, Judas Priest, and one called Every Mother's Nightmare. It was a long way from Duke Ellington and Benny Goodman. This stuff suggested the road to Armageddon. Then again every new generation is characterized as the one going to hell in a hurry.

"It's my grandkid's birthday," Shanahan said to the young, bearded guy behind the register, who looked at him curiously but benignly. Shanahan didn't know what he expected to find here, but it hit him between the eyes as he stood there—a ragged notebook on the counter, right beside the cash register. The page that stared him in the face was half-full of names and addresses, scrawled in various, barely readable handwriting. The mailing list.

"The kid's into heavy metal?" the guy asked.

"Lives for it. The heavier the better."

"Who's he into?"

"I'm not real sure." Shanahan glanced up to one of the posters. "I think I've heard him talk about Motley Crue."

"Not exactly the heaviest," the guy smiled. "But I've got 'em. CDs, records, cassettes? Maybe a T-shirt?"

"That's a good idea. You mind picking out a T-shirt for me?"

"Yeah, okay." The guy moved from behind the counter and began sorting through the rack of black T-shirts.

Shanahan flipped through the pages.

"All I've got is a large," the guy called out.

"Fine, he's a big kid," Shanahan said. "Bingo," he muttered as his eyes focused on the big box letters, "Moogie Swanson." Shanahan memorized the address. Sometimes the work is easy. He hoped he could do as well when he met with Bailey and Emilio Ramirez. Unfortunately, with the purchase of the shirt, he'd just cut into his fifty-dollar fee by ten bucks.

SHANAHAN WAS directed into Jennifer Bailey's conference room. Emilio Ramirez looked up, but didn't stop talking.

"...with their little plastic gloves and little plastic bags and little vacuum cleaners," he was saying.

"This is Dietrich Shanahan," Mrs. Bailey said to the youth. Ramirez stood and extended his hand. "He's helping with the investigation and will have some questions for you. Mr. Shanahan, please sit down. Emilio's apartment has had a thorough going-over by the police."

Emilio Ramirez wasn't what Shanahan had expected. Shanahan had pictured a kind of third-world Hispanic, a thick accent if he spoke English at all, a street tough, a former juvenile delinquent with a dagger tattooed on his arm, a broken-nosed punk for whom boxing was a legal way to vent anger and frustration.

Instead, he found a good-looking young man wearing one of those tennis shirts with a polo player on it. No accent, no tattoos. Even the young Cassius Clay didn't have a face that pretty. Maybe Mrs. Holland had had more than a motherly interest in the boy.

"Nice to meet you," Emilio said. "Thank you for agreeing to work on my case."

"Light heavyweight?" Shanahan asked, sitting down.

"Yeah, but I have to work pretty hard to stay at a hundred seventy-five."

"You training now?"

"Have to. Tomorrow night. At the Sherwood Club."

"What's your record?"

"Nine and O. You follow boxing?"

"On TV." Shanahan was going to tell the kid about boxing in the Army, but changed his mind. Not only was Jennifer Bailey's obviously disgruntled glare over the rim of her glasses an indicator that she thought there were more important topics to cover; Shanahan wasn't sure being a warm and friendly old man was a key to discovering the truth. He'd spare the kid the sports memories.

"We don't know the exact time of Sally Holland's death yet, but let's see if we can account for your time between, say, six p.m. and ten a.m. the following day," Shanahan said, sitting down and opening his notebook.

"I had dinner at six with my trainer, Charley Baker. At maybe eight I got home. I looked at a couple of magazines..."

"Did Charley Baker come back with you?" Jennifer Bailey asked.

"No. I watched TV. I went to bed at nine, maybe nine thirty."

"That early?" the attorney asked.

"I get up at five. Charley comes over and we do a few miles. At four in the morning I got a phone call. This guy—I don't know who—said that Sally wanted to meet me. Right away. I think he called it an emergency. Or he might have just said it was urgent. I got in my car and drove to meet her where this guy asked me to go."

"You didn't recognize the voice?" Shanahan asked.

"No. I didn't know who it was."

"Did you speculate as to whose voice it might have been?"

"No, I didn't. And I didn't think to ask. I was worried about Sally and about what it might have been about."

"What did you think it might have been about?"

"I had no idea."

"So you just obeyed some stranger? Without question?"

"I was asleep when the call came. All kinds of thoughts went through my mind. All I could think of to say was that I'd be there. Then he hung up."

"What kind of relationship did you have with Sally?" Shanahan asked.

"Friends. We are...were friends."

"Emilio...uh...obviously in ordinary circumstances..." Jennifer Bailey was having some problems with the obvious question.

"Were you intimate?" Shanahan interrupted.

"No. Absolutely not. She was married, a mother."

"How did you meet?"

"I know it's odd. A senator's wife and a boxer. We met at a fund-raiser for kids. We talked. We hit it off."

"You had lunches, dinners together, what?" Shanahan continued.

"Yes."

"Late night snacks?"

"Mr. Shanahan..." Jennifer Bailey interrupted.

"Let's all get something straight," Shanahan said. "I don't give a damn about Mr. Ramirez's private life. I don't care if he has intimate relations with a poodle. We've got to know at least what the police know. And I'm sure they've already asked these questions and some tougher ones as well."

"They have," Emilio said. "I met her late in the evening, maybe nine. We enjoyed each other's company. Her husband spent all his time in Washington, and because she didn't like it there, she stayed here. She was lonely. I was lonely." He glanced at Jennifer Bailey.

"What did you talk about?" Shanahan asked.

"Nothing that matters really. Innocent things."

"Innocent things?"

Emilio looked uncomfortable for a moment. The poor-lost-boy look gave way to a cool glare. "There are things between two people that should remain between those two people. Forever."

"If you are arrested, we might have to get back to those innocent things, Emilio."

Jennifer Bailey finally punctuated the long silence that followed. "Where did the man on the phone ask you to go?"

"Butler University. Holcomb Gardens, they call it."

"By the canal, near the river?" Jennifer asked him, but she looked at Shanahan.

"Yes."

"And university security saw you there?" she continued, her look conveying to Shanahan that she knew how serious this was getting.

"Yes, I talked the guy into letting me stay. I kind of...uh...made up a story. I told him I was having trouble with my girl and she was going to meet me there."

Shanahan was speechless. If the police didn't arrest young Emilio, they were fools. It was made to order. It was only a matter of time before the police and university security would hook up. That put Emilio at the scene, if not of the murder site itself, then close to the spot where the body was dumped. The cops wouldn't need a motive now. Hell, they had their pick. The girlfriend story was practically an admission. And Ramirez wouldn't fare any better now by saying it was a lie. Jennifer Bailey knew all this too and tried not to let her feelings show.

"You have a spare key to your apartment?"

"Yeah, a couple."

Shanahan asked, "Who has keys besides you?"

"Only Charley Baker. And the landlord, I guess."

"Can I have one? I'm not sure when I'll get over there. You mind?"

"After the police, who cares? The thing is, you really don't need a key. There's a rear door, up the stairs. They put the lock on backwards and there's a space between the door and frame. Hell, I can use my driver's license to push that little thing in and the door opens." He looked up, this time at Shanahan. He was trying hard not to give anything away, but he looked scared. "I'm looking good for this, aren't I?"

"I don't know," Shanahan said. He didn't know what to make of the kid. "Who knows about anything?"

But the idea that anyone could get in registered. Shanahan didn't bother with the key. Instead, he'd find out just how easy it was.

SEVEN

LYLE BRODY drove his leased, top-of-the-line BMW the few short blocks from his office to the renovated Silk Factory near Lockerbie. He could have walked, but the neighborhood was only half restored. He didn't want to have to look at the down-and-outers who still loitered in alleys or sat on the stoops of buildings with plywood windows and "For Lease" signs. In the past he believed he'd seen more than a touch of menace in the eyes of the transients. Looked as if they were measuring his worth or his ability to defend himself. Or both.

Brody was on his way to visit Jamie Brothewaite, the great granddaughter of drug king Ellis P. Brothewaite. Legal drugs. Ellis P. had founded one of the world's largest pharmaceutical companies, and Jamie, by quirk of being on the right branch of a convoluted family tree and getting the luck of the draw in equally convoluted legal maneuvers, found herself rich. She not only had a chunk of the old man's fortune—a man she never knew—but held voting shares that numbered in the hundreds of thousands.

Like many others who had made fortunes in Indianapolis, Jamie had homes in other places, but finances tied her to the city where the books were kept, the city where a battalion of accountants—corporate, private, and IRS—kept track of funds.

Lyle adjusted the rearview mirror to check his hair. Not good. It was never good. Though he had tried it one night in his apartment, he refused to torture his thinning hair forward. His fear of pain prevented him from going the implant route, and he refused to wear a "toupe," as he called them. He could always tell, he thought. So would others.

So far nothing worked. He could never figure out why it grew everywhere else—on his back, on his butt, on the back of his hands, but not on his head. Brody called 800 numbers, answered magazine ads, and even traveled to Switzerland in search of the "cure."

Once, he'd thought he'd divined his own solution. On a week-long ski trip he discovered that his beard grew less quickly on higher elevations. Less oxygen, he surmised. He was sure the converse was true. More oxygen would stimulate hair growth. Last year every evening for a month he'd sat for three hours wearing a skullcap connected by a hose to an oxygen tank.

Before Brody got out of the car, he patted his hair on the sides and poufed up a few sprigs where he could. It was as good as it was gonna get. He sniffed his lapel and hoped a little air during the walk from the car to the entrance would sap the strength of what he now realized was a too generous splash of Obsession for Men.

Jamie had purchased two of the condo units at the Silk Factory, one on top of the other, and built a stairway between. Lyle was convinced she could have bought the whole damn building and not noticed an appreciable difference in her bank statement. When she answered the door, she said she was on the telephone and suggested he wait in the living room.

He couldn't read anything in her face, but he'd gathered by the brevity of her message when she called that this wasn't to be a frivolous meeting. Perhaps she wanted to offer her condolences. After all, she knew Sally. And David.

Actually, though Lyle didn't know for sure, he'd heard from reliable sources that Jamie Brothewaite knew David Holland very well. Lyle chose to believe it. There was a stack of rumors that implicated Senator David Holland in various trysts. Though never substantiated, the sheer weight, the incredible number of rumors, suggested some of them must be true. Lyle was convinced that his brother-in-law would screw not only for fun but for campaign contributions.

He was also convinced that a wealthy woman like Jamie Brothewaite would contribute big for a toss in the hay with the likes of David Holland and still be able to convince herself she hadn't paid for it.

Lyle walked toward the wall of factory-style windows that looked out over the city. It was 7:00 p.m., but still too early for the sunset. Even so, the skyline view was impressive. A better view than his, and she was only two floors up. "Shit," he said under his breath. The woman never worked a minute in her life. The right goddamn sperm and the right goddamn egg, and she's worth millions.

He looked around. A place with a view like this in New York would cost more than a few mil. Jamie's place cost less than a tenth of that. Then again, you weren't exactly looking out over Manhattan. He sighed.

"I am very sorry about Sally," Jamie said.

He hadn't heard her come in. He looked at her for a moment. She wasn't exactly an attractive woman. While she bought expensive clothes with the most exotic labels, she didn't show them off to their best advantage, choosing styles that would look spectacular on runway models, but something less than that on this slightly horse-faced, horse-buttocked forty-two-year-old.

"Thank you, Jamie. It was all so sudden, so horrible."

"How's David taking it?" Jamie asked turning to an inlaid mahogany cabinet to fix a drink. Lyle could feel the blood rushing to his face and was glad she was occupied and wouldn't notice. "You have talked with him?" she continued.

"Yes. At the funeral home where he washed his hands of any and all arrangements."

"I meant how is his state of mind?" Lyle expected her to hand him the drink, but she took a sip and held on to it.

"I suspect he's more concerned about his reelection, if you want my opinion." Lyle thought about making himself a drink, but he didn't feel that much at home. He went to one of the twin sofas and sat down.

She smiled. "I suppose I did ask for it, didn't I? The opinion, I mean. Don't get too comfortable, Lyle. We have a little problem, you and I. You know the little statues I've laid out two point five million dollars for?"

"Yes. They're on their way, Jamie."

"Is that right. That's not what I'm being told. It seems that this little country in the Middle East somewhere is claiming that they were stolen umpteen hundred years ago. Why did I have to hear that from someone other than you?"

"All of that shit is stolen. Everything in every goddamn museum around the world was pilfered from one place or the other."

"That all may be so," she said. "But this little country is filing suit, and if they win someone will get the statues and someone else will get stiffed. I think that's the word. But then you'd know more about that than I would."

It was then he knew he wasn't going to get laid and that it had nothing to do with his cologne.

"IS THERE another way we can go?" David Holland asked the state trooper who navigated the stretch Lincoln back onto I-69.

"Nothing any quicker, Senator. We can switch over to Twenty-four, go through Wabash and catch Highway Thirty-one near Peru."

The trooper pronounced it "Pee'roo." Eric would've gotten a kick out of it. "Yeah, do that," Holland said. It was boring enough without having to see the same nothingness twice. You get a closer look on the lesser traveled highways.

"I'm from Peeroo," the state trooper said. "So's Cole Porter."

"Cole Porter? I've heard the name," Holland said. Maybe he had, maybe he hadn't, but he didn't want to have an extended conversation. He reached forward, asked the operator to connect him to the hotel, and asked the hotel switchboard for Eric's room.

"Eric Barton," came the voice.

"This is Holland. I want you out of the hotel, and when you get back to Washington, I want you to clear out your office."

"Look, David, I understand what you're going through. I'll resign right after the campaign, but..."

"Now, Eric. I don't want to see your face."

"David, get a grip on it. *After* the campaign. It would be political suicide to..."

Holland hung up. "Wabash then Peeroo, that right, officer?"

"That's right, Senator."

"Good." Senator Holland settled back comfortably in the plush back seat of the limo. It was as quiet as a ride to the cemetery.

LYLE BRODY WAS worried, all right. He thought about the situation all the way to the car. He'd already known about that lousy government over there making its claim; but he didn't know how she knew. Hell, she knew some big-time bankers, and the bitch was probably checking up on him all down the line.

"Serves her right," he said out loud as he pulled out onto the street.

The thing was he didn't know if he could get the money back. The deal had been struck, the money exchanged before the government put their stinking mitts on it. Natural treasure, my ass. Governments, all of them, are just like everybody else. They want it back so they can sell it. Confiscate. Don't pay a cent. Maybe he could get some of it back.

He smiled. He'd get his commission from the sellers. "Up her butt," he said, laughing.

Lyle Brody knew he'd be all right. Financially at any rate—even if the art deal hadn't come along. No, he wouldn't be having regular lunches at the Skyline Club, and he probably couldn't afford to get in the Meridian Hills Country Club. Couldn't meet the annual dues, let alone the initiation fees. But he was getting seventy-five grand a year sitting on his duff, wasn't he? Every year for the next fifteen, unless the chain outfit from New Jersey that bought his Cajun restaurant went belly up. Unless that happened, the check would arrive on the first of the month sure as the sun comes up in the morning.

There'd be other deals. Of course, it couldn't be a restaurant. That was part of the agreement with the Jersey folks. He could start a nightclub or something. A show bar. Wouldn't that embarrass the hell out of David Holland.

Brody shrugged. If he couldn't be in with the rich and powerful as an art dealer, then fuck, he'd rub tits with some gorgeous babes at some exclusive strip or lingerie club.

No. No. Brady shook his head. No, that's not what he wanted, goddamnit. He wanted a little respect. He was tired of being a toad.

He drove his car up the ramp that led to the parking area for his apartment building, took a couple of curves into the shade of the garage, and pulled his BMW into its assigned space.

THE AFTERNOON newspaper Shanahan picked up on the way home had a brief article on the front page stating, in effect, that the Indianapolis Police Department was working on "solid leads in the brutal slaying" of Sally Holland. There were, however, no suggestions of an impending arrest and absolutely no mention of Emilio Ramirez. That was all there was on the murder.

However, there was a major story, above the fold, with large side-by-side color portraits of Edmund Carem and David Holland, that ran under the headline: "What Now in Senate Race?" The gist of the story was whether or not Senator David Holland would withdraw in light of the tragedy. The color photographs were slightly out of register, reminding Shanahan of trying to look at 3-D without the funny glasses.

Eric Barton, who was described as Holland's senior aide and close friend, apparently tried to dispel the rumor. "In remarks to the press late last night, Barton said that the tragedy, more than anything else, points up the need for strong leadership in the battle to preserve traditional American values." There were no quotes from the senator himself.

The reporter raised the question whether Edmund Carem's "struggling and financially strapped campaign" would be helped or hindered by "recent events."

Carem reiterated his current moratorium on campaign commercials, saying, "I think I will forgo politics as usual and merely extend our heartfelt condolences to Senator Holland, who is trying to deal with one of life's great tragedies."

Robert Silvers, former prosecutor, now Indianapolis mayor, who pundits continually speculated would make a run at either the governor's office or any available senate seat, indicated this wasn't the time to address whether or not he would be a willing substitute should Holland decide to withdraw.

Inside, the newspaper gave a full-page story, virtually a eulogy, to Sally Holland, and a small, gray-toned sidebar outlined her civic interests.

Shanahan was surprised to learn that the conservative senator's wife had been involved in groups and organizations that seemed at odds with the senator's reputed agenda. She was concerned about whales, solar energy, rain forests, and world hunger. Sally Holland was decidedly against nuclear energy and anything at all having to do with the military industrial complex.

He also noted that besides David Holland and their daughter, Elizabeth, the only survivor listed was a brother, Lyle Brody.

While Maureen buzzed around in her worn terry-cloth robe, trying to get ready for her celebration dinner—an offer was made on the house and Maureen was counting her chickens—Shanahan turned to the sports page. There was nothing on Ramirez and tomorrow night's boxing match at the Sherwood Club. He looked at the National League standings to check out how farfetched it would be for the Chicago Cubs to take the division. Chicago was playing a night game, again at San Francisco. If they got back from dinner early enough, the two of them could catch most of it.

For someone who usually had plenty of time on his hands, Shanahan figured he was going to be real busy for a while. He couldn't forget Mrs. Schmidt's problems. So, in addition to checking out this "Moogie" kid, Shanahan also wanted to go over Emilio's place and later talk with Charley Baker. If anybody knows what a boxer is made of, it's his trainer.

"How 'bout a movie afterward?" Maureen asked as she breezed through the living room to find her purse. "Something sexy, to get us in the mood?" She leaned down, kissed him on the cheek, and ran away.

Shanahan thought he caught a waft of gardenia in her wake. He loved gardenias. He also figured there'd be no baseball tonight. Then again, it wasn't unusual for a Cubs game to go the marathon route and keep its fans up until the team lost in the eighteenth inning.

"I don't need a movie," he said. "Where are we dining this evening, Mrs. Smith?"

"Japanese, is that all right? I didn't want anything too heavy."

Shanahan folded up the paper and went out in the backyard to toss the tennis ball for Casey in the dying light.

He tossed the ball way up, over the treetops. He watched as the dog settled in under it.

God, Shanahan thought, if he catches it, it'll go right down his throat.

EIGHT

SENATOR HOLLAND had his bags brought from the hotel to the house. The governor had kindly provided three shifts of security, two state policemen for each eight hours. They would keep away gawkers, reporters, and other undesirables. The telephone company also cooperated, and Holland had a new unlisted number which he gave to his parents and the mortuary. Nobody else.

The house on North Pennsylvania Street seemed both immense and immensely quiet. He had second thoughts about firing Eric if for no other reason than that he was a great person to yell at. Holland went to the kitchen, poured himself a glass of diet Coke. He looked out of the window at the golden light of sunset. Beyond and barely discernible behind the sturdy pines was a rooftop and a window of blinking bluish light.

The real estate agents had referred to it as the "Carriage House," but that was pretentious. Built in the thirties, long after the demise of carriages and buggies, this was merely a three-car garage with an upstairs apartment.

It was Byron Jaegar's apartment, which he had rent-free in exchange for looking after the grounds and keeping a watchful, protective eye on Sally and Elizabeth. Though Holland had agreed to hire Jaegar four years ago when there was more than a little talk about David and the vice presidency, the senator rarely talked with the man.

All he knew was that Jaegar was a former secret service agent, retired early because of a bad heart, that he had a pension, that he didn't need a salary. Holland knew that Jaegar wasn't married, that he was the kind of private, unambitious guy who was more than content to live quietly over someone's garage.

Jaegar had talked with the police. He had heard, seen nothing on the night of Sally's death. He went to bed early, he said. He always went to bed early.

"You get what you pay for," Holland said out loud. He went through the rooms of the house. They were barely familiar. It was as if they belonged to some occasionally visiting aunt. A piece of furniture, a painting, and a few sentimental items were from the home they had in Fort Wayne when he was a congressman, but Sally had given most of the furniture to the Salvation Army when they moved to Indianapolis, where Sally grew up.

Though they agreed on the move, they did so for different reasons. Sally wanted to be near Lyle, her only living relative, something David found strange because they didn't appear to be very close. Hell, they didn't seem to like each other. For David, Indianapolis meant better airline connections, a larger media market, and a chance to expand the campaign contribution base.

The fact is that during his tenure as senator, David did little more than sleep over after some political function of some pressing social—meaning potentially financial—engagement. Instead, Holland found that the real power and money were to be found inside the Washington beltway, though the national press did little more than ignore him, favoring the senior senator from Indiana, who presided over the higher profile committees.

Holland continued his tour through the bedrooms upstairs. There, in Elizabeth's room, he discovered that his daughter was a reader—that she was fascinated by Egypt and King Arthur. There was a whole collection of illustrated classics, books he remembered he was supposed to read in school but had found boring. Instead of reading them, he'd paraphrase chubby little Howard Whitaker's book reports.

Holland found his daughter's thick diary. In the suddenness of her departure, she'd left it open on her small pale-blue desk. Her handwriting was small, compressed and without margins. He sat on his daughter's bed and began to look through the diary. He'd glanced at it before. But there were, no doubt, more current entries.

Elizabeth sounded so adult for a ten-year-old, he thought as he rummaged almost idly through the pages. Then he saw the phrase, "mother's friend, Emilio." He stared at the name for a while, then moved on. He turned on the light by the bed and lay back. She'd written quite a bit more since last he'd looked at it.

ON THE DRIVE to Sakura's, the Japanese restaurant on Keystone Avenue, Maureen started talking about Harmony, how great his loft space was, how he reminded her of the early sixties, and how, if she were twenty again, she'd fall madly in love with him.

"Yeah, that's great, Maureen, but your little flower child has made life difficult. Technically I'm withholding evidence, and if Rafferty wants to, he can pull my ticket to the golden years."

Maureen was quiet.

At the restaurant Maureen ordered sushi.

"Adventurous," he said. He ordered the large bottle of Asahi and agedashi dofu, an appetizer of braised tofu and seaweed. Maureen looked at him approvingly until he finished off by ordering chicken teriyaki.

"Chicken teriyaki?" she asked in tortured disbelief when the waiter left. "We drove all the way over here so you could have chicken teriyaki?"

"Don't be a snob, Maureen. The fact is we are eight hundred miles from the Atlantic and twenty-five-hundred miles from the Pacific. The last I heard, no one had caught a tuna in White River.''

''I'm sorry. I just wanted things to be exotic. I don't know whether I am supposed to tell you this.'' She paused, still debating about whether to go ahead. ''In June Harmony happened to be somewhere where he shouldn't have been and he did something he shouldn't have done.''

''Go on.''

''The police were arresting some guy, and Harmony said they were beating the hell out of him. Harmony had his camera with him and videotaped it. One of the cops saw him, and he had to talk pretty fast just to keep his camera. They took the tape.''

''Okay...''

''Harmony went to the police station and filled out a report stating what he saw. He said everybody there was pretty decent to him and said they'd look into it. He thought everything would be fine, but then he started seeing a police car around his place. At first he thought he was just paranoid until one day the car pulled up beside him and he saw the cops who took his tape. One of them said, 'Hi, kid. Taken any good pictures lately?' ''

''Pretty scary stuff,'' Shanahan said sarcastically.

''The other one alluded to the fact that Harmony lived in a pretty rough neighborhood—that he should be careful where he walked and make sure he locked up real good when he went to bed at night.''

''I see,'' Shanahan said.

''He called the police the next day and said that he'd changed his mind about the report. I think he thought you'd think he was chicken or something.''

Later, when the waiter brought the food, Maureen looked at her food a little anxiously. ''Look, Shanahan,'' she said, ''there are at least twenty-five Japanese eating sushi in here, so it must be all right.''

"Sure," Shanahan said, "unless they were all born in Ohio."

AFTER DINNER Maureen begged off Shanahan's offer to stop by Harry's tavern, saying she wanted to keep "the mood." Indeed, she had apparently found a cassette of Japanese music which she put on as Shanahan climbed into bed.

"What's this?"

"Now, what we do," she said, sliding in beside him, curling her leg over his thigh and letting her hand slide across and then down his chest, "is this." Her hand slid lower. "We are someone in the mountains, near Kyoto. I am a Japanese princess and you are a handsome navy lieutenant."

"I'm too old to be a lieutenant . . ."

"Look, Shanahan, I'm not even sure there are princesses in Japan. Okay? You can be a goddamn general for all I care."

"Admiral. Navies don't have generals."

"Shut up," she said. There was the slightest taste of plum wine as her lips touched his. He felt her breasts pressing against his chest. He could feel himself respond to the warmth of her body, the caresses of her fingers.

A lieutenant, sure. A handsome young navy lieutenant. Why not? he thought.

IT WAS nearly eleven when Holland finished Elizabeth's diary. He closed it, tossed it on the bed as he got up. Three things disturbed him, one of them his daughter's delicate hand forming the word "Emilio." The second was more upsetting. He had been struck by the fact that he had had absolutely no idea who his daughter really was—what she liked, disliked, what she believed in—nothing, before he began reading her diary. The third and most startling realization was that in all those words, all those pages, Elizabeth never once mentioned her father. About that he had very mixed feelings.

It was dark now, and the flashing light of Jaegar's TV blinked somewhere on the periphery of his vision. He looked out of Elizabeth's window. He could see Jaegar through the window, apparently asleep, arm dangling at his side, looking a little uncomfortable in the recliner.

The poor schmuck, Holland thought. A real exciting life this guy must lead. Falls asleep watching TV. Sally would have been better off with a Doberman—hell, a Lhasa Apso.

Holland went to his and Sally's bedroom, then decided he didn't want to sleep in there. He went down the hall to the guest bedroom, talking himself out of a glass of Scotch. He'd been good so far. No need to botch it now. It was important to have a clear head. He realized that he hadn't eaten all day, even turning down Mom's honey-baked ham in Fort Wayne. He wasn't hungry then. He wasn't hungry now. Why should he eat?

"YOU ASLEEP?" Maureen's voice sounded like velvet in the darkness.

"Nope."

"It's only eleven. You suppose the game's still on?"

"I don't think they carry the game over here on the mountaintops of Kyoto. Besides, it's already tomorrow here."

"Are you sure it's not yesterday instead?"

"If it's yesterday, then we've already seen the game."

It was too late to object. She'd pointed the little plastic box toward the set and clicked. The room lit up in a burst of gray light.

"Okay, okay." He sat up, fluffed the pillows up behind his back. "Wait a minute," he told her as she was about to change from the news on the local channel to Chicago's WGN on cable. "Turn up the volume."

A picture of Senator David Holland was in the little backlit frame behind the newscaster.

"In a move triggering renewed speculation about the withdrawal of David Holland from the senate race, acting campaign manager, aide, and close friend Eric Barton has apparently resigned, this according to sources close to the campaign. Mr. Barton refused to confirm or deny the rumors, saying only that he was returning to his home in Washington and wasn't sure how long he would need to take care of what he would refer to only as personal matters."

Shanahan took the remote from Maureen and switched on the Cubs game.

"What's going on?" Maureen asked.

"It's getting curiouser and curiouser." The Cubs announcer was saying the game was already two hours old and they were only in the fifth inning. The score was 13 to 9 in favor of San Francisco. "Looks like we missed the fireworks," Shanahan said.

"Did we really?" she asked.

HOLLAND HAD absolutely no idea what time it was when he woke. It was still dark. Traces of dream lingered, however. His father was playing a trumpet and Elizabeth was dancing. Holland was trying to get her to stop, but she couldn't see him. He called out to his father, who continued to play the trumpet. They were dead or he was dead. That's all he could remember.

He was wide-awake. He got out of bed and, still in his boxer shorts, went downstairs to the kitchen. He thought maybe a glass of milk or some cereal might help him get back to sleep. In the dark, as he entered the kitchen, he was struck by the eerie blue light in the window. It was coming from behind the pines. He moved closer to the window. At first he was relieved. It was only Jaegar's TV. He looked at the clock on the stove. Nearly 5:00 a.m.

People often went to sleep with the television on, didn't they, waking up either by the sound of static or morning programming? He poured himself a glass of milk and went back to the window.

He put down the glass, went through the pantry and out the side door. A fingernail moon in the clear sky lit the drive surprisingly well. He walked slowly toward the garage. Perhaps it was merely a reaction to the gruesome days or the unusual dream, but a strange feeling crept over him. He could feel the outer edges of his vision grow dark as his eyes focused on the one open garage door. Once inside, he moved to the stairway, up the wooden stairs. Holland felt a sudden cold. He was chilling. There was a sudden tingling in the center of his forehead.

Through an instinct he would never be able to explain, Holland knew there was absolutely no need to knock.

NINE

AFTER TALKING WITH the state policemen parked in front of his home, David Holland walked back up the drive. The warm blacktop was still soft and glowed as if there were light beneath it.

Holland glanced up at the moon. He hadn't been aware of such a clear night since he was Elizabeth's age. Fantasy days then. Fantasy nights. A very slight breeze stroked a few stray wisps of hair. "King Arthur," he said, smiling and thinking of Elizabeth, and then of himself at ten when things were important, worthwhile—when good and bad were simpler constructs.

"No compromises," he said out loud and laughed. Then he felt a wave of shame and sadness. He was drowning. Pulled under.

He wasn't sure how long he stood there looking at the sky. He wasn't even sure what he had been thinking when bright headlights nearly blinded him and the sounds of car doors slamming brought him crashing back to reality, a world lit in red and blue lights. The almost mystical spell of the quiet night was shattered, and for a moment Holland felt he had been transported to the great Las Vegas strip.

"DON'T YOU EVER wear any clothes?" Shanahan asked a bleary-eyed Harmony at eight thirty in the morning.

Harmony, standing there in his underwear, wiped the long, stray strands of brown hair away from his eyes. "I put these on to answer the door," he said. "You never know, it might be a Jehovah's Witness."

At the far end of the room, there was someone lying in the rumpled sheets of Harmony's bed. The body moved, wrapped itself in a sheet, and scurried away.

Harmony looked at the ghostlike figure nervously, then back at Shanahan. "I always thought somebody ought to get the addresses of every Jehovah's Witness in town and knock on their doors early in the morning."

"I've got a couple of questions," Shanahan said.

"Okay," Harmony said. "I'll get my robe. Mary can make us some coffee."

Then it dawned on Shanahan who this apparition was. Mary was Harry's granddaughter. He'd met her twice at the bar and knew that she and Harmony planned to marry. He wondered if Harry knew they were sleeping together. Didn't matter. Friends or no friends, Shanahan wouldn't be the one to tell him. And what were he and Maureen doing if not shacking up?

"So ask me," Harmony said as he and Shanahan sat at an old chrome and formica kitchen table, the kind people were giving to Goodwill ten years ago and the kind people were clamoring to find these days. Shanahan didn't like them then. He wasn't too fond of them now, but it seemed to fit in with Harmony's strange but appealing sense of decor.

"So tell me. But first, Maureen told me why you didn't want to call the police. I don't blame you. Unfortunately, we might have to disclose that to keep me from losing my license. I say 'might.'"

"I don't want you to get in trouble."

"Why you were there?" Shanahan asked.

"I made it in the microwave, hope you don't mind, Mr. Shanahan," Mary said, bringing in three cups of coffee and sitting down with them.

"It's fine. Nice to see you again."

"I look horrible in the morning."

"I'm sorry to wake you. I probably should have called, but I didn't have the number and I was on my way somewhere else when I decided to stop by and talk with Harmony."

"Should I go in the other room?" she asked.

"Not on my account," Shanahan said.

"No, not at all," Harmony said, pressing his palm on her wrist. "I'm making a music video, Mr. Shanahan. What I mean is I'm making a video and a local rock group is providing the music. It's a project for them, actually. I spent my freshman and sophomore years at Butler, and that area seemed to fit my idea for the visuals. That's why I was down by the river. And why I had the video equipment."

"Can I see it? What you taped?" Shanahan asked.

"You mean the part where I taped the body?"

"All of it, if you don't mind."

"No, I don't mind. We can watch it and I'll make a copy of it for you at the same time. You have a VCR?"

"Yeah."

"VHS or Beta?"

"I don't know."

"Well, I'll make a copy anyway."

The three of them moved to another part of the room.

"How long is it?"

"Twenty minutes altogether. I need to shoot some more, but I didn't want to go back out there."

They watched in silence, and when it was done, something troubled Shanahan. The images that Harmony had captured before discovering the body in the water were disconcerting. More than disconcerting, Shanahan sensed something ominous, frightening, something strangely dark in the bright August noon.

"Tell Mr. Shanahan what the name of the song is," Mary said in the quiet moments that followed the close-up of Sally Holland's nude, floating body.

Harmony was quiet. It was apparent to Shanahan that this wasn't something the young man would have volunteered. "'Meet Your Maker,'" Harmony said.

"Isn't that ironic?" Mary asked the two of them.

SHANAHAN HADN'T BEEN to Woodruff Place in many years, though, in fact, it wasn't far from where he lived. Woodruff Place, where Emilio lived, was an area of once-fine upper-middle-class homes that consisted of three long, wide streets, each with a grass median broad enough for fountains and statues. The fountains, Shanahan guessed, no longer worked. And the statues had been painted white to halt the already visible effects of age and acid rain.

The house he hunted for was on Middle Drive. It was a large yellow-brick home in want of a little care. In front, however, there were flowers, colorful dahlias and a few other annuals, which indicated that someone was not opposed to starting fresh every spring. Because there was a "C" beside the street number on the little sheet of paper Emilio had given him, it was clear the house had been divided into at least three apartments.

Shanahan went in the front entrance, saw the buzzer marked "Emilio Ramirez," and pressed the button. When there was no answer, Shanahan went around to the back. He was curious about this trick back door.

From his discussion with Emilio, Shanahan surmised he needed to climb the outdoor stairway. Once at the top, he was shielded from the sun by cheap wooden latticework, which would have easily hidden someone maneuvering a body out. And with a car, pulled up to the bottom of the stairs, one could dump a body into a trunk without being seen. Especially in the dark.

At the top of the stairs there was a door, the top half of which was glass. Shanahan could see the kitchen. He knocked again, then tried to turn the knob. Emilio was telling the truth. Shanahan didn't even have to use a credit card. All he had to do was jiggle the door with some force and it opened.

He was now inside the apartment of Emilio Ramirez, and he took a quick tour. It wasn't much of a place. The kitchen was the main room, though it obviously had been an upstairs screened porch originally. There was a small cranny for Emilio's bed behind the kitchen, and a bathroom with a tub, commode, and sink—all different colors and from different eras. Probably from a salvage yard.

The floors of all the rooms were covered in linoleum that was supposed to look like brick. There was a long, narrow, dark hallway, which led to the other entrance. Shanahan opened the door and found the main hall to the upstairs of the house itself, probably also subdivided into God knows what configurations.

He wondered what the police investigators had seen. Apparently, not much, because Emilio was still free. Of course running lab tests on the contents of the vacuum bags would take a while. Shanahan took the small tour of Emilio's place again, looking into the shelves above the bed. Underwear, socks, T-shirts. Nothing unusual.

The bathroom was clean and orderly. Nothing beyond the usual shaving cream, deodorant, toothpaste, mouthwash, aspirin, and a few salves and whatever for aching muscles. Nothing unusual.

The kitchen was the living room, after all. Aside from a fairly neat countertop and some small cupboards—housing very little food, just staples like salt, sugar, and a box of Rice Krispies—it wasn't much of a kitchen either. Obviously the boy ate out.

The refrigerator was small, so small that it rested on a countertop. It was a bar fridge or a cabin fridge. Inside was a half gallon of milk, two packages of butter, Heinz ketchup, Miracle Whip, and some assorted fruit.

The kitchen table would sit two comfortably, though he doubted sitting on the folding chairs would be really comfortable. He imagined Emilio sitting in the well-worn chintz overstuffed chair by the window. A floor lamp stood guard beside it. So did a blond veneered cocktail table, which supported a whole stack of books and magazines.

The magazines were predictable: *Ring* and assorted other boxing magazines. The books, however, were not so predictable. A quick perusal showed that each was related to the Catholic faith in some way. Shanahan opened up a book called *Ancient Fears, Autobiography of a Zen Seminarian* and read the opening paragraph, the last lines of which were:

I have been silent, diligent and spend nearly every waking hour in prayer. Yet, though I have been taught He is a loving God, there is clearly hate in my soul. I sense it in the silence, when the only sound I can hear is the violent hammer blows of my heart against my ribcage. It is as if this blood-gorged muscle seeks to escape its bony cell and consummate its passion upon God Himself.

What troubled Shanahan was not so much that passage, pretty circumstantial evidence of the state of Emilio's mind—soul maybe—but the fact that there was little else. No letters. No pictures of Mom or Dad. Indeed there were no *Playboy* magazines, no TV listings, though there was a small black-and-white TV and a telephone. There was no stereo or radio, however. There was nothing unusual in Emilio's belongings; it was hardly normal to have nothing unusual. Boxing and religion. That was it.

As he went back down the stairs, something else bothered Shanahan besides the sudden, oppressive heat.

There were no boxing trophies, no belts, ribbons, or scrapbooks. Didn't the kid have an ego?

IT WAS quicker to stop by Harry's place than home. It was nearly 11:00 a.m.; and Harry was setting up for what usually amounted to a pretty paltry lunch crowd.

"You want a corn dog, Deets?"

"Can't say that I do." Shanahan looked up. Geraldo Rivera's face was four feet tall on the TV above the jukebox.

"Try one. I've just added it to the menu."

"You're not cutting out the Lobster Rockefeller, are you?"

"You never know," Harry said.

"No. I never do. Can I use your phone?"

"Well, Mr. Hoity Toity, it's *may* I use your phone."

"If I had one, I wouldn't be asking to use yours," Shanahan said, going behind the counter and pulling out Jennifer Bailey's card. "By the way, you can forget the Mister, just call me Hoity." Shanahan held the card under one of the bar lights but couldn't make out the number on the card.

Harry took off his glasses and handed them to Shanahan. "Look through the bottom of the lens, Hoity."

"It's dark in here."

"No, you're going blind. You're no spring chicken. Get you some glasses. They got 'em at the drugstore for ten bucks. Here, gimme that." Harry read the numbers.

Shanahan dialed. The secretary said that Jennifer Bailey was out. He left the number of Harry's place.

"If you're settin' up shop here, you can help pay the rent."

"You watch that crap, Harry?" Shanahan asked, nodding to the television.

"Deets, that's the most fascinatin' thing ever. It's crazy, man."

"Man? Who have you been hanging out with?"

"Used to be when I was a kid you didn't talk about the things they talk about now in polite company. I mean my mother never even knew what 'transvestite' meant. She would have thought it was a brand of luggage. I'm hooked, Deets. Hooked on Geraldo, on Donahue, on Oprah. I'm gettin' real sensitive to women's needs, you know?"

There was a glimmer in Harry's eyes that meant he wasn't exactly searching for sensitivity but the right words to say to appear sensitive.

"You ought to be real sensitive by now. You've had five wives. You watching the soap operas too?"

"No soaps, Deets. I swear. But it does get lonely around here sometimes."

That was the closest Harry ever came to self-pity. Shanahan wondered if the gregarious soul had made a mistake in buying Delaney's old bar. "You have today's paper?"

Harry tossed it on the counter. "This ain't a library," he said, recovering from his moment of weakness.

"No, the library probably has some customers. How about a cup of coffee?"

Shanahan took the paper and the coffee to a booth by the window, one bathed in a wide swath of light. Perusing the paper, Shanahan found no indication of an arrest in the Holland case. In fact, there was no front-page story. He thumbed back through the pages and after checking the ball score—having fallen asleep while the Cubs and Giants were tied in the fourteenth inning— found a tiny story buried—or perhaps a hasty, last-minute insertion—at the bottom of the local news.

All he could think when he saw it was "curiouser and curiouser."

Byron Jaegar, 55, was found dead early this morning in the carriage house behind the residence of
Senator David Holland. Police say Holland reported the death at 4:47 this morning to the state
police, who were providing the senator with security. The state police reported it to the Indianapolis
Police Department.

Holland, troubled by the recent and brutal death
of his wife, told police that he did not know Jaegar
personally, but that he had rented the small apartment over the garage for about two years. Police are
investigating, but believe the man died of natural
causes.

Shanahan turned to the obituaries. Though Sally Holland had had quite a spread in yesterday's paper, she was
nonetheless listed today along with the appropriate times
and places of the funeral. There was also encourage-
ment to skip the flowers and make a donation to an Indiana wildlife organization.

"Harry, I'm going to need your help," Shanahan
called out to Harry, who was wiping the empty bar for
the third time.

"What's new?"

"We've got to break into a house tomorrow afternoon."

"Easy for you, but I've got a bar to run. You'll have
to find somebody else to play with."

"There isn't anybody else," Shanahan said, then realized how to hook him. That was one of the benefits of
working with somebody off and on for nearly fifty years.
Shanahan knew Harry was a sucker for celebrities. "I'm
working on the murder of Sally Holland."

"No, you're not," Harry said, rounding the bar in a
real hurry and heading toward Shanahan's booth.

"Yes, I am."

"You think you can get Maureen to watch over this place?"

"Maybe," Shanahan said, smiling.

TEN

Feeling as if he was getting somewhere, finally, Shanahan grabbed the telephone and called Maureen.

"You want to see a fight?"

"Not right now, I'm busy. Just don't get hurt."

"Boxing. Tonight."

"Tonight?"

"You'll like it. Lots of sweaty young men in shorts."

"That's the good part, but the bad part is that they beat the hell out of each other," she said.

"Also, do you have time to watch the bar for Harry for about two hours tomorrow afternoon?"

"I don't have a bartender's license and I can't make exotic drinks."

"I doubt if it's a capital offense, and Harry doesn't allow exotic drinks anyway. All you have to do is pour whiskey and open beers."

"What's this all about?"

"Harry and I are going to pay a visit to the Holland household while the senator is at his wife's funeral."

"Oh, God," she said weakly. "If I take the bar gig, do I have to go to the fight?"

"No, of course not. You don't have to do anything."

Shanahan glanced up at the television. There was a whole row of long-haired rockers on Geraldo's step-up stage. "You really don't want to go tonight, do you?"

"I'm sorry."

"It's fine. I'll probably be running late so you'll be going solo on dinner. I have a possible date with Moogie and Francine."

"Good."

"Good?" He'd expected "Who."

"I've got a quart of Häagen-Dazs Vanilla Swiss Almond, and I wasn't keen on sharing."

SHANAHAN DECIDED he was truly a dinosaur. What other fool would sit in an automobile without air conditioning in ninety-degree heat and wait for some kid he wouldn't recognize to come out of a house he might not be in. This was not what made good investigators, let alone rich investigators.

"C'mon, Moogie, come out, come home, do something."

He was glad he hadn't brought Casey along. This oven was no place for a dog.

That exhilarated feeling he'd had at Harry's was slipping into depression. He began to doubt he could help Jennifer Bailey in what was not only a serious murder case, but a hopeless one at that. What Shanahan was, he thought, was a mom-and-pop investigator without the mom, much more suited to the trials and tribulations of elderly women concerned about their granddaughters' choice of boyfriends.

The real professionals had long since developed high-tech surveillance—bugging, wiretapping, microphones that when properly directed could pick up conversations miles away. Through windows and walls. The world was going electronic and Shanahan wasn't. Simple as that.

He never was a surveillance expert anyway. That was Harry's specialty. But Harry was pretty long in the tooth and hopelessly behind in the world of electronics. Mom and pop, definitely. The only thing he was any good at was snooping around somebody's house. You got a measure of a person's character, beliefs, interests. While it rarely provided the essential evidence, it often told him where else to look, whom to talk to.

There, he felt better, but not good enough to want to continue the murder case. This involved a U.S. senator, for God's sake, and Emilio, guilty or not—and Shanahan thought he probably was—deserved someone with better investigative resources.

Shanahan had just turned on the radio when he saw a skinny kid in a black leather jacket come out of the house and get into a '57 Ford. Could be Moogie, could be Moogie's brother. Could be anybody.

The car, in good condition, seemed to have been primed for a paint job and left that way. A dull matte gray with darkened windows, it looked like something out of *The Road Warrior,* a movie Shanahan now remembered Maureen had walked out on.

Shanahan followed the car from Dearborn and Michigan north and into Broad Ripple Village, a place where the vestige of punk, new age, and otherwise trendy mingled, oblivious to each other. He followed the car back into the village itself, where old homes had been converted into feminist bookstores, interior design shops, and travel agencies.

The possible Moogie pulled his car into the parking lot of "Second Time Around," a small video and record shop across from a new brew pub. Shanahan waited a few minutes, then went in. There was a counter, some unslick magazines Shanahan guessed were about rock 'n' roll, and a few T-shirts.

The guy behind the counter was drawing something on a big white pad and didn't bother to look up. Shanahan went through the doorway and found rows of videotape boxes with numbers on them. The guy he followed was looking through the records that occupied bins in one corner of the room. Shanahan managed to get a little better look. About five feet nine, black hair, spiked on top, nothing on the sides but ears, and at least one of those pierced.

Shanahan wandered along the rows of videos. While he recognized a few movie titles, most were lost on him. Some, he discovered, were French, German, or Italian. There were rows of forties' and fifties' horror and sci-fi films with lurid images on the covers. Many of the others were music videos, and he recognized some of the names from his venture into Malibu Trash earlier.

Shanahan hung around the door when the dark-haired kid was leaving.

"Hey, Moog," the guy behind the counter said, "I heard you guys were recording next Tuesday."

"Yeah, if we can get Dizzy to make up his fuckin' mind."

Shanahan was sure the kid wasn't talking about Dizzy Dean, let alone Dizzy Gillespie. He heard the door shut, waited a couple of counts, and followed. When his now-confirmed "Moogie" went into a place called Future Shock, Shanahan decided to end his stakeout and go home. He'd definitely stand out in a shop that looked as if it specialized in stud bracelets and T-shirts with skulls on them.

Shanahan looked at his watch. He could be home by 6:00 p.m., then he'd call Jennifer Bailey and let her know she should hook up with someone else. He was pretty sure she'd be there. She wasn't the nine-to-five type.

LYLE BRODY stood in front of the mirror in his bedroom. Should he wear a black suit or merely a dark one to the funeral tomorrow? Maybe his gray Boss suit. The funeral was in the afternoon. If it were winter, he could wear a turtleneck. Maybe he'd better wear a tie. He *was* family. And the press would be there. He imagined a photograph in *USA Today* that would include him, the senator, and the little girl. He went to the closet and took the gray coat off its hanger.

Connie Blakely hadn't confirmed she'd go with him to the funeral. "The bitch!" he said out loud, and nearly ripped the jacket taking it off. He wasn't tan enough to pull off gray. He didn't like Connie anyway. The two of them had different ideas about the meaning of oral sex. She always talked when they were fucking. More than once he was tempted to put a pillow over her head.

He pulled another suit coat out of the closet. It was black. He'd gotten it at Barney's in New York, and he kind of liked it when he reached inside for his wallet and the label would get noticed. He looked in the mirror again. It didn't make him look any better and maybe it was too black, too evening wear. Could he tone it down with a blue shirt?

He wished he could have gotten more sun or was more disciplined about going to the tanning studio. What was it that Onassis said: Never use your own money, pay it back on time, and always have a tan. Maybe that wasn't it exactly, but it was close—at least the part about the tan.

Brody searched through his ties. What color should he wear to a funeral, for God's sake? Black probably. Holland wouldn't have this problem. He'd have his aide call some fucking protocol broad or something, the bastard. He'd leave it all up to them. He hated Holland, and he wasn't too happy with the drug heiress either. Would she dare come to the funeral? "Yes, she would," he said to the mirror as he held up first one tie, then another. "C'mon, Connie," Lyle said out loud, "I want that Jamie bitch to see your tits."

Now he couldn't get Jamie Brothewaite out of his mind. That fucking business with the statues. She could afford to lose the dough. He couldn't. Then again, if that fucking government did sue, it'd be national news, international news. *The New York Times!* He laughed. "The fucking *London Times!*"

Lyle was elated. He could figure out tomorrow morning what he should wear. He went to his Rolodex and looked up the number of the tanning parlor.

DAVID HOLLAND was startled by the telephone. It hadn't rung since he'd been in the house. He hadn't heard a sound since last night's clamor in the driveway.

It was the President's chief of staff.

"First, David, let me express our condolences here at the White House...."

"I know. I know."

"Hey, it's okay. I just wanted to tell you that the vice president will be there for the funeral."

"Good. He can serve the punch."

"Just promise to be civil. I've been asked to ask you if you've reached a decision on the campaign."

"I'm not making promises," Holland said, "and I'm not making decisions."

"David, I know a doctor. I can have him out there in a couple of hours. Give you something to steady your nerves."

"Yeah, I'll bet." Holland hung up.

"DO I LOOK PITIFUL?" Maureen asked. She was sitting on the sofa in the living room. Weird voices, strange sounds, and the classical music background of cartoons blasted from the bedroom. Before her was a quart of ice cream, actually just the carton, which contained only a shiny spoon.

"Yes. You do."

"Good."

"The prospect of a night without your navy lieutenant do that to you, Princess Ming?"

She smiled. "That's Chinese, I think. No. It is the prospect of utter and complete doom. The new and fickle world of real estate, Shanahan. The sellers rejected the offer of the buyers, and the buyers didn't want to counter. A thousand tiny dollars separated them.''

"What did you expect? To make a sale the first time out?"

"No. I expected to cry a little and then you'd come and put your arms around me and say something like 'There, there, my darling.'"

"You really expected that?" Shanahan said. "From me?"

"No. Not really. Casey already consoled me, and for two spoonsful of ice cream even Einstein pretended to care." She got up from the sofa and took the empty carton to the kitchen. "What's new with you?"

"Well, I've located Moogie, but I have no idea what to do next."

"That's good. Who's Moogie?"

Shanahan followed her into the kitchen and explained. "I'm also thinking about suggesting Jennifer Bailey hire someone else on the Holland murder."

"Why?"

"This is a big case, an important one, and I don't think she needs an old fogie who's ten—hell, twenty—years behind the times to muck it up for her." He poured about two fingers' worth of J. W. Dant bourbon into a juice glass.

"There, there, darling," she said with no little sarcasm.

"I see."

"She called. Wants you to call her. You got the message."

"Both of them."

"I suspect there was a reason she called you in the first place, don't you think?"

JENNIFER BAILEY, as Shanahan had guessed, was still in her office.

"The warrant for his arrest has been issued," she said.

"You talk with the police?" Shanahan asked.

"With the prosecutor on the case, a D.A. by the name of Howard Nesbitt."

"Don't know him. Is that good or bad?"

"I don't know," Jennifer Bailey said. "In some ways I'd rather have Silvers. I think I'd rather face a cut-throat, publicity-seeking shark like him than a consci-entious law-clerk nerd like Nesbitt."

Shanahan laughed. "I've never heard you talk like this before. It's almost like you're . . ."

"Human. Right."

"Is Ramirez with you now?"

"He's in the other room. Fact is, he doesn't mind be-ing arrested as much as he minds the timing. He wants to box tonight."

"What finally made them decide to arrest him?"

"Two things. The university security guard, for one."

"The second?" Shanahan asked.

"Emilio has said all along and, I might add, in a sworn statement to the police that Sally Holland had never been to his apartment. Laboratory evidence strongly suggests otherwise."

"What does Emilio say?" Shanahan asked.

"He's sticking to his story. 'Impossible,' he says. I don't know exactly what the lab has, but Nesbitt says it's more than a strand of hair. Her being there, he said, is irrefutable. He will tell me after Emilio is indicted by the grand jury. He will too. He will play everything by the book."

"And that means Emilio will be arrested the moment he sets foot in the club."

"Yes. That is the least of my worries, but yes, I'm afraid so. We are faced with a flimsy alibi, laboratory evidence that catches him in an outright lie, and a wit-ness who puts Emilio at the scene."

"Two outright lies. He told the security guard that he'd been having trouble with his girlfriend. Then again, maybe it wasn't a lie." He waited for Bailey to react. She didn't. "Plus," Shanahan added, "a believable weapon, fists easily capable of inflicting death and a relationship so vague that an imaginative jury will have a ball filling in the details."

"Thanks for cheering me up."

"It's a special knack I have."

"I'm sorry. You're right." Jennifer sighed.

"All he'd have to do is change his story and admit she had visited him there. The whole thing is still circumstantial."

"I tried that. He will not change his story. I'm temporarily at a loss, Mr. Shanahan."

"Look, tell Ramirez I'll see if I can convince Lieutenant Swann to arrest him after the fight."

"Not a priority. I don't much care about the fight, Mr. Shanahan."

"Well, he does. Let's take one step at a time. We have a little time. Don't we?"

"I think so. Nesbitt is a stickler for details. He indicated he was pressured into making the arrest to soothe the savage press, but that he wouldn't jeopardize the case by rushing the trial."

"He told you he was pressured? He told you all that?"

"Nesbitt hasn't got a competitive or ambitious bone in his body. But he is a highly competent clerk. He will simply shut every possible escape hatch before the trial because he has accepted that responsibility on behalf of the people. He will do his job."

"That's refreshing."

"Is it?"

ELEVEN

SHANAHAN HOPED the tons of onion on his hamburger wouldn't upset his stomach, but he knew it would. He'd be tasting the White Castles until tomorrow morning. He stared at the stark white interior of the restaurant, sipped his coffee, and wished he'd been able to overcome this periodic, overwhelming craving for the little square burgers.

He had a couple of other wishes, too.

One was that the decidedly unlovable Max Rafferty would be the one handling the arrest of Emilio Ramirez ringside tonight instead of the more likable Lieutenant Swann. Swann would play it by the book. Rafferty might be induced to bend the rules—something he did often enough if it was in his own best interest—and wait until the match was finished. Given the possibility—however remote it might be—that Ramirez hadn't beaten Sally Holland to death late one dark night, why not let him have the match he'd trained for?

Shanahan also wanted to go to Sally Holland's funeral—see who showed up. Unfortunately, he couldn't be two places at once. He needed to be at Holland's residence while the funeral was going on, and he needed to have Harry there too. There were two places to search—the main house and the apartment of this Jaegar fellow who died mysteriously, maybe conveniently, a few days after Sally Holland.

He looked at his watch. Six forty-five. He needed to be on the far southside well before seven-thirty. Shanahan put down the last of his miniature hamburgers and went outside to the telephone booth, dialing information first, then the number the electronic voice gave him for Howard Cross.

"What are you doing?" Shanahan asked Howie after several rings.

"Sittin' here lookin' at my checkbook," Howie said. "I got forty bucks. Do I get my teeth cleaned, buy a bottle of Chivas Regal, go to P.T.'s and tip the strippers, or do I want to eat the rest of the week?"

"You want to earn a quick fifty?"

"Sure," the thirty-five-year-old former policeman said. "Tell me two things. What I gotta do. And who in the fuck are you?"

"Shanahan and you have to go to a funeral."

"Mine?"

"Not this time."

"Sorry. I didn't recognize the voice. The only people who call me anymore are aluminum siding salesmen. Oh, and the Goodwill people. I have to tell them I'm a customer, not a donor. You responsible for buying mourners for this gig or what?"

"I need to know who shows up."

"Okay. Tell me who, where, when, not that the when matters much. My calendar is clear until April twenty-first, two thousand and three, when Oliver Hogsmith says the world is coming to an end."

"Who's Oliver Hogsmith?"

"My neighbor. That's when he's eligible for Social Security, and since he's lost money in every investment he's ever made, he knows the world is gonna end the day before his first Social Security check arrives."

"Tomorrow. Sally Holland's funeral at the church and then the ceremony at the grave. You have a camera and film?"

"You been gettin' the high-profile cases lately. Well, I haven't hocked the camera yet, and a couple of boxes of film and half a jar of mustard are the only things in the fridge.''

"Hold the mustard, Howie."

Having worked out the details with Howie, who was having his own bout—only with the bottle—Shanahan headed for the Sherwood Club where Emilio Ramirez might or might not climb into the ring with some guy who wanted to beat *him* up.

LYLE BRODY hung around his office after he'd made his two phone calls—one unsuccessfully trying to track down this supposed lawsuit that could jeopardize the multi-million-dollar deal with the statues, and one successfully trying to get Connie Blakely to accompany him to the funeral.

Connie came around when Lyle mentioned the press. "This isn't just the local newspapers, Connie," he'd told her. "This is *USA Today*. Who knows, maybe *Current Affair* or *Hard Copy*." That got her.

She pretended to be unimpressed at first, but Lyle noticed she started talking faster and her voice went higher. By the end of the conversation she'd stopped using that tone when she said "Lyle," the tone that suggested that Lyle was some kind of pest, and started saying, "Lyle honey," like maybe she'd be rubbing up against him if she were there.

But she turned him down for dinner anyway. Said she had to get some things ready. Lyle was in the mood to go out to dinner, but had to satisfy himself with carry-out, maybe Chinese. Another night like the rest. A TV tray and Larry King on the tube. Things were changing, though. They had to.

SENATOR DAVID HOLLAND wished things could just go back—back to the way they were. He sat in the kitchen of what, in his mind, would always be Sally's house, drinking a bottle of carbonated water. Those early days, when he was the handsome freshman senator from Indiana, when everything was in front of him, were the best. Sally was not only willing but excited about living in Washington. She was as much a star as he was. The ideal couple. Nothing seemed impossible, including a new Camelot with Sally as first lady.

The days were full of meeting the powerful folks of D.C. The evenings were spent at dazzling parties where he'd met writers, actors, but, more important, discovering the power behind the power. The money people were the real power. They were the people who truly made things happen.

It had been good. The weekends were spent on sun-drenched golf courses—the best in the country—or at *the* country clubs playing tennis, where he impressed those same people with his athletic ability. He'd had dinner with legends.

Where had it gone? One minute he was a gnat's eyelash away from the vice presidency. The next minute he might as well have been living in Zimbabwe, wherever the hell that was. He had played the card that should have guaranteed him the spot on the ticket. And it was working. Goddamnit, it *was* working. Then poof. Up in smoke.

Holland's mom and dad would be there any minute now, with Elizabeth. He loved Elizabeth, but he wished she weren't coming, that they weren't coming. He wished it would all just go away, that he'd stayed with his dad at the plumbing company years ago. Kept his life simple. No, he couldn't have done that. Be real, he told himself. Working side by side with his dad for twenty years? He'd have never measured up.

He became a goddamn senator of the United States, and in his dad's eyes, he still didn't measure up. Damn, he wished they weren't coming. He wished he hadn't fired

Eric. Eric would've handled them. Eric was smart. Smarter than he was. Eric had told him not to threaten them. He was right. If Eric wasn't fucking queer as a three-dollar bill, *he* could be vice president someday.

SHANAHAN HAD HAD no idea the place would be packed. The parking lot out front of the far southside club was full, and he ended up parking his green '72 Chevy Malibu illegally at the end of a row. Inside, in the long hall, he paid fifteen bucks for a seat. The lady told him he was lucky he was alone. There weren't two together anywhere.

Shanahan handed his ticket to the man a couple of steps away who ripped it in half and told him, "C 14." Shanahan headed toward the noise—rock 'n' roll turned up higher than the stereo equipment could handle. He had expected more of a gymnasium with bleachers around the edges and folding chairs up near the ring. What he found was the ring surrounded by folding tables, hundreds of them, all occupied.

Above the ring was a mirrored ball, suggesting the space also accommodated proms for the southside high schools. Also hanging from the ceiling were chandeliers, the crystal pendants having been replaced by the kind of tinsel one normally tosses on Christmas trees.

The attendees, mostly young, mostly male, and all Caucasian, were drinking draft beer, munching on tortilla chips covered with yellow melted cheese. Some of the folks were hunkered over paper plates, gobbling up fried chicken, mashed potatoes, and cole slaw. The aisles were filled with people on their way to one of the bars or the rest rooms. Shanahan noted an abundance of beards, baseball caps, and Harley Davidson T-shirts.

On his way to the bar he looked around, found Section C, where he was assigned according to his ticket. He also looked around for the cops and the rooms where the boxers might be changing.

"Not here yet," Lieutenant Rafferty said, putting his arm on Shanahan's shoulder.

"He'll show."

"I figure he will too. Buy me a beer?"

"Okay," Shanahan said. He'd had a speech prepared about letting Emilio Ramirez get in his rounds before being dragged off. But he couldn't remember it. "Rafferty, why don't you let the kid have his fight?"

"Kinda irregular, ain't it?"

"So's drinking on duty," Shanahan said, handing the clear plastic container of draft to the corpulent cop. Rafferty was dressed more for a funeral than a boxing match.

"Good point. I haven't been to a fight in years. I imagine me and the boys could enjoy ourselves a little bit." He looked around the crowd. "Nothin' but big bellies and bad haircuts." He looked back at Shanahan, waiting for the obvious big belly comeback, but the older man was quiet. "Kinda mellow tonight, Shanahan."

Just then a rather buxom blonde passed by them, happily self-conscious.

"A lot of sail for such a tiny craft," Rafferty said, trying to imitate W. C. Fields.

The music came up louder yet. Shanahan could hear some of the lyrics. He could make out "danger zone." A couple of big guys in colorful silky trunks climbed in the ring, followed by their corner men.

"Come on over, sit with me," Rafferty said. "I'm up close. Got plenty of room. The boys are wandering around."

Rafferty had been a sport about things; the least Shanahan could do was sit with the guy. Maybe he'd learn something.

"You have room?"

"Yeah. Flashed a badge, got us a whole table."

The two in the ring were heavyweights. Of that there was no doubt. Whether either of them had done any sit-ups in the last five years was in doubt. Their trunks were pulled high. A few sloppy punches and the silk trunks sank under their guts, and their jelly bellies would shake when they gave or received a roundhouse.

Rafferty laughed throughout, but paid attention to the card girls, the scantily clad women—dancers from a strip bar—who seemed to enjoy the whistles and catcalls as the cards they carried announced the number of the next round.

"Hey, you in the blue shorts!" Rafferty yelled at one of the boxers. The boxer looked down and got nailed by a punch a blind man could have seen coming. Rafferty laughed again. "Got to get this thing over with. In this case, the dumb one loses."

The second fight was between two trimmer boxers, though they too offered more hostility than skill.

One, the one with the pony tail and the two days' growth of beard, was the local favorite. Shanahan would have called it a draw, but with the crowd roaring at every imagined tap by their man, the judges declared the favorite a winner by unanimous decision.

Fortunately, the bad fights went only four rounds. According to the program, there'd be one more four-rounder before Emilio Ramirez climbed into the ring for six rounds. There were two more fights after that, the main event and a four-round final.

The two who entered the ring now looked like a mismatch of the first order. One was a tall, skinny white kid. He had long reddish hair and arms thin as coat hangers. The other guy, shorter, more fully built, looked as if he was carved from black granite. Both had worked up a sweat, and the white guy was bouncing and moving as though he'd had too much coffee.

"This ought to last about thirty seconds," Rafferty said. "Betcha ten the white kid don't make it to round two."

Shanahan didn't take the bet. When the bell rang, the white kid danced in, slinging three sharp jabs before the body builder felt the first one.

"Jesus," Rafferty said, then, turning to Shanahan, "Glad you're the shy type."

The only punch that landed on the skinny kid in the whole round was a body shot that raised a big pink welt on the pale white flesh around the kidney. The body builder was slow, too slow, and while he never got nailed with the big shot, his right eye began to swell, his face having been riddled by jabs.

The second round wasn't a repeat. While Rafferty consumed his second order of nachos and cheese, the skinny redheaded boxer didn't go after the swollen eye as one might expect. Instead he worked the body.

Shanahan thought he was making a mistake. The black guy's washboard belly looked like it could take punches all night long and not feel it. And while the kid was concentrating on the body, the black boxer got in a punch that sent the skinny kid back to the ropes.

It was obvious the all-white crowd was rooting for the white guy, and Shanahan hoped it wasn't for the wrong reason. The fact was that the white boxer, though he didn't look the part, was a better boxer. If there were any doubts, the skinny kid repeated the body shots and came out of the third unscathed.

During the fourth and final round, the skinny boxer went back upstairs, jabbing his way in at will. He was no doubt ahead in points, so the fight was his unless the muscular boxer got in something lucky. Suddenly the white kid pummeled his tired opponent with an incredible five-punch combination, the last one catching the black kid's head as it went down to kiss the canvas.

He got up before the count, but was so lost and so dazed that the referee mercifully stopped the fight.

The crowd gathering to congratulate the winner obscured for a moment the arrival of Emilio Ramirez and his opponent, Bob "the Brawler" Babinski from South Bend, Indiana.

Once the ring cleared, the announcer stepped in. There was quiet applause for Emilio Ramirez. However, Bob "the Brawler" had apparently brought along a cheering section. When he was announced, there was a rambunctious barrage of hoots, hollers, and whistles. From the looks of him, Babinski was no pushover. He looked bigger than Emilio, who was having trouble staying at 175.

Ramirez must have waived Babinski's pounds beyond the limit—all twenty of them. Babinski, according to the announcer, weighed in at 195. Thing was the Brawler wasn't fat—just big. Every inch of his body was solid, and Shanahan could tell as the Babinski guy danced in his corner that he was pretty quick for a big guy.

Both fighters were undefeated, but Babinski had had more fights. He had seventeen to Emilio's nine.

The twenty-pound difference seemed like even more as they stood next to each other getting the referee's instructions. Babinski was broad and his biceps were thick and hard. Emilio had a sleek body, more like that of a swimmer or diver than a boxer.

"Even money," Rafferty said. "I'll take the Slav and the cute broad holding the cards."

Shanahan ignored him and, as the boxers went back to their corners, noticed a guy with a video camera setting up just outside the ring. He wondered if it was one of Babinski's fans. The camera didn't look professional enough for the local TV station. But then again, Shanahan didn't know much about these things.

"Thanks, Rafferty, for letting the kid box," Shanahan said.

"Hey, what kind of guy do you think I am?"

The bell rang, and Shanahan was glad he didn't have to answer the question.

TWELVE

SHANAHAN WAS TIRED. The noise, the cigarettes, the beer, and Rafferty were all getting to him. He'd put in a full day already. Now at nine in the evening, with the rock 'n' roll music blaring, Shanahan really preferred bed to boxing.

He noticed that one of the guys standing with Emilio Ramirez in the center of the ring as the announcer talked to them was a large black man. That had to be Charley Baker, Ramirez's trainer, because the other guy—a pale kid with dishwater blond hair who looked in need of a meal—was too young.

The two boxers went back to their corners and the bell sounded. Babinski rushed in, his heavy right hand crashing in on Ramirez. Even though Ramirez managed to get his glove between the fist and his face, his head rocked nonetheless, and the South Bend cheering section rose.

Shanahan felt his own blood rushing now as the heavier fighter's left came punching to Ramirez's kidney. The crowd was roaring as Babinski flailed away. It didn't seem to matter that nothing but the kidney punch landed—Ramirez catching the rest on his gloves and finally moving away—the crowd had already smelled the kill.

Ramirez stayed away from him the rest of the round, dancing back, then to one side, then to the other, Babinski's powerful shots either glancing blows or landing on Ramirez's gloves. No doubt, though, the points were going to Babinski if for no other reason than that he was the aggressor, the only one throwing punches.

Shanahan watched the corner. Charley Baker didn't seem upset. In fact, he said nothing to Ramirez, who looked surprisingly calm. Babinski charged in again at the bell and met a straight jab that surprised more than hurt him. He caught another, then another. Shanahan couldn't tell where the next punch came from. All he could see was how it lifted Babinski off his feet.

It was so quiet that the people ringside could hear the thuds as Babinski's back, then his head hit the canvas. The referee started the count, then dropped to his knees and looked around the ring, obviously for the doctor.

Within thirty seconds of the second round, Emilio Ramirez had dispatched his opponent with five left jabs and a right to the chin.

Rafferty smiled. "Well, will you look at that!" he said while the crowd was too stunned to make a sound.

"There you go, Lieutenant," said the guy with the video camera, who dropped a large video cassette in front of Rafferty. "Looks like you got a winner."

Shanahan looked up, suddenly understanding why Rafferty had let Ramirez get his fight in.

"Rafferty, I'm a fool and you're an asshole," Shanahan said, getting up. He felt sick. It would have been far better for Ramirez to have been beaten. Now the jury would have some means of measuring the power of Emilio Ramirez, who knocked out cold a boxer twenty pounds heavier with one stupefying punch.

"I just got lucky, Shanahan. Hell, I thought big ole Babinski would've put Ramirez away real quick. Then we'd a had nothin'."

He scooted away from the table, heading toward Emilio's corner to join what appeared to be three plain-clothesmen. Seven or eight uniforms were coming down the crowded aisles, also heading toward Ramirez.

"What'd he do, kill him?" someone in the crowd said, referring to Ramirez's sudden and surprising victory over Babinski, who still hadn't moved a muscle.

SENATOR HOLLAND'S MOTHER was in the kitchen, cleaning the refrigerator.

"Where are the trash bags?" she called out to her son.

"I have no idea," he shouted back from the living room, where his father sat with Elizabeth in front of the TV set, both seemingly engrossed in a baseball game. The senator sat staring in the general direction of the screen, trying to seem part of this strange family who occupied this strange house.

Elizabeth had been polite with her father, but he could sense her tensing up when she arrived and he attempted to hug her. Instead she clung close to her grandfather.

"Now look at this, Lizzie," Holland's father said. "The pitcher has given up only one hit in six innings, and now they're gonna take him out 'cause some guy blooped a single into left. In my day a pitcher pitched nine innings, for Christ's sake."

"There's some perfectly good ice cream in the freezer," Mrs. Holland said, standing in the doorway to the living room. "No sense in letting it go to waste."

Holland got up, went to the kitchen, not for the ice cream, but because he was bored with the game.

"I used to tell Sally to get a new icebox," Mrs. Holland said, "one of those frost-free kinds. Told her to go to Sears."

"Doesn't matter, Mom."

"Of course it doesn't. I just remembered the two of us standing here that afternoon, talking about it. That's all."

THOUGH A FEW PEOPLE followed the officers leading Emilio Ramirez out the main entrance to the club, most remained to see the main event. Shanahan was among those who followed the police, hoping to get a chance to talk with Charley Baker.

What Shanahan hadn't expected were lights, cameras, and throngs of reporters, no doubt notified by Lieutenant Max Rafferty, opportunist extraordinaire. Ramirez, minus gloves, was allowed only his robe. His hands were still bandaged.

Shanahan, who caught the scene as uniformed police created a wedge through the crowd to the waiting patrol car, saw only the back of Ramirez, arms to his sides, making no attempt to cover his face.

It was a major coup for Rafferty politically—within a few days police had not only nabbed the killer, but created a media event of the nabbing. Certainly Ramirez had unwittingly cooperated by winning the match. But he had done more. He'd done so convincingly on videotape, dramatically showing Ramirez's cold, brutal power. What message would that convey to a jury?

"I'm not a reporter," Shanahan said to Charley Baker, who shrank back from the crowd.

Charley Baker didn't respond.

"I'm working for Emilio's attorney, Jennifer Bailey," Shanahan continued. "I need to talk with you."

"I don't have nothin' to say," the man said.

"You want to help Emilio?"

Charley Baker remained silent, but his glare made it clear he wasn't in the mood for conversation. He turned, forged his way back through the crowd.

IT WAS ALMOST LIKE fireplace light, except that the flickering color on the white walls and ceiling of Lyle Brody's bedroom didn't crackle or provide heat. It was the Sony Trinitron that bounced shadows and light. He'd pushed the mute button.

He'd also punched in number 7 on his telephone and through the magic of electronics was connected to the 900 number of his choice. The person who would answer didn't need to hear the moans and cries of pain on his videotape.

He gave his telephone number, complete with area code, to the woman who answered. She asked him if he wanted to use the credit card on file. Yes, he did.

"This is Melissa," said the new voice on the other end of the phone.

"Sure it is, bitch," Lyle said. "Three fucking dollars a minute, I don't need to know your fucking name." It wasn't her real one anyway. He knew that.

USUALLY IT WAS Shanahan who got up first. He would make the coffee, play ball with Casey in the back while it brewed. But this morning, when he woke up, the space next to him was empty. The indentation Maureen's head had made in the pillow was there, as was the trace of her body on the sheets next to him.

That impression made him think of Sally Holland—that strange shape along her outer thigh and hips where it appeared her flesh had decomposed more quickly. He shook off his thoughts and climbed out of bed.

He remembered Maureen and he had argued before going to sleep. He'd told her about the fight, how Ramirez had dispatched a much bigger guy and how the prosecution would use that against him in court. One thing led to another and Shanahan wasn't sure why. Perhaps she was still uptight about losing the sale on that house.

He was grateful to find Maureen very much among the living. She was weeding around the peony bed. The blooms were gone, but the bush itself was still green and healthy. She wore her khaki shorts and white short-sleeved shirt with the long collar that formed a V, exposing a tasteful amount of lightly freckled cleavage.

She hadn't seen him come out into the yard, and he relished these moments—looking at her when she wasn't aware of it, feeling lucky she was with him. Maureen was so much unlike his first wife, Elaine. Elaine would have plastic flowers so they would stay nice and the petals wouldn't mess up the tabletops.

Maureen would select fresh flowers from the garden, carefully, so they wouldn't be missed. She was still in awe of nature, noticing the little gray and yellow birds that came to the birdbath. She had, in fact, built the bath from a broken bowl and stones she'd found in the yard. Somehow she made it beautiful.

Once she brought in a small brown frog she'd found and, after showing Shanahan, took it out again by the front door so Casey couldn't get it. Elaine wouldn't have touched it. Maureen would stand out on a starry night and just look. Elaine would have been inside doing needlepoint.

Casey brought Shanahan the smudgy green tennis ball, ready for his morning workout. That's when she saw him.

"I wanted to get out here while it was still cool," Maureen said. "I think this will be the hottest day yet."

"You're not mad at me about last night?" Shanahan asked her.

"No. I was worried you were mad at me."

"No. I don't think I've ever been mad at you."

"It's your job," she said, tossing a handful of weeds in the compost pile. "You have to believe he's innocent. I should just butt out."

"I don't exactly believe Emilio Ramirez is innocent either. But you're right. I have to assume he might be or I can't do what I'm hired to do. That was all I was trying to say. And I was puzzled about why it upset you so." He wished he had never mentioned anything to her about Ramirez.

"I just don't like big, strong guys who make a living beating up other people. Or abuse women, that's all."

"If he did it," Shanahan said, regretting immediately. Damn, he was stubborn. But so was she.

"Sometimes, when people are arrested for a crime, it's because they did it. Let me get you some coffee."

There was something more to Maureen's anger, but now wasn't the time to talk about it.

"I can get it," he said, tossing the ball for Casey.

"No, I have to go in anyway and get ready to flirt with the guys at Harry's bar, remember? Why are you laughing?"

"I was just thinking about the guys who come in that bar."

"Oh? You never know who just might wander in out of the heat." She grinned.

They both stopped talking when they heard the low rumble of Harry's van as it pulled into the driveway.

LYLE BRODY let the hot, pulsating shower revive him from an uneasy sleep. Have to do something about this body, he told himself—the same thing he told himself every time he took a shower. Join one of those health clubs, get himself a stair stepper or a Nordic Track, maybe some weights. The hard force of the hot water turned his pale sagging flesh pink.

He'd meet Connie at the church for the service, then the two of them would ride out in his BMW to the burial. Maybe they'd have lunch. The Skyline Club would be the place, but he hadn't gotten anyone to sponsor him. They'd have to do the Columbia Club. If he played it right, if she got excited about all the celebrities, all that power at the funeral, he could coax her into the sack. He

wished he hadn't called that 900 number last night.
Maybe it would hinder his performance.

The hot water and steam seemed to clear his head, and
he'd decided to wear the gray suit, the pale blue shirt, and
the silver tie. Mourning in the morning, he thought, and
laughed. You wear gray in the morning. He was pretty
sure of that.

Lyle turned off the shower, dried himself off, then
wiped the mirror so he could see himself well enough to
shave.

"Yes, it is a great tragedy," he said to his image in the
mirror, practicing what he would say to others at the funeral. "She was not only my sister, but my best friend."
He shook his head. "It is a great tragedy. I don't know
how many people understand what a wonderful woman
she was."

He nodded, patting on the shaving cream. He thought
that was better. The best-friend comment didn't sound
right. "We all wonder why the good die young." No.
"She was doing wonderful work for the environment."
That was better, he thought.

HARRY, in his blue work pants with matching shirt and
baseball cap, stood in Shanahan's kitchen.

"You check your lawn mower? Does it work?" Shanahan asked.

"Yep." Harry nodded and took a swig of coffee.
"Don't you clean up nice so early in the morning," he
said to Maureen.

"Natural beauty," she said, tossing her hair back and
grinning, "enhanced only slightly by a forty-five-minute
indulgence in the subtle art of makeup. Otherwise I'd
look like a bloodhound. Thanks just the same."

"Don't mention it. Nothin' to running the bar. I'll get
you set up before we head out to the senator's place. Oh,
and, Maureen, don't be too disappointed if the custom-

ers don't stay too long. Not knowing you and all, they might feel uncomfortable. They're kinda used to me tellin' 'em stories, you know, guy bullshit and all."

"I'll try not to drive all your business away, Harry."

"I'm just sayin' this so's you won't get your feelings hurt, that's all."

"We've got to load our mower too," Shanahan said, coming in, wearing a tan getup similar to Harry's.

"I've got a question for you two desperadoes. It's broad daylight. The police are on the property. How do you plan to break in? You gonna mow 'em down?"

"Something like that," Shanahan said.

SENATOR DAVID HOLLAND could smell it even before he started down the stairs. He knew what it was. His mother was fixing breakfast and had heated maple syrup. The smell made him nauseous.

"Look what I found under the sink, Davey," she said, looking up from the stove where she jabbed a fork into crackling strips of bacon. "A waffle iron. And I figured that's just what Davey needs to face the day."

"That's not what Davey needs," he said to his mother sharply. "Davey needs a cup of black coffee."

Holland's father shot him a quick, angry look. But he didn't say anything. David Holland scooted in between his mom's empty chair and that of Elizabeth, whose only acknowledgement of his arrival was a brief glance. She poked at her waffle. There was a pool of syrup in the middle with remains of butter floating in it. She had cut off a corner, but it was still on the end of her fork.

"How are you, honey?"

"Okay," she said flatly, and looked down at her plate.

Holland couldn't tell anything by her face, a gift—if that's what you called it—she got from her father. Her mother's face gave away everything.

"Sally doesn't...didn't go in for a lot of sweets. That's why the waffle iron was hidden away," the senator said.

"Something sweet every now and then won't hurt," Mrs. Holland said, sliding a plate in front of her son. He looked down at the waffle, the steam carrying the nauseating scent of syrup up his nostrils. "Your father got up early, went out and got the groceries, Davey, so you can just eat a little bit. We're still your parents."

In one motion David Holland stood up, grabbed the plate, and flung it toward the sink. The edge of the plate took out a pane of glass in the window above and the waffle slapped against another pane and slid slowly down the window and wall, leaving an oozing trail of syrup.

"For Christ's sake!" His father stood up, but David Holland was already out of the kitchen.

"Honey," Mrs. Holland said to her husband, "this isn't easy for him."

"A fucking goddamn senator of the United States and he acts like a goddamn three-year-old." He looked down at Elizabeth, then realized what he'd said. He almost cried. "I'm sorry, Lizzie. It'll all be over in a little while."

Elizabeth put the bite of waffle in her mouth, but didn't seem to be in any hurry to chew it.

THIRTEEN

SHANAHAN'S PLAN wasn't foolproof. What he and Harry had to do was convince whoever was left at the house that they were the lawn service. And as far as Shanahan could figure it, any member of the household or anyone else who'd likely know about the lawn care of the Holland home would be at the funeral, except for the state police he had seen when he drove by yesterday.

The black van went by the house. He saw two state police cars out in front, parked on the street, and a long black stretch limo in the driveway. He and Harry drove up to the Café Patachou on Forty-ninth and Pennsylvania and had a cup of coffee.

"Why in the hell can't we be electricians or something?" Harry asked in his complaining tone. "That way we wouldn't have to mow a whole goddamn lawn. In this heat, Deets, you'll get a stroke or something."

"Thanks for your concern about my personal welfare, but if we were electricians, one of the cops is liable to wander around the house with us. This way they won't even know we're inside."

"We have to mow the back too?"

When they drove by the Pennsylvania Street residence again, the big, black limo was pulling out. Shanahan counted four people besides the driver. One was a young girl, who peered out of the open window for a moment before rolling it up, her face almost disappearing behind the tinted glass.

Harry drove, at Shanahan's instructions, back into the Butler-Tarkington area, where Howie Cross lived, but more important, where Emilio Ramirez was i.d.'d. They drove several blocks west on Forty-sixth street, by Hinkle Fieldhouse, turning into the university and eventually down the steep, curved drive into Holcomb Gardens.

"We'll give them a few minutes," Shanahan said. "Make sure they don't come back for the family Bible or something." He got out of the van and walked halfway across the wooden bridge that spanned the canal.

He came back to the van. "Harry, it doesn't figure. The campus police report talking with Ramirez down here. The body is found in White River a long way down from here. Half a mile at least."

"The river's just down there a piece," Harry said. "Could've tossed her in and the body floated down. That's the way the current runs. South."

"Yeah, but why didn't he just drive down Michigan Road and toss her off that bridge directly into the water?"

"Maybe he did. Maybe he just met her here. He punches her here or there don't make no difference. Drives to where you say or some other bridge, tosses her in."

"Yeah, but there's no second car. How'd she meet him here? And it wasn't at Emilio's place, either. He had to have taken her to his house, killed her, put her in the trunk, then driven her back out here. Why would he have parked here, Harry? Was she already in the trunk? If so, why was he here? If he'd already dumped her body, why was he here? Doesn't make sense."

"Looks to me like however it happened, he's the one," Harry said, shaking his head.

"Yeah, not everybody who's arrested is innocent," he said, thinking of Maureen's words earlier. But something else bothered him. "The water's real calm in the inlet, where she washed up...if she washed up. I'd think if she was tossed into the current, the body would've just kept floating down the river, not into that inlet, then all the way to the shore.''

It didn't pull together right.

TWO STATE policemen were chatting by their cars, parked on the street in front of the Holland residence. When the black van pulled into the driveway, the heavier of the two cops raised his hand, showing a dark ring of perspiration under the armpit of his tan shirt.

"Whoa, boys!'' he shouted. He sauntered up to the window as if he were on a Sunday stroll. "What's cookin'?''

"With this heat, looks like our brains gonna do some cookin','' Harry said. "Lawn service.''

Shanahan didn't mind letting Harry take the lead when it came to talking them in or out of trouble. Harry was a master bullshit artist.

The officer looked in to check out Shanahan. The other officer, younger and thinner, came up behind.

"Probably not a good idea today, gentlemen,'' the man said. Shanahan could see two bright images of Harry's face in the officer's mirrored sunglasses.

"You damn right it's not a good idea,'' Harry said. "A fellow could get heat stroke out here. And it's gonna get worse.'' He looked at Shanahan. "I told you, Gruber. Nobody oughta have to work on a day like this.''

"The ticket says today,'' Shanahan said.

"It's a ticket to the morgue, I tell ya.''

"All I know it's what's in the contract,'' Shanahan continued. "We don't get to do it, they pay our boss anyway. But we don't get paid.'' Shanahan sighed. "It's the only job I have this week.''

"C'mon, Jasper,'' the younger cop said. "What's the harm? They'll be done in a couple of hours.''

THE SERVICE AT the church on Monument Circle was mercifully short. Closed casket. The priest spoke of her good works for "the community of mankind." Perhaps it was the choir or maybe the light coming in through the stained glass, maybe the overwhelming number of people who came—the local big shots, senators, congressmen, even the vice president of the United States.

Whatever it was, Lyle Brody felt the tears well up in his eyes. He wondered if they'd stay that way when people filed out of the church. It was important for them to know he grieved for his sister.

He looked at Connie. She listened attentively. She had chosen her dress appropriately. It was nice, expensive; but sedate, respectful.

Also seated in the first pew was the vice president, who was on David Holland's left. Holland's daughter flanked the senator's right side, followed by his mother and father. The other senator from Indiana and the governor were also in the first row, as well as a few people Lyle didn't recognize.

Lyle Brody craned his neck, looking back over the crowded church. Standing room only. He recognized a few people. The reigning newspaper publishing family was represented. Senator Holland's political opponent, Edmund Carem, was there with his wife and two kids— make that his lovely wife and two darling children, Brody thought.

Christ! There was Jamie Brothewaite in one of her funny dresses. She sat with some guy Lyle thought he recognized, but wasn't sure.

He spotted several men in dark suits who looked to be secret service. Probably were.

As they left—the intimate relatives and super dignitaries first—Lyle noticed Elizabeth ducking from David Holland's arm to retreat back to her grandfather.

Outside, Lyle Brody was struck by the harsh, wet heat. "Christ," he said.

"Oh, God," Connie said. Lyle put his arm around her waist.

"The car is air-conditioned." He looked around for the car, saw that the four street entrances to the brick-paved Circle had been blocked off. It looked like a car show at the Convention Center. Only the cars were shiny black limos, nose to nose, occupying all three traffic lanes that circled the monument.

He wondered how anybody could make sense of it. But there were state troopers and they seemed to know what they were doing. It dawned on him that something was missing. He looked round again. Where in the hell was the press?

A state trooper ushered Lyle and Connie to a limo. They were third in line. The casket first. Senator Holland and his family second. He didn't like following the senator, but the idea that the vice president rode in the car behind him took the sting out of it.

THEY HAD ALREADY clipped the hedges and bushes around the house, checking for a security system as they went and, surprisingly, finding none. With only half the long front lawn mowed, Harry's face was already beet-red and shiny with perspiration. He'd taken off his work shirt, and the silver-gray hairs on his chest showed through the sleeveless T-shirt. He turned off his mower, wiped his brow with his forearm, which did little more than move the sweat around and sting his eye.

He walked over to Shanahan, who was mowing the long sliver of lawn on the other side of the drive. Shanahan shut off his mower.

"The young cop headed out," Harry said.

"Lunch, probably. Good."

"The other cop probably wants to stay out here and guard the drive."

"Why don't you go over there and tell 'em we're gonna take a break in the backyard, out of the sun."

Shanahan picked the lock to the back door and found himself in the kitchen. It was quiet, cool. At first he thought the only sound he heard was the air conditioner, but it was the refrigerator. Like the stove, the white Hotpoint was at least thirty years old, at least as old as his.

He looked around for some evidence of a desk or something that would contain papers or bills. People often keep important papers in the kitchen, but a quick search found nothing out of the ordinary, except a broken pane of glass over the sink and sticky goo on the window frame and the wall beneath it. Looked like someone tried to clean it up but wasn't very successful. There was also a strange trash receptacle. It was in four sections, each one labeled: paper, plastic, glass, metal.

Walking quickly through the first floor, he noticed nothing unusual there, either. It was clean, orderly, yet homey. He'd expected to find something grander. There wasn't even a den or library for the senator. He checked the half-bath downstairs. Clean. Nothing revealing in the medicine cabinet, but then he really hadn't expected anything there. The upstairs bathroom would tell any tales that needed to be told. Shanahan went up the stairway, taking two steps at a time, but careful not to leave a sweaty palm print on the railing.

He went to the bathroom first. The medicine cabinet. Cough syrup. There were two small brown plastic containers with prescription labels. One was for 500 milligrams of penicillin. The refill expiration date was long overdue. The other was for some kind of Tylenol you apparently needed a prescription for. Shanahan knew it wasn't likely someone on cocaine or heroin would keep their stash in the medicine cabinet. Those who get addicted to prescription drugs often do keep them there. It legitimizes the habit. But nobody was going to get high on these.

The cabinet also contained the usual hygiene products—toothpaste, mouthwash, and so on. What puzzled Shanahan was the can of Noxzema shaving cream. There was a throwaway safety razor that looked fresh out of the cellophane package of six or eight. But there was a ring of rust around the bottom of the shaving cream and another circle of rust on the metal shelf, off center from where the can was. If that was the senator's shaving cream, then perhaps he hadn't been home in a while—at least not long enough to worry about shaving—until recently.

He went down the hall to inspect the bedrooms. There were four. In two, there were opened suitcases. In the closet of the big bedroom, the one Shanahan would've thought belonged to the senator and his wife, there was clothing for a man and a woman. However, there were two suitcases on the floor and one on the bed.

There was a crumpled *Sporting News* on the floor beside the bed and a copy of *Modern Maturity* on the bedside table on the other side. The shaving kit had a can of talc, a brand he hadn't seen in years. In the woman's overnight bag he found denture adhesive. An older couple, he thought.

In one of the smaller bedrooms, he found what had to be the senator's suitcase and suit bag. The bedroom had the look of a guest bedroom. It didn't look lived in. The senator, a guest in his own home. Shanahan carefully but quickly went through the suitcase. Nothing.

The next one of the rooms looked to be an office, but not likely the senator's. Elaborate illustrations of various flora and fauna occupied one whole wall. On the desk were envelopes from Greenpeace, The Sierra Club, and similar organizations. There was Sally Holland's personalized stationery, her name—Sally Brody Holland—and address along with an imprint of a blue spruce tree.

Shanahan scanned the desk drawers and found very little. Her checkbook revealed only the most modest of purchases and the most modest of balances. There were also several statements from her accountant, which showed only debits and credits on a more sizable but hardly significant bottom line.

The fourth bedroom was most certainly the daughter's. It was smaller yet and done with great care. He was just about to write this room off when he saw the diary on the little desk. He used the pick he'd used for the back door and sprung it open without scratching the metal clasp or breaking the lock.

He looked in front and saw that the diary went back two years. He decided to work from back to front. He skimmed, but didn't have to go far to pick out the name of Emilio Ramirez. It was an entry dated the previous night. Unlike the rest of the entries, it was written in pretty, self-consciously large, round letters.

It isn't fair. It was like the three of us were friends. My mom and Emilio and I. All of a sudden both of them are gone. It was God's will, grandpa told me. God took my mom. The police took Emilio. Grandpa says the police think he killed her. I know by the way he and grandma talk that they won't let me see him or talk to him. I told them he was a nice person, that he wouldn't do anything like that. Grandma said that sometimes people aren't as nice as they seem. I didn't tell her I knew that already. Grandpa didn't say anything, but I think maybe he believes me.

There were other, earlier references to Emilio. At the zoo. At the Hispanic Center, at Eagle Creek and Brown

County last fall. But more important than any other reference was the one telling about strolling along the canal with Sally and Emilio.

So it was clear that Ramirez was at least somewhat familiar with the area.

The girl's writing was very happy when she talked of the three of them. At one point she had written: "If I were older he'd be my boyfriend for sure. I like to think of him as my brother."

According to the diary, Emilio told her stories, was teaching her Spanish, and lent an ear when she was having trouble at school, which was often. The girl also corresponded with Ramirez in some way. One of the girl's entries said: "Emilio loved my card with the penguin on it. He told me he laughed a lot."

From Shanahan's quick scan, she seemed a lonely girl. No mention of close friends at school and no mention of her father, either positive or negative. When she wasn't talking about what it would be like to own a horse farm when she grew up or her complaint about Mrs. Blakely at school, she talked about herself and Emilio and her mother, sometimes referred to in the diary—oddly in Shanahan's mind—as Sally.

There were several empty pages yet to be filled in. On the last, though, was Emilio Ramirez's address.

Shanahan glanced at his watch. He'd been there for twenty minutes.

"Damn," he said.

FOURTEEN

THE FOUR OF THEM—Holland, his daughter, mother, and father, hidden from view by the tinted windows—rode without speaking in the cool, somewhat darkened interior of the limo.

If someone were to ask him later what he had seen on that drive or what he had thought, he wouldn't be able to tell them. He was not thinking of Sally Holland or of Elizabeth or of the political campaign that continued to swirl around him despite his lack of participation.

His father glared at him, but Holland took no notice. His mother looked at him, the worry lines on her forehead deeper than usual, her mouth curling under as if she were on the verge of tears. The senator did not notice, nor did he even sense the despair of his daughter, who stared, like her father, blankly into a space others could not see.

The sleek black limo passed through the stone gates of Crown Hill Cemetery, then beyond the gate house that looked like an old, rural train station. The car cruised the curving lanes as smoothly as an ocean liner on calm seas, through the grassy knolls where the grand, granite markers of past lives looked like miniature cities.

As SHANAHAN eased himself out of the back door of the Holland residence, he heard Harry's voice.

"...so I tell him, if dogs are so damn smart, how come every time a dog farts, he jumps like it's some big surprise?"

Laughter. It came from just around the corner. Harry had intercepted the police.

Shanahan rounded the corner and moved up behind Harry. The younger cop held a white paper bag, no doubt lunch.

"We're just about ready to mow back here, don't want to get grass in your burgers," Shanahan said.

Harry turned back, an expression of great relief on his face. "I was just tellin' 'em how your dog jumps every time he farts like he don't know what hit him."

More laughter.

"We can eat in the car, Jasper, turn the air conditioner way up," the younger cop said, and they both headed back down the drive toward the street.

"Where in the hell have you been?" Harry asked angrily. "Taking a nap?"

"Reading, Harry."

"Damn." He wiped the sweat from his face.

"Why don't you go up and check out Jaegar's place over the garage. I'll go out and finish the front. You hear the mower go off, you'll know somebody's coming, so get the hell out of there."

"We got to mow the backyard too?"

"Not much here. Look funny if we didn't."

LYLE STOOD THERE. The back of his shirt was wet from sweat. He could feel it. He wondered if it showed through his suit jacket. He should've worn black so the sweat wouldn't show through.

He looked around. It could damn well have been a burial for the Queen of England. There was an American Legion Honor Guard all dressed up. There were some uniformed police in their dress blues. There were hundreds of people, distinguished people. Even in death her shadow overwhelmed him.

There was Jamie Brothewaite. She stood just outside the white canvas canopy, amid the flowers. Beside her was the man Lyle thought he knew. Still the identity mystified him. Lyle turned away, catching small bits of the priest's monologue—a word here, a phrase there. His eyes locked onto Senator David Holland, still looking fresh in the hot sun. Is the man so goddamned perfect he doesn't sweat? There wasn't a trace of emotion on Holland's face.

"Damn!" Lyle had almost said it out loud. Alec Malone. That's who it was. That's the guy with Jamie Brothewaite. The actor, Alec Malone, who always came to Indy in May for the race. She's always got to be one up on somebody, Lyle thought. He looked at her. She had been looking at him. She didn't turn away, just scowled. He could tell by her eyes. She was still pissed about the statues.

"Fuck her," he said under his breath.

As the coffin was lowered, Lyle Brody felt suddenly and profoundly alone. Holland's parents were there. All the friends and associates. But his own, his and Sally's parents were dead. No family. No real friends. None at all.

LAST NIGHT Emilio Ramirez had remained awake listening to the sounds of prison. Hushed whispers, an accidental clanging of something metal against the bars. Once in a while a barking cough rose above the quieter sounds. Somewhere—down the corridor—the subdued cadence of two unsynchronized breaths, heavy and deep, gave the darkness a strange thickness.

Early this morning two guards had come to take his cellmate away—a heavyset guy with a reddish beard, hairy hands, and a missing front tooth. Emilio didn't know why they were taking him or where. If the redhead knew where he was going, he hadn't said. He hadn't said anything to Emilio during the brief time they shared the small space. For that Emilio was grateful.

Now it was quiet. He looked out past the bars of his cell, across the range—a wide corridor between his cell and the outside wall of the Marion County Jail—and through the little barred window. All he could see was a small patch of blue-white sky and a billboard with a black cowboy holding a pack of cigarettes.

For a moment Emilio felt a wave of bitterness. How unfair life was! That surprised him. He'd thought he already knew that. He'd thought that he'd already come to terms with the way life was, not just for him, but for everyone. He resented...was bitter about being bitter. It wasn't so much that he'd been imprisoned for something he hadn't done. Being blamed, punished for something he didn't do, was something he'd dealt with, successfully, finally he thought, as a child.

It was more than that. It was that someone, for some unfathomable reason, took the life of someone so good. It wasn't for himself he grieved. It was for her. He smiled at his ability to fool himself. No. He grieved for himself—her death was his loss, not hers.

Emilio took off his shirt and pants, dropped to the floor and began doing pushups. "One, two, three..." His body rose and fell effortlessly. "...ten, eleven, twelve..." He could deal with prison. "...seventeen, eighteen, nineteen..." They would never have his body, let alone his mind. He was as free in a prison cell as he was in his small apartment. "Thirty, thirty-one..." He would read and sleep and exercise. Be inside himself. Perhaps it would be better than struggling to pay the rent. "...sixty-two, sixty-three..." It would be good. He would not be caught up in things of the world. He would be a monk, without the superficial trappings of some false orthodoxy, closed-mind, didactic, religious order. "...ninety-two, ninety-three." He would be more in control in prison than out.

Well beyond one hundred pushups, his body began to release sweat. A light sheen gathered over his smooth olive skin, and his thoughts began to evaporate.

DAVID HOLLAND felt numb. He wondered if he was holding his daughter's hand. No, he wasn't. Elizabeth's arms were down at her sides, limp arms, not resisting gravity. She seemed pale, but there was an alertness in her eyes.

Then gradually the world moved away from him. The whole panorama of tombstones, little green hills, and people dressed in black seemed set back, moving away from him. The priest's lips were moving, but Holland could not hear him, could hear nothing but the semblance of speech as one hears while underwater at a public swimming pool.

Someone nudged him. He tried focusing his eyes outward and saw that everyone was looking at him. They expected something.

"The rose, Davey," his mother said, nodding toward the grave.

"Oh, yes, yes," he said. His legs were weak. The right knee buckled. He heard a huge chorus of voices all making the same sound. "Ooooh."

"Oooohh," David Holland could hear himself saying too as he realized he was no longer in control of his body and that somehow it was pitching forward.

"WHAT THE HELL is this!" Harry said.

Shanahan followed his friend into the bar, the cold rush of air conditioning chilling the sweat on his forehead.

Since Harry had taken over Delaney's bar, there had never been more than two or three customers at a time except on Friday and Saturday nights. There was more than a dozen at two o'clock on a weekday afternoon, the boisterous noise of their conversation not quite muffled by the gravelly voice of Louis Armstrong singing on the jukebox: "...munching on some cheesecake..."

"You're all pink," Maureen said to Harry, then looked up at Shanahan, who shrugged and sat at the bar.

Shanahan thought she looked particularly radiant. The customers were Harry's regulars, but instead of straggling in as they usually did for a cold one and then leaving, they apparently decided to stay and soak up some of Maureen's sun.

"Go home, Harry," Mulrooney shouted from the end of the bar.

Maureen brought each of the new arrivals a beer. For Shanahan the tall, long-necked, clear bottle of Miller High Life. For Harry his bottle of Rolling Rock.

Shanahan took a deep gulp; once it settled, he could feel its inebriating effects immediately. Two beers after all that sun, he thought, and he'd be a stumbling drunk. He decided to go slow.

The afternoon had been fruitful, he supposed. Harry, who canvassed Jaegar's closed-up and therefore stiflingly hot apartment over the Holland garage, wondered why a man who supposedly had a heart condition also had a complete set of weights.

He said that the man's bookshelves were full of books about various government agencies, namely the FBI, CIA, NSC, and the Secret Service—nonfiction about Kennedy, his assassination and alleged connections to organized crime; Nixon's ties with Bebe Rebozo. There were articles Jaegar had cut from the tabloids about the current President's mysterious ties with some Florida hoods and the like.

Harry's conclusion, bolstered by the fact that the man had retired early, suggested he had worked for the government in some capacity. Jaegar also wore a size forty-eight suit. A big man.

Shanahan went to the end of the bar and stood by Harry, who was perusing the green in the little compartments of his cash register.

"I'm going to use your phone," he said to Harry, and waited for some sort of nasty reply.

"Sure, Deets, go ahead."

"It's wonderful to see a happy man, a man with dollar signs in his eyes."

He dialed Lieutenant Swann. Eventually, after a series of bored voices, he was connected to someone who wanted to know what he wanted with the lieutenant.

"Tell him it's Doctor Ruth and it's about . . ."

"This is Swann, Shanahan."

"You're screening your calls?"

"Lieutenant Rafferty's idea. He wants to handle anything dealing with Mrs. Holland. You're not going to talk to me about that, right?"

"Uh . . . right. I wondered if you could check on a couple of juveniles for me. A Moogie Swanson and a Francine Schmidt."

"Moogie," he said in his deadpan tone.

"Probably a nickname."

"You have a real name?"

"All I have is Moogie." Shanahan was surprised that Swann would even consider looking him up.

"This isn't Mayberry," Swann said dryly. "It'll take me a little time."

"I appreciate it," Shanahan said. "I do have a question about Sally Holland." Silence.

"Lieutenant Swann?"

"Shanahan, I've got these plastic bags. One of them, a little one, contains hair fibres from the victim's head. Another contains particles of skin. Both from the kitchen floor of one Emilio Ramirez. In another I have photographs of the face and neck of Sally Holland. The important fact here is the one on her face. A bruise, singular, the good doctor says, didn't come from a sharp instrument, but from something blunt. In all probability a fist, because the varying depths of the bruise would match a man's knuckles.''

"I see," Shanahan said.

"I've got folders, too, Shanahan. One contains a statement from Elizabeth Holland, who says, among other things, that Sally Holland and Emilio Ramirez spent time together. Another contains a sworn statement from a Butler University security guard who recognized a photo of Emilio Ramirez and stated that beyond a shadow of a doubt Ramirez was the man he saw in the middle of the night in proximity of the crime scene. He can also tell you precisely what hour and what minute he saw him. I have a copy of his own security report, time and date duly and professionally noted, which clearly identifies the suspect's car and license-plate number. Also in the report the security officer says Ramirez said he was depressed. That he was having trouble with his girl-friend.''

"Is that all?" Shanahan said sarcastically.

"I've got still another folder with a statement from Mr. Ramirez who can't tell us who allegedly called him to set up a meeting at this strange hour of the night and who denies that Mrs. Holland ever set foot in his apart-ment.''

"And you have a videotape of Emilio Ramirez," Shanahan said, "knocking out a guy twice his size in the ring?''

"That was Rafferty's touch," Swann said. "Have I answered all your questions?''

"I've got two more. Any evidence of rape?''

"Probably no. At least there are no signs that he . . . uh . . .''

"Okay," Shanahan said, amused at Swann's uncop-like prudery.

"What's question number two?"

"You ever talk dirty?" Shanahan asked.

"No. That it?"

"Sounds like manslaughter at best."

"I guess you don't read the papers," Swann said. "His bail was set at nine hundred seventy-five thousand. Murder in the first. I'll get back to you on Moogie and Francine."

Shanahan dialed the number to Howie Cross's office. A computerized woman's voice said: "We're sorry. The number you have dialed is no longer in service."

Shanahan dialed Cross's home number, then looked up at the big TV screen to see Cubs' first baseman, Mark Grace, foul off a pitch. "We're sorry. The number you have dialed . . ."

FIFTEEN

THE DOZEN OR SO people at Harry's place booed as Maureen made her exit with Shanahan.

"I'm going to drop you home, then I'll be out for a few hours," he said. The heat of the afternoon and the effects of the beer made him want to change his mind and go back and sit in the bar until nightfall.

"This is Friday," she said.

"That's true."

"Tonight is Friday night."

"So far, you're making perfect sense."

"Dinner," she said. "A night out, a good restaurant, something maybe a little romantic. You buying all this?"

"You buying dinner?" he asked her.

"I buy, I pick."

"It's a deal, but I've got to see Howie first."

HE'D BEEN spending a lot of time in Howie's part of town. It wasn't all that far from the Holland residence on Pennsylvania Street, and it wasn't more than a half-mile from the Butler University campus where Ramirez was seen in his car and where Sally's nude body had floated in the still inlet.

Howie's neighborhood was an older section, older even than where Shanahan lived. He'd read somewhere that the Butler-Tarkington area had been integrated since something like 1926. Blacks and whites had lived comfortably there together for more than sixty years.

Unlike the frame houses in Shanahan's section of town, these homes were well kept. They weren't huge homes, most of them—miniature colonials, Tudors, Cape Cods, and some assorted Mediterraneans—all about the same size and set back an equal distance from the street, but each home distinctively different.

For the most part they had manicured front lawns, very green despite the merciless August sun. Flowers bloomed. Young parents pushed strollers and chatted. Sprinklers were on; their little metal arms twitched. Small green boxes near the curbs were filled with recyclables and were ready to be picked up. The Jeep Cherokees and lower-priced models of BMW graced the blacktopped driveways.

Howie's place didn't fit in. In front, a beat-up VW bug was parked at a careless angle to the curb. Well-worn, irregularly placed stone steps, half hidden by weeds that had grown to the size of small trees, cut up the slope. The house, barely visible even at the top of the steps, was set way back. The grass in the yard was so tall it had flowered. Shanahan walked along the path between four cedar trees tilted dizzyingly south, until he reached the gate, which drooped to one side, connected only by a single rusted hinge. The gate was open, its lower edge embedded in the earth.

Shanahan wondered if Howie Cross recycled.

"Congratulate me," Howie said at the door.

"Congratulations."

"I have been sober for thirteen hours," Howie said, stepping aside for Shanahan to enter. "Let's have a drink and celebrate."

"I'm already a little lit from two. I'll pass. I tried to call."

"The main benefit of having your phone disconnected is that they can't call and bitch to you for nonpayment. They've cut off their noses to spite their face, er, faces. Whatever."

He pushed aside several magazines and a half-empty bag of Ruffles. He put an empty can of Van Camp's Pork & Beans on the top of the TV, which flashed from the final scenes of a soap opera to a woman holding up some feminine hygiene spray.

"You sit here," he said. "I've already carved a space for me. Isn't this comfy?"

"Comfy," Shanahan said, sitting, pretty sure the blond detective wasn't caught up in the green movement.

"You hear about Holland taking a dive?"

"What?"

"The junior senator from Indiana, the one who isn't the Rhodes Scholar, did a swan into the grave of his dearly departed wife. He was carted off to the hospital."

"You get the photo? Could be worth a fortune."

Howie Cross not only hadn't gotten the falling Holland; he hadn't caught any photos of the funeral service or the graveside ceremony. Security for David Holland was more than heavy; it was impregnable, Cross told Shanahan.

"The veep was there with an armed division of conservatively dressed storm troopers. It says something about our elected officials when there's that many people who want to blow them away. Anyway, no photos. But I do have the list."

"The list?"

"The list of every soul permitted to cross the police barricades. There are some cops on the force who don't hate me."

"Good," Shanahan said. "That may be better."

"Yes and no."

"Tell me the no part."

"I'll show you the no part." Cross stood up and went to a pile of stuff on the floor, picked up a copy of *Play-*

boy. Underneath it were some Xeroxed copies. "Here, read 'em and weep."

There were seven pages, each three columns wide, containing names. At least seven hundred names, Shanahan guessed.

"Christ," Shanahan said.

"Everybody who was anybody was there. But I don't remember seeing a long-haired guy on a burro."

HOLLAND WAS getting dressed, the little containers of food and drink and the sectioned plate on his hospital tray untouched.

"They want to run some tests, Davey," his mother said.

"They always want to run tests," he told her. "That's how they make their money."

A nurse came in, set flowers on the windowsill. "What are you doing, Senator?"

"Exactly what it looks like I'm doing."

She left quickly.

The senator's father was out in the hall talking with a patient who'd been walking in the hall, plastic tubes coming from his forearm to a metal contraption that held plastic bags of clear liquid. Elizabeth was sitting in one of the Naugahyde-covered guest chairs in Holland's room, her body hunched into itself, eyes staring blankly at her knees.

As Holland sat on the edge of the bed, slipping on his dark wingtips, a silver-haired man wearing aviator-styled eyeglasses and a white coat came in.

"You haven't been released," the doctor said.

Holland gave him a brief glance of disgust and slipped on the other shoe.

"We'd like to run some tests. It may be heat, maybe stress. Maybe you're dehydrated. We could run them, probably have you out of here later tonight, tomorrow morning. In any event, you could do with the rest."

"Thanks for your concern," Holland said, standing, tucking in his blue button-down shirt. His tone wasn't one of sincere appreciation, rather dismissal.

"Davey... better safe than sorry," his mother said.

David Holland ignored her, went to Elizabeth, and kneeled down in front of her. He took her hand. She didn't look at him. "I've not been a very good daddy, have I?" he asked her. She didn't respond. "For a while," he said, speaking very slowly, looking at her eyes, trying unsuccessfully to get them to meet his, "you can stay with Grandma and Grandpa. I'm going to try to change things, try to make things better. Okay?"

Finally she looked up. Holland was hopeful. Any response was better than none, he thought.

"What about Emilio?" she asked.

Holland felt his heart drop into his stomach. "I don't know about Emilio," he said. He thought for a moment he was going to cry. He stood up and walked out quickly. In the hallway he caught his father's eyes for the briefest of moments. His father's look was one he'd seen a thousand times. "I know who you are," it said. "I know your dirty little secrets."

BECAUSE HE WAS so close, Shanahan decided to check on something. He drove his green '72 Malibu toward the Butler University campus, took the street by Hinkle Fieldhouse, where the movie *Hoosiers* was filmed, turning right past the landscaped pond, past the observatory, then another right to the curved, smooth, blacktopped road back down again to Holcomb Gardens.

It was late afternoon and, though it was not exactly cool, it was cooler. A few cars were parked on the large cul-de-sac, the same area where Emilio Ramirez would have parked. There was a young couple out walking their dog, some strollers in the long garden rows.

Despite the heat, Shanahan saw a few joggers on the path on the other side of the canal, and two bicyclists were moving slowly down the same path.

Shanahan parked, got out, walked slowly over the little arched bridge that spanned the still, mud-colored water of the canal. He could feel the ribbed wood of the bridge under his feet, and was more secure when he reached the gravel of the path.

He walked south, still a mile, perhaps more from where the body had floated. There were smaller pathways, some gravel, some paths just dry worn earth, all leading through a large field, away from the canal and eventually to the river. He walked on, still by the canal, until he found a wide path to the river with an easy descent.

It soon narrowed, twisted through some high weeds into more trees. It was maybe a hundred yards from the path to the river and still far short of the spot where Sally Holland had been found by young Harmony.

The river indeed flowed south, but though the current was rapid, the water was shallow. Now, with a view of the river all the way down to the big Michigan Road bridge, he realized a body dumped this far north didn't have much of a chance of floating into the inlet. There were enough rock shallows, earthen islands, and tree limbs to have snagged it.

Sally Holland was not put in the river anywhere near where Emilio had parked his car. Shanahan wanted to rest a moment before he finished his hike from where Emilio had been spotted by the university police to where her body had floated in the still waters of the inlet.

Shanahan sat down on the cool earth next to a tree. Someone had carved a heart and the beginning of a name in the weathered, rough, corduroyed bark. Beneath the heart a large black shiny ant carried a much larger and apparently dead beetle.

Shanahan walked back up on the path and continued south. It was a long walk already, one he would have to repeat to get back to his car. He passed a few people on the banks, simple fishing poles in the water, fishermen oblivious to him. There was an occasional sweating jogger, sometimes a pair of them. Finally he crossed Michigan Road and the large bridge that spanned both the canal and the river, where they came closest to joining, where he had parked that morning, where Harmony had parked the morning he discovered Sally Holland.

He was sure this was where the person who dumped her body had parked. But why had this person not tossed the body off the bridge? Why had someone taken the trouble to walk farther down the canal path, then down an even narrower path, through bushes and low limbs to place her where she could still be found?

And of course they had walked down that very path. His dog Casey, returning from sniffing around the corpse, had sniffed high in the air that day, his nose not on the ground trying to catch the scent of a raccoon or possum, but high up on the low branches where Sally's body would have brushed against the leaves.

"Damn," he said. "Why would anyone go to so much trouble?"

Shanahan looked at his watch. He should get back, take Maureen to dinner. He didn't need to revisit the last sighting of Sally Holland before the morgue.

IT WASN'T THAT the food was worse than gruel, which it was; it was that there was so little of it. Emilio Ramirez could put breakfast—the taste of pasty, bitter gravy smothering a soggy piece of white bread—out of his mind. He considered it fuel. Simply fuel.

He, like the others, went to the end of the cellblock to wait for the trustees to shove the metal tray under the bars. There would be cold coffee and warm milk—sometimes a doughnut. A couple of hard souls would trade him milk for his coffee. That helped.

Lunch had been an attempt at Mexican. Beans, some chips, and some salsa, but not a whole lot of it and about as South-of-the-Border as a Twinkie. The guy in the next cell had dozed off when lunch came. No one woke him. Instead, there was a minor fight over how his rations would be split.

Now Ramirez sat on his bunk with dinner. The cold mashed potatoes went down hard. There was a small slice of meat loaf, a slice of white bread. There was milk, thank God, and a small chunk of dehydrated cake.

It would do him no good to exercise all day, he thought, if he couldn't get enough calories to sustain himself. He'd have to figure out the proper ratio of food and sit-ups or find out how to get more food.

Jennifer Bailey didn't know when his case would come to trial. As she told it, they reduced the bail and he was lucky to get bail at all. Didn't really matter. A million and a half dollars versus several hundred thousand. It's a lot like not being able to swim and finding yourself in seven feet of water. Might as well be a thousand.

Worse yet, there was a good chance he'd never get out.

SIXTEEN

LYLE BRODY looked at the grainy photo on the front page of his favorite national newspaper. He shook his head. It was just like the fucking asshole to steal the show, he thought. The shot, obviously taken from a camera with a high-powered telephoto, showed Senator David Holland inside the grave, spread-eagled across his wife's casket.

To add insult to injury, Connie had ditched him as soon as they left the cemetery. "Too upset," she said. She was going to bed. Alone.

Then, this morning, before he could even have his first cup of coffee, Jamie Brothewaite called. He could imagine her big hips in some fifteen-thousand-dollar antique kimono while she bitched at him about the statues.

"Like I told you, Jamie, we have to wait," he said.

"This is your responsibility, Lyle. And quite frankly, this is looking more and more like a con game. You have two and a half million of my money, and it looks more and more like the statues are heading home."

"I don't have your money. I don't have one fucking cent of your money," he said, wishing he'd left the "fucking" out of it. It didn't pay to piss her off any more than she already was. "The brokers have it."

"Then get it back. We'll just call the whole thing off."

"We can't do that," he'd told her, though he wasn't sure that was the truth. Maybe he could. But if she got her money back now, he wouldn't get anything out of this. He'd counted on his commission. "I say wait."

"It doesn't matter what you say, Lyle. Haven't you figured that out yet?"

"Oh, yes, it does, sweetie," Lyle said, but saying it didn't make him feel as good as he'd thought it would.

"Lyle?" she said softly.

"What?"

"I'm going to New York for a few days. When I get back, you better have something for me." She hung up.

"I'll have something for you all right," he yelled into the phone. But only the dial tone replied. "Son of a fucking bitch," he said out loud, throwing the paper across the room.

SHANAHAN WAS UP before Maureen. Out in the backyard he was trying to give the dog his workout before the onslaught of the heat. He had given the dirty green tennis ball its final trajectory when Maureen in her worn terry-cloth robe, juggled two cups of coffee and the screen door. The door lost and slammed back with a sharp crack. Casey took his eyes off the ball for a second and it popped him on the head.

Shanahan knew better than to laugh. Casey did not like to be laughed at.

Maureen sat in the recently painted—she'd done it herself—Adirondack chair, setting both steaming cups on the flat, wide arm.

"Sorry, Case," she said, grinning.

Casey, seeing Shanahan head toward Maureen, sensed the game was over, and, displacing his anger, sunk his teeth into the ball, violently jerking his head back and forth as if he had a possum by the neck.

Shanahan took his cup, took a sip, glanced down to see the lightly freckled flesh in the V of Maureen's robe. She looked up, smiled.

"So where was that gleam in your eye last night?"

His extended trek up and down the canal had left him exhausted. He'd passed out on the sofa shortly after dinner.

"I must've lost it somewhere down by the river."

"You went back?" she asked.

"There are a lot of things that just don't make sense."

"What?"

"Why Emilio, if he killed her, was just sitting in his car near the scene, yet not near the scene."

"Maybe he was going to dump her in the canal, but saw the police first. Had to change his plan."

"Could be. Why would someone carry a hundred and ten pounds a long way into the woods in the dark when he could have dumped her off the bridge?"

"Maybe he was afraid a car would pass. We are saying 'he,' aren't we?" Maureen asked, eyes smiling.

"Have to be a pretty strong woman. But you're right. If he pulled off the road...if he had the body in the trunk, he could have backed in, taken the body, and even a car passing wouldn't see him."

"See?" she said, smiling. "You're trying really hard to make him innocent."

"I think I need to find Charley Baker."

"Who's Charley Baker?"

"Emilio's trainer." He remembered how the man had evaded him after Emilio's last fight before his arrest, the bout the police videotaped, capturing the potentially lethal power of the young boxer's punch. Shanahan figured if anyone knew what Emilio Ramirez was made of, Charley Baker would. Now all he had to do was find the guy and get him to talk.

Shanahan found no Charley Bakers in the phone book. There were sixteen Charles or Chas Bakers, and even eliminating the all-white or upscale neighborhoods, it would be difficult to find anyone home at this hour.

Instead he called one of the local boxing promoters. Finally getting by the receptionist—who could tell him nothing but was determined to help anyway—Shanahan got in touch with the guy who ran the operation. He was a busy man, he said, and wasn't an information service. He became real friendly, though, when he heard Shanahan was a P.I. Usually Shanahan got the opposite reaction. More than likely this guy wanted in on the gossip.

"Don't know how you can get a-hold of Charley. He don't much like people gettin' a-hold of him." There was a laugh. "He's an odd bird, that Charley. Ramirez is the only fighter in ten years he's looked after. We all thought Charley Baker was dead. Then we find out old Charley took the kid in off the street. The kid was thirteen or something. Charley raised him. Sent him to school. Taught him to box."

"What about the guy who works the corner with Charley?"

"Nobody regular. That night it was Seth Bostick."

"Might be the guy," Shanahan said.

"Skinny shit, no ass. Can't keep his pants up?"

"That's him," Shanahan said, remembering. "You have his phone number?"

"Nope. So how you figure to get Ramirez off?"

"Don't know."

"Shanahan, there's two kinds of boxers. The kind who's only mean in the ring. A lot of 'em's pussy-whipped, you know... well, what I mean to say is that they are sweet guys wouldn't harm a fly until they hear the bell. Then the adrenaline gets 'em off. You'd think they had an iron bar in their gloves. You know, like them stories of women being able to lift a car off their kids? Anyways, the other kind, that's the flip side, gettin' physical is the only way they know."

"So what kind of fighter is Ramirez?"

"Good question. You look at his face, he don't show you nothin'. Maybe Charley knows. Problem is, even if he does, he probably won't tell. They're a pair, Charley and Ramirez, cool and quiet."

"They're close, those two?"

"Who can tell. I don't think I ever seen 'em talkin' to each other."

"You ever see Ramirez with a woman?" Shanahan asked.

"Can't say that I have."

"Never with a woman?"

"You're not saying the kid's a little light in the loafers, are you?"

"No."

"Oh, you mean like with the senator's wife?"

"Yeah."

"No. The kid's all business. I seen him three, maybe four times. Don't say nothing. First round, figures out what he's up against. Then bang! Atlantic City, Las Vegas stuff. You know? The kid's got a chance. Did have a chance, huh?"

"Who knows?"

"Yeah, who can figure. Does he have a good lawyer? I know a couple of guys...."

"He's taken care of."

"Who is he? Maybe I know him."

"Jennifer Bailey."

"A chick? Jeez."

LYLE BRODY had showered, shaved, and slipped on a pair of Calvin Klein boxer shorts. Now he was faced with what was always his most difficult decision of the day—what to wear. He'd already ventured out to the balcony to water the miniature palm and a huge rhododendron. He could have cut the air with a knife. He needed something cool. If he didn't have an image to keep up, he'd wear a T-shirt.

"That's it," he said, the solution suddenly dawning on him. He had a beautiful yellow silk T-shirt. That was it, the expensive yellow T with his gray suit. He scurried over to the bureau, pulled out the drawer, and lifted the prize with care.

He set it on the top of the bureau so gently one would have thought it easily breakable. That's when he heard the sound. Nothing could make a sound in his apartment, except maybe the ice-maker. But this wasn't ice dropping. When he entered the hallway, he felt something on his forehead. For a second there was a bright light, like someone flashed a strobe inside his brain. Then the light went out.

SETH BOSTICK'S phone number was in the book. However, Bostick's wasn't the voice Shanahan heard. Apparently, the young corner man's circuits went the way of Howie Cross's, disconnected. He heard the same electronic lady's voice saying, "The number you have reached..." Shanahan thumbed back through the book and wrote down the address.

A quick check in his street guide indicated a location somewhere in or near Greenwood—a rapidly growing town south of and virtually swallowed by the city. At one time the community had been the butt of jokes having to do with rednecks driving pickup trucks with gun racks. That was hardly the case now, at any rate, though the majority of residents were still likely to be church-going, white families.

Shanahan stood on the steps, tapping the metal-framed screen door of the pink-and-gray house trailer that seemed to fit the earlier stereotype. The light outside was too bright and the light inside was too dim to see in. Through the windows, he could hear a twangy guitar and a deep, countrified voice singing something about lonely women making good lovers.

"What can I do for you?" The voice was friendly. Seth Bostick was now visible on the other side of the screen. It was the guy.

"My name is Shanahan. I'm a private investigator."

"Listen, I already told 'em they could come and get it," the kid said without malice.

"I'm here about Emilio Ramirez."

He laughed. "I thought you was the guy from the collection agency. C'mon in." Bostick opened the door and stepped aside. He was shirtless and barefooted. A pair of blue oil-smudged work pants hung precariously on his bony hips.

"I just have a couple of questions," Shanahan said, stepping into the tiny room that smelled of spoiled milk. A child, not more than two or three, clutched an empty milk bottle, blue eyes staring up at the intruder.

"Don't work anyway," Bostick said, nodding toward the huge television set. "I knowed you wasn't picking up the TV 'cause of what you were driving, so I wondered what the hell was goin' on." He laughed. "Sit down."

"Thanks, but I won't be but a minute. You worked with Emilio often?"

"That was the first night, the night he got arrested. I was working the corner for another boxer, and old Charley asked me if I'd help him out."

"Charley Baker?"

Bostick nodded.

Remembering the promoter saying Charley hadn't managed a fighter in ten years, Shanahan wondered how a guy this young would know him.

"You work with Charley before?"

"He managed my ol' man. I knowed him when I was a kid no bigger than Dwight here," Bostick said, pulling up his pants and nodding toward the kid. Dwight's diaper was slipping too.

"A chip off the old block," Shanahan said.

"Yep."

"So you know the fight business?"

"No, just like to hang around, pick up a few bucks."

"You hung around Charley Baker a lot then?"

"Back maybe a ways. Me and my ol' man used to go fishin' with Charley. Two of 'em sit there and not say nothin' for hours and hours."

"That right? They'd fish around here?"

He nodded his head. "White River, mostly."

"Yeah, I've seen people around there, also the canal. I never could figure what people caught in that still water."

"Carp mostly. Ain't much good eatin' really. Charley seemed to like them, though."

"You know where I can find Charley Baker?"

"I don't know his address or nothin', but I think I can show you how to get there."

He went to a little table in the dinette, grabbed a blunt pencil and the envelope that had once held his light bill, and began to draw. "This here is Meridian Street, right?"

"Right..."

SEVENTEEN

LYLE BRODY thought his head was going to explode. His ankles hurt. He was hot and he felt like he was upside down. When he opened his eyes, he discovered he *was* upside down. Below him, seventeen floors below him, traffic had stopped. A crowd had gathered. He looked up. His feet were tied together, and the rope was tied to the balcony. And it seemed like his belly had slid up to his throat.

I'm going to have to diet, he thought to himself.

THE DOORS OF THE OLD but immaculate white frame garage were wide open, looking like short wings on a stubby bird. A heavyset black man in a summer T stroked a rough-edged handsaw across a six-foot length of fresh two-by-four.

Even at his age—and Shanahan guessed Charley Baker to be a contemporary, maybe seventy—there was strength in his sweaty arms.

"Whatchou want?" Baker asked as the pine snapped, fell from the sawhorse, making a hollow clunking sound as it hit the cracked asphalt.

"You remember me?"

"Man lookin' for answers to questions he got no bidness askin'."

"That *is* my business, Mr. Baker."

"That a pretty poor way to have to make a livin'." He picked up the piece of wood he'd just cut, gripping it at one end as if it were a club. "It's too hot to hurry, but you could start mosying back to your Chevy 'bout now."

"Mr. Baker, I'm working for Jennifer Bailey."

"Don't mean nothin' to me."

"She's defending Emilio Ramirez in the murder of Sally Holland."

"Still don't mean nothin' to me." He glared at Shanahan.

"I'm not sure you understand. I'm trying to help the kid."

"That your bidness." Charley Baker reminded Shanahan of the presence of the piece of two-by-four by crossing it in front of him, letting it tap the palm of his other hand.

"You are his trainer?"

"I was that."

"His friend too, I'd think."

"Who say that?"

"They tell me you practically raised him. I thought maybe the two of you went fishing."

"I think maybe that jus' what you're doin'." Baker turned away, put another length of wood on the sawhorse.

Shanahan strolled past Baker's big shiny old Oldsmobile. It was as well-kept as the house and garage. He was sure he wasn't going to get any more answers. And pressing Charley Baker didn't seem like a good idea, two-by-four or not.

But some things troubled Shanahan. If Charley Baker didn't like Emilio Ramirez, why would he have come out of retirement to train him, work with him day after day? Baker didn't seem like a man who'd suffer fools kindly. And if he did train Ramirez solely because he thought he had a real contender, wouldn't he want to keep his man out of prison?

He would unless, of course, he honestly thought Ramirez had done it. He'd have to be pretty damn sure, Shanahan thought.

WHEN THEY LET Lyle Brody out of the hospital—he'd been there only two hours—he returned to his apartment by way of one of his favorite "dance" bars, one of the sleazy ones. This was the first time he didn't bother teasing the girls. Instead, he picked up a shiny, pearl-handled, snub-nosed .38 from the day manager.

Danny Mitchum, who was by day a full-time go-go herder, guided the more ambitious girls to more lucrative performances at night. He owed Lyle for not one but two no-shows. He couldn't blame the girls because they no doubt got wind of Brody's reputation. He got a little rough sometimes. Even so, he still owed Brody.

Normally it took Mitchum a couple of hours, at least, to round up the desired hardware. But Lyle was in a hurry, and he wasn't a "fucking collector," he just wanted to be able to blow someone's brains out. Mitchum, taking note of Lyle's mood, decided not to bullshit him, even if that meant giving up his own gun.

When Lyle finally arrived at his apartment, he self-medicated by chugging three shots of Stolichnaya neat. The fourth he poured over ice, feeling the pain in his head recede. He picked up the phone and pushed the button programmed for Jamie Brothewaite, often glancing at the door as the phone rang.

"Jamie, please," he told the male voice that answered.

"I'm sorry, she's away for a while."

"What the hell does that mean. Away? Where can I reach her?"

"I'm sorry," the voice repeated. "Who is this calling?"

He started to tell the guy to go fuck himself, but he paused to gather a little calm. "My name is Lyle Brody and...uh...it's urgent that I talk with her. Now."

There was a long pause.

"You still there?" Brody asked.

"Yes, yes," the voice said nervously. "I'm sorry."

"Quit fucking saying you're sorry." Brody just couldn't hold his anger.

"I'm sorry. I mean I'm not sorry. Can I give Miss Brothewaite a message should she call in?"

Jamie Brothewaite obviously had some goddamn list of people she was willing to talk to. And Lyle Brody's name wasn't on it.

"Yeah, tell her that little rope trick cost her two hundred thousand dollars, and if she plays it again . . ." Lyle stopped suddenly. What a stupid ass I am, he thought.

"I'm sorry, what?"

"Fuck it," he said, and hung up.

He sipped his vodka, looked at his watch, trying to figure out what time it would be in Greece and whether the guy who answered Jamie's phone came with the condo.

SHANAHAN FOUND a note from Maureen when he got home:

"Be back around eight. Will bring Chinese."

He let Casey out, not letting the spotted, speckled mongrel bark Shanahan back out into the heat for an impromptu afternoon ball game. Instead, he rummaged through his cluttered desk for Jennifer Bailey's phone number.

When he picked up the phone and started to dial, he heard, "Hey, it's me."

"Who's me?"

"Sounds like one of those Eastern Religion questions. Howie Cross. I didn't hear it ring."

"It didn't. I'm psychic."

"Cool. Then you know what I'm going to say."

"Don't deprive me of the pleasure of your voice."

"Thought you might want to know something. Lyle Brody, the brother of the senator's recently demised wife? They found him hanging off his seventeen-floor balcony."

"Suicide?"

"Well, if that's what he wanted to do, the fool got the wrong end. He was hanging by his feet. He is very much alive. I ran into the cop who gave me the funeral invitation list at Dick's Dogs, and he couldn't wait to tell me about it."

"So tell me."

"Brody says it was some guys playing a practical joke. He wasn't going to name names, let alone press charges. But it doesn't wash because he has a lump on the back of his head the size of a tomato. They wanted to take him to the hospital, and the medics had to wait thirty minutes while he fussed about what he was going to wear. What do you figure?"

"Sounds to me like he's made some trouble with somebody who knows how to make trouble back."

"Yeah. If not retribution, then a warning of some sort."

"Howie, do I have to pay you for this? It'll be on this evening's news."

"Not the way I told it."

"Then to earn your keep, you mind finding out a few things for me?"

"On the payroll, you say?"

"How can I get to the senator?"

"Go to the airport and get on the plane marked Washington, D.C. He's outta here as of this afternoon, so says Channel Thirteen last night. What a fool I am! Now you see why I never have any money? Oliver Hogsmith thinks I ought to be an official UFO investigator. Says I might not earn much right way but that there's a great future in it. I've told you about my neighbor, Oliver

Hogsmith, haven't I? He thinks a group of aliens are just waiting for the right time to take over, say as soon as all the nuclear weapons are destroyed, they'll walk right in."

"Could happen," Shanahan said, finding Jennifer Bailey's phone number.

"He says never mind the Trilateral Commission, it's…shit, I can't remember the name of these beings, but they lived here once some place in the Pacific Ocean. They found better digs in another galaxy and took off. Sank their own goddamn country, he said. Meanwhile, they're the force behind the Republicans."

"Sounds reasonable," Shanahan said, flipping through the white pages for Lyle Brody.

"Oliver is reasonable. He can program a VCR. Anybody can do that has superior intelligence."

"Thanks, Howie," Shanahan said, spotting the "Lyle R. Brody," with a downtown address. "Where are you calling from? I thought you were disconnected."

"All my life. Public phone. I'll be putting the fifty cents on my expenses."

"It's only a quarter, Howie."

"I dialed wrong the first time. If only I were as smart as Oliver Hogsmith."

"Is he a real person, Howie, this Mr. Hogsmith?"

"God, I hope so. I'm too old to have an imaginary friend. Then again…"

Shanahan thanked him, wondered for a moment if Howie had been drinking, then remembered talking to him when he was sober. He couldn't tell the difference. Shanahan decided to make another call. He dialed, squinting his eyes to make out the number scribbled on the piece of paper he held in his hand.

Jennifer Bailey's male secretary, who used to regard the detective's calls as nuisances, promised to get her right away. He also called him "Mr. Shanahan" without the usual sneer creeping into his voice.

Shanahan had planned to tell the attorney about Charley Baker and hope she could get something from Emilio about what happened between the young boxer and his trainer. Also, to warn her Baker could be an unfriendly witness. Now he would fill her in on Lyle Brody's circus act and an idea that had just occurred to him.

EMILIO RAMIREZ sat in his jail cell, holding a letter from the only person who ever wrote to him, other than those who addressed him as current resident.

Dear Emilio,

Tomorrow is the funeral. I am very sorry you cannot come. Mom would have wanted you there more than anybody. You didn't do it. I know that. I wanted you to know that for sure. Grandpa says that sometimes the police make mistakes and that's why they have courts and judges. Then the truth comes out and the people who do wrong go away for a long time and the people who didn't do it are let go.

Grandpa always tries to tell the truth. But I am worried. It seems that not everything is fair at all. Things that aren't nice seem to happen to people when they didn't do anything wrong. And sometimes the people it happened to can't do anything about it.

Anyway, I miss you, Emilio. If they let you write letters, please write to me. I'm in Fort Wayne now. The address is on the envelope in case you forgot.

Love,
Elizabeth

Emilio folded the pages carefully, slid them into the envelope, and tucked it under the mat on his bunk. His only letter, and it had been opened before he got it. Opened, examined, and probably copied.

He shook his head. He could imagine them calling Elizabeth to the stand.

"Now don't be frightened. Just answer the questions and you can get down. How many times did Emilio Ramirez visit your house when your father wasn't at home?"

That's what they'd ask, something like that. And Elizabeth would tell them. Poor, sweet Elizabeth. It wasn't over for her, either.

SHANAHAN DISCOVERED Jennifer Bailey knew next to nothing about Lyle Brody. She reluctantly okayed the expenses Shanahan would incur pursuing his idea. She was a little more excited about Lyle Brody's dangling rope trick.

She also said Emilio was emphatic about Sally Holland's never having been in his apartment.

"He told me she didn't even know where he lived. That the only person who ever set foot in his apartment was Charley Baker, who went with him on his morning run."

"Maybe she found out where he lived, was lonely one night, and showed up unexpectedly. In the dark, he thought..."

"No," Jennifer had said, "he would have told me."

"Are you getting a little too close to this?" Shanahan asked, almost calling her "Jennifer."

There had been a long pause at the other end of the line, punctuated finally by a very tired voice saying, "Maybe."

SHANAHAN PULLED HIS Chevy to the curb in front of the tallest of the three towers that made up the complex. He remembered when they were built. A big deal then. Years ago. They were going to build an entire community—a bunch of towers, a bunch more condos. They were going to dig a lake big enough for small sailboats in the middle of the city. Never happened. The towers stood there amid the low-rises like three spikes in a sidewalk.

"Who is it?" came the curt response to the button near the mailboxes in the little space before the lobby.

"Dietrich Shanahan. I'm a private investigator working for Jennifer Bailey. Defense counsel, Mr. Brody."

"You got papers?"

"No."

"Get lost."

EIGHTEEN

SENATOR DAVID HOLLAND sat at his large oak desk on which there was a scattering of papers and a framed triptych of photographs of his family placed at such an angle that visitors could see them better than he could. Slightly behind him, against the wall, an American flag flanked one side of the desk. The Indiana flag stood at the other. On the walls of his Washington office were hundreds of pictures. One was the formal portrait of the President. The others, all photographs, framed in the same thin black frames, presented David's life in the flattering manner of an authorized biography.

His graduation picture. One with him and a group from Junior Achievement. Holland receiving a college debate trophy. His college football team with the young senator-to-be's face prominently circled with a light blue tint. The rest, the bulk of them, were celebrity shots. Holland with movie and TV stars. Holland with former Presidents and other politicians who'd achieved some sort of legendary Washington, if not national, status.

Holland had been sitting there for hours. Expressionless. He was not sure what he was thinking or, in fact, if he was thinking. Suddenly he smiled. He got up and walked into the staff room. It was only half staffed because Congress wasn't in session. But he called aside one young man who'd been there six months.

"Carter, I want you to get hold of that public relations firm...oh, shit, what's their name...Beaton, Burns and Farnsworth."

"Keaton, Burnside and Farnsworth?" Carter said.

He, like Eric Barton, wore suspenders and tortoise-shell glasses. These aides, the senator thought, they were interchangeable.

"The very ones. Set up an appointment for tomorrow."

"Yessir," Carter said too enthusiastically.

The others looked apprehensive. It occurred to Holland that while they knew something was up, they didn't know what. A firm like Keaton, Burnside and Farnsworth was used not only to deliver good news but to handle the bad.

"If we want to be around six more years, we'll need some help, won't we?" he asked them.

To his surprise, they applauded. He felt tears welling up. The flow was stemmed just as quickly when he thought they might merely be applauding for their jobs.

"Good news, huh?" he said to them. He was back to reality.

SHANAHAN HAD retreated from the apartment tower entrance, but only so far as his green Malibu. The sun, fortunately, was on the other side of the building, keeping his metered parking space in the shade. In less than fifteen minutes a lady with a cloth bag full of groceries headed toward the entrance.

Shanahan got out of the car, dropped two quarters in the meter, and followed.

"Let me get that," he said as she removed her key from the lobby door and started to push in.

"Oh, thank you. If I'd known it was this hot, I would have stayed home."

In the elevator she asked Shanahan if he lived in the building. "No," he replied. "Visiting a friend. Lyle Brody. You know him?"

"I've lived here fifteen years," she said, "and I know maybe three people who live here. I don't think I've ever met your friend."

"He was the one hanging from the balcony," Shanahan said.

"Oh, goodness. What a terrible thing. Is he all right?"

"That's what I'm going to find out," he told her as she got off on fourteen.

Shanahan understood how you could live in a building like this for years and not know anyone. Just long halls with doors, much like a hotel. Then again, Shanahan had lived in his house for more than a few decades and couldn't name any of his neighbors.

The lady's concern about Mr. Brody's current state of health was answered when the door opened. Lyle Brody was all right enough to handle a gun. The shiny .38 snubnose was pointed right at Shanahan.

"You the guy buzzed me?"

"Shanahan. Working for Jennifer Bailey."

"What do people think I am? A goddamn washrag? I say no. No, like in no visitors."

"I don't know, Mr. Brody. I just thought it would be easier talking to you here than getting some sort of court order and you having to come to some stuffy office when you're feeling bad."

Brody, in his pale ivory silk pajamas and silk robe, lowered the gun and stepped aside. He gave Shanahan a good look. Whether he was looking for signs of a weapon or merely judging him by the less than expensive cut of his cloth, Shanahan didn't know.

"What I'd like to know is why you'd be interested in me." Brody followed Shanahan in, sat on the leather sofa. "Sit," he said, "and explain to me what you want. I wasn't there when it happened. I never met this Ramirez guy. She never even told me anything about him. I got nothing to give you." He got up, picked up his drink from the table by the door.

Shanahan glanced around the room. A far stretch of city could be seen through the glass doors that led out to the balcony. The furniture inside was moderately expensive. Contemporary. The place was immaculate. On the glass-topped cocktail table was a stack of magazines. *L'uomo, Vogue, GQ,* and a couple of others he couldn't see but guessed were men's fashion magazines. He thought about Cross telling him Brody took half an hour to get dressed for the hospital.

"Well?" Brody said, sitting down again, putting the shiny .38 next to him, on the sofa. "Well?"

"What was your sister like?"

"Christ. I hope this doesn't take forever. Okay. A good kid. A do-gooder. A little sentimental maybe. Literally, and I mean literally, she wouldn't harm a fly."

"You think she could have had an affair?"

"With that boxer? You kidding? She did some work with the what-do-you-call-it—the Hispano Center. Probably ran into the guy there. Probably trying to help him in some way. Teach him to read, or get him some education. Maybe he hits on her. I didn't mean it that way. Maybe he falls for her. She doesn't want any part of it. Bam! Then he hits on her for real." He smacked his fist into his palm, then shrugged, as if to say, "Could be, how should I know?"

"Did you like your sister?"

"What is this? C'mon. Don't play shrink. Uh. Of course, I liked my sister. She's my sister. Why wouldn't I like my sister?"

"Anything odd in the family? She and the senator . . ."

"Like anybody else married for a few years. Things cool off, you know. He's got his career. She's got her interests, whales and shit like that."

"People say David Holland's a real great guy."

Brody laughed. "Yeah, well, people'll say anything. I mean sure he's a regular guy. Nothing special. Good looks. With a little luck could be anybody sitting up there."

"Pretty straight guy. Good husband. Good father, that sort of thing? That's what I heard, anyway."

Brody grinned, sipped his drink. "Yeah, well, what politician isn't a good family man? They work pretty hard to keep things under wraps. You know, no drinking problems, no domestic quarrels. Go to church on Sunday—after they tell the press what time they'll be there. Every politician's a saint, right? Don't believe the press releases."

"I checked. Nothing in the scandal sheets."

"Not high enough profile. Anyway, they got plenty with the Kennedys, don't they?" Suddenly he leaned forward. "Listen, you tell anybody I said this and I'll deny it. Off the record, huh?"

"Yeah, sure."

"Hill fever. You know what that is?"

"No."

"It means that once you get to Washington and you get yourself into the Senate or the House, the women come out of the woodwork. The women come fluttering to the hill like moths to a porch light. Guys, you know, like a looker, right. Don't have to be nothing between the ears. Just good legs or tits or whatever their thing is. You see these beautiful women, right? Half the time they're with some old toad. So you become a senator or something. And suddenly you're glowing with power. And then all that power you got goes right to your pecker."

He laughed, took a sip of his drink.

"Is that right? So the senator likes to play around?"

"You know the power people? Here in the city? The ones that make things happen? The ones that build the museums and donate a bundle to politicos?"

"I doubt it."

"Well, it's not the people who get their names in the newspapers or magazines. It's a quiet group, the money group. And I'm pretty sure—hell, I know—David Holland will hop on the merry-go-round with any one of them if there's a possibility for a campaign contribution. And the rich bitches—man, they think he's Mel Gibson or somebody." Brody took another sip.

"Just gossip probably."

"I'm fucking well sure of one," Brody said. "You heard of Jamie Brothewaite? Of course not. Worth a ton, though. This one came from reliable sources. A real bitch, that one." His hand dropped down over the .38. "She'll fuck him up, that's what she'll do." Brody stared out the window as if in another world for a moment. Then he shook his head. "Women," he said with disgust.

"How'd you end up hanging off the balcony, Mr. Brody?"

"You know about that? Just a prank. I got some friends. They play some pretty rough practical jokes, you know?"

"They practically broke your skull. I'd think about making some new friends."

"I hit my head on the railing. They were so busy laughing they didn't notice. I mean, I'm not pressing charges or nothing. No big deal."

"Is that why you answered the door with a gun in your hand?"

"Listen," he said, laughing. "I'm not sure why I'm being so nice to you. I hope they fry the spic bastard!"

SHANAHAN DIDN'T LIKE what was happening to his investigation. Instead of narrowing in, things were broadening out. He had more questions than answers.

Driving home, Shanahan was still pretty sure Ramirez was guilty. And that could explain why Charley Baker seemingly washed his hands of the kid. And Brody getting dangled off the balcony could be explained by the guy's less than likable personality, but it wasn't likely. He wasn't buying the prank story, but it wasn't difficult to imagine a guy like Lyle Brody doing something that really rubbed somebody the wrong way and not merely with his abrasive personality. But he'd like to know who Brody was rubbing, if that was the case.

He checked his watch. Maureen wouldn't be home for a couple of hours yet. He'd stop by Harry's, he thought. He remembered the woman who unwittingly let him in, the one inquiring about Brody's health. That made him think of Mrs. Schmidt. Maybe he'd drive by Moogie's first.

NINETEEN

HE DIDN'T SEE Moogie right away. But the hood was up on the '57 Ford, and a black leather jacket was on the roof. Shanahan slowed, inched up until the window of his car was even with the slender youth hunched over the engine.

"Moogie?"

The kid looked up, perplexed. Trying to place the face. Couldn't.

"Who the hell are you?"

This wasn't Shanahan's day for friendly greetings. At least Moogie wasn't carrying a gun.

"Shanahan. I'm a friend of Mrs. Schmidt."

"Who...oh. So?"

"I want to talk with you."

"She sick or something?"

"No."

"Francine all right?"

"As far as I know. But that's what I want to talk with you about."

"She don't want me seeing Francine. That it? Tough shit, mister." Moogie turned, put the air filter back in.

"I just want to talk for a minute," Shanahan said.

"Nothin' to talk about. And I don't have the time even if there was. I'm late."

"Won't turn over?" Shanahan asked, nodding toward the car.

"No. Don't even try. Just a click."

"Try the horn," Shanahan said.

"What?"

"Try the horn."

Moogie gave him the kind of look you'd give someone who told you to do something disgusting. He tried it anyway. No sound. Nothing.

"Shit," Moogie said, leaning back against the car. "It's the fucking electrical system."

"Maybe just the battery."

"It's ninety degrees out here. How could it be the battery?"

"Check the cells, see if they aren't dry."

Moogie did as he was told.

"You're right," he said. "Three of them. Not a drop." He ran back toward the house, returning with a hose, water barely coming out.

"I still want to talk with you," Shanahan said.

"Look, thanks for the advice, okay? Hey, pay back later, okay? But not now. I gotta run."

"You need a charge," Shanahan said. "I've got cables."

"I do too," the kid said, smiling.

"What are you going to hook them to?"

Moogie looked around. "Good point."

"Mrs. Schmidt. Can you be nice to her?"

"Who is she to you? Are you Francine's uncle or something?"

'I'm a private investigator. She hired me to check up on you."

"C'mon," Moogie said.

"Doesn't matter, anyway. She's a nice lady. She's kind of living in the past, you know?"

"Tell me."

"What I'm trying to say is that the world has kind of moved ahead. And she hasn't. She's not up on what kids wear these days. I mean you're running around looking like a savage, and Francine comes home with her nose pierced. This scares the hell out of a woman like Mrs. Schmidt.''

"Man, this is the way I wear my hair.''

"I'm not telling you to get a haircut. You can paint it purple for all I care. Just say hello to her. Ask her how she's feeling or something. You're going to get old someday.''

"Not me, man. I'm blowing out my last candle at twenty-nine. No shit.''

"Yeah. That's what every guy says when he's your age. But you'll grow up to be an old fart like me. Then you'll have hair growing out of your ears, your ass will get all bony, and you'll have trouble taking a piss just like the rest of us.''

"Man,'' Moogie said, shaking his head. "You're a kick.'' He ran his hand over his hair, grinned. "You carrying a gun?''

"No.''

"A private eye. No shit?'' He shook his head.

"So I'm just trying to make her feel better. Talk to Francine. It doesn't hurt to be nice to the woman.''

"Like be a real phony, a real nerd. How are you today, Mrs. Schmidt. My, you look fine. Like Eddie Haskell or something.''

"The world's pretty scary for her. Help her out. Won't cost you anything.''

"What you want me to do? Bring her flowers and shit.''

"Maybe. Pretend she's your grandmother or something. Are you nice to your grandmother?''

"They're dead. Both of them.'' He reached for his jacket, pulled out a pack of Marlboros, poked the package on his hand until he could get his fingers on a cigarette. "I knew one of them. She was okay. I think she knew she had a shithead for a son.'' He lit his cigarette, took a long drag.

"So you and your dad don't get along?"

Disgust showed on Moogie's face. "Man, the guy goes to work, comes home, eats, burps, sits in front of the tube, and goes to bed. And then he's got the balls to say I ain't gonna amount to anything."

"So what do you want to do?"

"Music."

"So do it."

"My old man says I'm just goofin' off. Won't fucking even listen to what I'm doing. You got kids?"

"Yeah," Shanahan said. "A son. A pretty old kid by now, I guess."

"You guess?"

'I haven't seen him in a while."

"You don't like him or something?" Moogie asked, head cocked to one side as if verifying his belief that fathers don't care about their sons.

"It's a long story," Shanahan said. "Let's get your car running."

SHANAHAN HADN'T thought about his son, Ty, since the day he called to say Elaine had died. And Shanahan pretty well cut short that conversation. One phone call in thirty years, and Shanahan blew it. Probably be another thirty years before he heard from him. If he had his son's number, maybe he'd call him. But he didn't even know where the kid lived. Kid? He'd have to be forty by now.

He didn't want to think about it. At times like these, Shanahan was glad he had something else to occupy his mind. And right now it was the curious Mr. Brody who could do that for him.

Instead of heading directly to Harry's bar, which was closer, he continued north to visit Howie Cross. Howie, with his police connections, however tenuous they were, might be able to get some information Shanahan couldn't.

Just as he pulled up to Howie's place, the Indiana Bell Telephone van scooted away.

"It's a good thing this is summer," Howie told him, clearing the debris off the sofa so Shanahan could sit. "Because it would narrow down to a choice. Do I want to freeze to death or do I want to spend three hours on the phone with my mother?"

"Tough choice."

"No, no, listen. Get this. I can't afford to pay my phone bill, right. So they go bang, no service. Okay, I'll buy that. But to hook you back up costs you a fortune. So you get more in the hole. If you're running your bank account near empty and you happen to bounce a check— whamo, they hit you with a big fee 'cause you don't have enough money. Then, when you go to the grocery, you can't afford to buy much, so you buy the little cans, the little packages, which cost more per pound or ounce or whatever than the big ones that you can't afford to buy. Those who can afford it the least pay the most." Cross slumped back in the sofa in mock despair. "You want to hear another?"

"I get the picture, Howie."

"No, one more. You know how I could afford to get my telephone hooked up?" He picked up a bag of Ruffles, offering them first to Shanahan, who declined.

"I give. Tell me, how did you pay your phone bill?"

"By repossessing a couple of cars for some dude at a finance company that charges a kazillion percent interest. Now the poor schnook can't go to work, so now he won't make his mortgage payment, and so they'll take away his house." He tossed the bag on the TV set, threw up his hands. "To get on my feet, I had to cut someone off at the knees."

"You mind doing something a little illegal?"

Howie smiled. "As long as it's not throwing cats in front of seeing eye dogs, at this point, I'll probably do it.

But Jesus, the whole world is embracing capitalism, and I think I'm become a socialist. My timing is lousy, don't you think?"

"Lyle Brody. I want to find out how he earns his money, and I want to find out who he talks to."

"Used to own a restaurant. Sold out to a big chain. Probably still living on the proceeds. That's your first answer. And in case you're wondering, I used to date a waitress who worked there."

"I don't believe this," Shanahan said.

"Don't forget, I was a cop. I've dated a lot of waitresses. And frankly a lot of waitresses worked for old Lyle. He didn't like ones he couldn't screw, and he didn't like the ones he did screw after he screwed them. Then they were really screwed. He isn't a nice man."

"Did your date ever talk about Lyle and his friends?"

"No, she wouldn't have picked up on that. And I don't recall him getting into any serious trouble with the police."

"You have any connections with the phone company?"

"If I did, would they shut off my service? Actually, I do." He rubbed his hands over his eyes. "I'd have to lay out some money, Shanahan. And about the best I could do is long distance outcalls. Nothing sophisticated." He stopped talking for a moment, sat down on the arm of an upholstered chair. "A hundred, maybe two, if I'm reading the question on your face right. Is it worth it to go on a fishing expedition?"

"If only I knew what I was fishing for," Shanahan said. "Do it." He hoped Jennifer Bailey agreed. If not, he could be fishing for his dinner—he and Charley Baker.

BY THE TIME Shanahan stopped home, left a note for Maureen, and arrived at Harry's bar, it was nearly six. It was like stepping into a dark refrigerator. When his eyes adjusted, he noted the usual number of usual people were around the bar. Regulars. There was a stranger at one of the tables eating a bowl of stew. Obviously, the guy wasn't a regular. The word on Harry's stew had gotten out pretty quick.

Harry had a long-necked bottle of Miller High Life on the bar as Shanahan sat down, looked up at the big screen in time to see a bowling ball miss a lone pin.

"Can we watch the news?" he asked Harry.

"Listen, Deets, the news ain't good for business. People drink better to sports."

"The action on now is pretty hard to tear yourself away from, I know. But it's important."

"CNN?"

"Local."

"Something cooking on the senator's wife?" Harry said, switching the channel to 13.

"Emilio Ramirez's goose."

"Just because you're on the case don't mean he didn't do it."

"That's Maureen's line."

"Well, she's right as rain."

"Maybe," Shanahan said.

"Why?"

"Because," Shanahan said. He took a big gulp of beer. The taste wasn't important at the moment, just the cold.

"Why? C'mon, let me drag it outta you one word at a time," Harry said sarcastically.

"Harry, look. He says Sally Holland has never been to his apartment. Never. The police have next to absolute proof that she was there. Yet he won't change his story even at the urging of his own defense attorney. It's against his own interest to keep saying that."

"Maybe he's stupid."

"Maybe he's stubborn," Shanahan said, noticing the video of a person dangling from the balcony of a high rise.

"Well, and you're an expert on that."

"Turn it up Harry."

". . . in a bizarre incident today at a downtown apartment building," said the newscaster's voice-over, "the victim, Lyle R. Brody, former owner of the Louisiana House restaurant, said that it was merely a prank gone wrong. Police and fire officials at the scene had no comment. And the prosecutor's office said there was little they could do unless Brody files charges. Brody, who is the brother of the late Sally Holland, could not be reached for comment, though he has been released from the hospital with only minor injuries."

The camera switched back to the studio. A back-lit photo of Senator David Holland was superimposed on the wall behind the dark-haired, mustached newscaster.

"In related news Channel 13 learned today that Senator David Holland will comment on speculation about his reelection campaign. There has been increasing concern that he might bow out because of the deep personal tragedy. A formal announcement is expected within days. Meanwhile, polls show increasing support for former state congressman Edmund Carem."

Shanahan drank his beer, only half listening to the anchor talking about the likelihood of the popular, former Indianapolis mayor stepping into the race.

"You mind if I use the phone?" Shanahan asked, fishing a crumpled piece of paper out of his pocket. He unfolded it and squinted. "Why is it always so dark in here?"

Harry put the phone on the bar, watched his friend punch in the number. "Because we ain't performin' surgery in here, Deets. We're trying to set the proper mood. You understand mood, don't you?"

"Yeah, I'm feeling pretty romantic, how 'bout you?"

Again he was connected with Jennifer Bailey with dispatch. "I'm running a check on Lyle Brody and it's going to cost a few bucks."

"The brother?"

"Yeah."

"Why not?" she said, sounding tired or depressed or both.

"What's up?"

"The prosecution has Elizabeth Brody's diary. In it, apparently, she mentions Emilio on about every other page."

"I know."

"You know? How do you know?"

"Oh, I imagine. He's a nice-looking young man, and she's at that impressionable age."

"Well, it's clear he has visited her at her home. Several times."

"We knew that, didn't we?"

"Yes. They probably did too. But a diary, Mr. Shanahan. It's written. The jury will be impressed by it. I don't know." Shanahan could hear her sigh. "I don't know what we have to counter any of this. The evidence is mounting every day, and I don't even know what to tell you to do or where to look."

Shanahan knew that all they had at the moment was the standard, ineffectual, I-was-framed defense.

"We'll figure out something."

"Charley Baker is the only character witness, and now you're telling me he's not too eager to help."

"Doesn't appear to be," Shanahan said. "Do they want to make a deal?"

"They couldn't if they wanted to," she said.

"Unfortunately, if it's a frame—and, Ms. Bailey, I'm saying 'if'—then we have to find the framer or framers."

"I don't believe he could have done it," she said it in her cold, professional voice. "I'd stake my career on it."

He took her tone as an admonishment. Negativity, with regard to Emilio Ramirez, wasn't to be permitted. The thing was, she wouldn't have to stake her career on it. She'd not only make the papers, she'd get national coverage. And given the situation, losing wasn't better than winning. But it was better than not being part of it at all.

"You are going to Washington then," she continued. All the real weariness, fear, vulnerability he'd glimpsed earlier had completely vanished.

"Yeah. Tomorrow, I think." He chose not to run down the complete list of evidence Lieutenant Swann had reiterated for him. She was probably all too painfully aware of it. "Would you make me a copy of the diary and send it over to my place?"

"Shanahan. Emilio hasn't had an easy life."

He wanted to tell her Charles Manson had a pretty terrible childhood too, but he didn't.

TWENTY

IT WAS STILL an hour or so before Maureen would arrive home. He decided—if he kept his dehydrated body on the bar stool, he'd get lit. He put two bucks on the bar and told Harry he'd see him later.

Tonight he'd fix dinner. The two of them would climb into bed and watch the Cubs. The game was in L.A. Another late night at the ballpark thanks to an orbiting satellite.

Her Toyota was in the driveway. Inside, he found her in the bedroom, wrapped in a towel, looking under the bed for something. She'd just stepped out of the shower, the little beads of water catching gleams of light.

He wanted to ask her where she'd been. But he'd promised himself he'd never do that. He never wanted her to leave; he was more sure of that one thing than of anything else. Still, it was one day at a time. Limit the expectations.

"I thought I was supposed to meet you at Harry's." Her face, scrubbed clean of cosmetics, nevertheless seemed to glow.

"What did you lose?"

"Oh." She laughed, got up, and sat on the edge of the bed. "I forgot. My marbles, I guess. A harried day. Oh, yes! My other slipper. I think Casey took it. I think he's trying to make me think I'm going crazy like Rex Harrison did with Doris Day."

"Dinner in?"

"If you're cooking." She looked up at him. "You have that look, you know."

"What look?"

"Like you are finding me absolutely, devastatingly irresistible right now or..."

"Or?"

"You mean that's not it? Then it can only mean you have something to tell me that you think is going to upset me, even though it never does."

"I'm flying to Washington tomorrow."

"And you don't want me to come?"

"You want to?"

"That's not what I asked," she said, grinning.

"It's work." He *was* finding her irresistible.

"So you don't want me to come?"

"Yes, I do. Maureen, why don't you come with me?"

"I can't. I listed a house this afternoon."

"Then we'll celebrate," he said, glad she was happy, but gladder still that he knew what she had been doing all afternoon.

"Then afterward we'll have dinner," she said, standing up, kissing him, gently tugging at her towel until she could feel it slipping away.

LYLE BRODY was still bitterly disappointed about his failure to make it on the front page of *USA Today* in the expected dignified photo of the grieving family. It was as if the senator's all too photogenic swooning dive into his wife's grave wasn't enough.

Nor was it enough punishment to miss, at least—at the very least—a mention in Donna Mullinex's society column for handling the city's largest art transaction.

No. No, his fate was to be forever remembered as the chubby guy in his boxer shorts, tied by his feet, dangling from the balcony of his seventeenth-floor apartment.

It was early morning. Barely light. Still in his pajamas and robe, Lyle Brody was on the phone, waiting for the phone to ring a few thousand miles away, listening to that eerie silence as the signal climbs to a satellite and bounces back to earth in Brussels. He'd already called their office in Athens. The only thing he'd understood after he asked for the senior partner was the word "Brussels." Fortunately he had their stationery, which listed that number as well.

They were legit, these art dealers, but business was business and he wasn't sure they'd be willing to take a loss. Hell, he wouldn't. But then these guys were big international guys. They had a reputation to think of.

"Bonjour," came the voice finally.

He asked for the man whose name appeared first on the letterhead, the man he'd talked with earlier, before he was shunted down to some lower-level functionary.

"Who is speaking, may I ask?"

"Lyle Brody. I'm calling from the United States."

"T'ank you. One moment, please."

"Ah, Mr. Brody," the man said cheerfully. "So good to hear your voice again."

That was a good sign, wasn't it? He was eager for signs of hope. He was nervous. He'd never been nervous talking with people before. Despite the fact that he kept his apartment extremely cool in the summer, he was already perspiring.

"Thank you. My client, Miss Brothewaite, has learned something disturbing."

"Yes, yes," the man said, his voice filled with concern. "It is so terribly unfortunate. I learned of it only a few days ago, myself."

"That's what I wanted to talk with you about. Miss Brothewaite feels that this situation certainly...uh... compromises the agreement we had with you and your client."

"It is truly devastating news. I can say that we here are all terribly disappointed, and our client has expressed his concern over your situation."

"My situation?" Brody said. Oops. They weren't going to take any responsibility. But he felt a sudden dislike for the man he was talking to, the phone courtesy and expression of sympathy. He'd rather the guy would just say, "Buddy, you're screwed to the wall."

"Perhaps your attorneys could contact ours and arrange for a little assistance on this side of the Atlantic, Mr. Brody."

"No, no, what this means is the deal is off. Obviously your client didn't own what he sold."

"I understand your frustration, Mr. Brody. And we will do all we can here to help you through the complicated laws in this part of the world. Perhaps we can…how is this best to say?…retrieve this from the fire. As I said before, perhaps we can be of some advisory assistance in this regard."

"How can you sell what isn't yours?"

"Mr. Brody, please. Let us keep our fine relationship. There is considerable room for an appeal. It is not set in stone."

"Fire, stone, what the hell. A court case could take years and be very expensive, especially trying to do this from the U.S. I believe handling that sort of thing is your or your client's job. Not mine. I'd appreciate your wiring the money immediately."

Brody already knew the answer. But it was worth a try.

"I couldn't do that, even if I wanted to. Like you, we are only intermediaries. Please take a moment to read the agreement. There are situations that apply to the transaction with regard to responsibilities for prior claims. I am sending along your commission on the sale, Mr. Brody, as indicated in the agreement, and I shall include in a cover letter the name of our attorneys and how to contact them should you decide to pursue this matter, whether in a spirit of cooperation or not. Good day.''

"Goddamnit, you knew that fucking government was going to come after the statues. That's why you were in such a fucking hurry to..."

That was it. The phone went dead. Lyle Brody knew he was in trouble. This same thing had happened to a couple of local folks a few years earlier in a deal for some mosaics. Somebody had to eat a million on that one. If Jamie Brothewaite didn't cut his balls off, she'd sue his ass off. The commission check, handsome as it was, would be a mere drop in the bucket just in the legal fees to defend in a suit he probably wouldn't win.

The feeling of powerlessness was familiar. He'd felt it all his life. As a kid, it was always Sally. She was so pretty, so nice, so bright, so fucking perfect. And he was a toad before he set foot in kindergarten. Even his mother kept her distance, always sided with Sally. He'd been screwed over by women all his life. And here it was happening again. Jamie Brothewaite was about to destroy him.

THE FLIGHT WAS SMOOTH, though he felt a sickening, sudden emptiness in his stomach as the plane made its steep descent into Dulles International. It was the same feeling he had when he was younger, driving on the old highways and feeling the abrupt dip in the road. The same, only worse.

Short as the flight was the quiet hum of the engine and the stretch of all too heavenly clouds gave Shanahan time to think. What he thought about was how hopelessly far he was from having any useful information at all. In his mind he ran through the list of odd characters whose stories didn't add up.

The list wasn't long. Charley Baker. Lyle Brody. Perhaps, just perhaps there was David Holland himself.

That's why he was heading to D.C., wasn't it? To talk with the senator. Surely to God, the police had checked his whereabouts that night. That would be the first thing. He would make a call to Lieutenant Swann to verify that. Then, there was, of course, Emilio Ramirez, which would make all this running around an expensive lesson in the art of goose chasing.

While thumbing through a current issue of *Time* magazine, Shanahan saw two stories that intrigued him. One was the ongoing perplexity of the Kennedy assassination, the possible involvement of the CIA in a convoluted tale of setups, betrayals, and murder. The other was some accusations of dirty tricks in the current presidential elections.

Byron Jaegar. He'd almost forgotten. The renter who was found dead in the senator's coach house.

"Christ," he said. The gray-suited man beside him turned. Shanahan wasn't aware he'd said it out loud. To the man, who continued to stare, he said, "I think I left the iron on."

The man gave him a strange smile, but obviously didn't want to talk about it.

No way, Shanahan told himself, this time without moving his lips. But the idea made more sense than he wanted it to. Somebody wants to keep Senator Holland in line. He doesn't want to be in line. There are threats. Not believing they would be carried out, Holland ignores them. Threats are validated by the Sally Holland killing. Assassin gets assassinated and the deed is covered up nicely. Overweight man dies of heart attack.

Nothing suspicious there. Ramirez, a "dumb" boxer, with no connections and no money, has been seen with Sally Holland. He is called in the middle of the night to meet in an area where security is known to patrol. The body—no, better yet, something to imply her body—hair, clothing, fabric maybe—is dumped at Ramirez's place.

The body is dumped in the inlet in the area where they set up Ramirez to be spotted.

Maybe the daughter is next on the list. Senator gets in line. Maybe they—whoever "they" are—don't want the senator to run. He has a ready out. Grief for his wife's death. And now he has a child to raise.

Still reeling from the implications of his thought-filled trip, Shanahan walked through the crowded airport in near shock. At the car rental counter he could barely focus on the forms.

"How will you be paying?" asked the woman.

"Cash."

"Fine," she said. "But I will need a credit card."

"What?"

She looked at him as if he might be a space alien. "I'm sorry, but we do require a credit card imprint. When you return the car, you can pay in cash, Mr. Shanahan. We'll simply tear up the invoice."

"I see," He said. Apparently no amount of cash—and Shanahan had brought the amount of his last pension check in cash, and more than he had ever imagined needing—could be used as a deposit.

"Is this the first time you rented a car?"

TWENTY-ONE

SHANAHAN CHECKED INTO a downtown hotel that sounded like it was named after the looney weather man on the *Today Show*. He'd already gotten over the price he'd pay for a room—Jennifer Bailey's secretary had made the reservations and booked the flight, using the firm's American Express—and now he merely felt uncomfortable in surroundings more plush than he'd grown used to.

It was also Bailey's secretary who straightened out the rental car fiasco. Shanahan now felt indebted to the young man whose ears he had once wanted to pin back. Shanahan was feeling more than a little out of touch with the world. He also thought about how he had told young Moogie to be kind to Mrs. Schmidt because the world had passed her by. He might as well have been talking about himself.

Shanahan had brought along his only suit, the dark one. He extricated it from his luggage and hung it in the closet, hoping that by merely hanging there, the wrinkles would go away. He sat on the bed and picked up the phone. He had the hotel operator guide him through the long distance procedures. When finally he reached the Indianapolis Police Department and asked for Lieutenant Swann, he was put on eternal hold, and his mind ran back to the thoughts he had had on the plane.

Shanahan wasn't much for conspiracy theories. With the exception of Kennedy's death in Dallas, conspiracies largely fell into the same category as the "I was framed" defense. But if there was any truth at all to his perhaps paranoid speculation, Emilio was dead meat.

Also, if there was any truth in it, then the case was too big for Jennifer Bailey. Certainly, it was much too big for a retired detective trying to fill in where his military pension left off, which was usually after a few friendly beers at Harry's. He couldn't imagine what Jennifer Bailey, or better yet Lieutenant Swann, would think about such a theory.

WHEN THE barred door slid open, there was the usual commotion, crowding at the end of the long hallway, bartering, arguing, spilled coffee. Lunch at the Marion County Jail.

Emilio Ramirez never looked at anyone. He'd catch a glimpse here and there out of the corner of his eye. It was important to figure out who might be trouble, who wasn't. So far, nobody bothered him.

They read the papers, knew who he was. They already had targets. One was a skinny, effeminate kid with carrot hair and bad teeth. He didn't want to think about what they had him do. The other was a rich roly-poly unkempt guy with glasses, frames held together with dirty adhesive tape. The guy had a slow, whiny voice.

Both the kid and this guy ended up with pretty sparse meals. The chubby guy complained. The skinny kid must've felt lucky to have anything at all.

Ramirez had gotten his tray without hassle. He sat on the thin mat that covered most of the concrete platform that was his bed, the tray on his knees. He dipped the soft, doughy bread in the lukewarm gravy of what some might call a stew. The chubby guy was crying. Survival of the fittest.

It was the same on the outside, he thought. This is just a place where it's all pared down to the essentials. If you're weak in here, you serve the strong. If you're weak out there, you're preyed on just the same. A gang, an employer, the cops, the politicians. If you're not part of the power, you're under it.

He'd always known that. The only thing that got him through the day on the outside was developing his body, using his mind to train his muscles to forge his way out of servitude. That, and only that, kept him going.

Now, somebody, some strange person or people, had plucked him from his world for their own unfathomable reasons. No, they had snuffed two lives, hadn't they? His and Sally's.

"No pity. No self-pity. No self-pity." He kept saying it, as he pushed the fork into his hand.

"SWANN HERE," the voice said, jarring Shanahan back to the here and now, and, he hoped, his sanity.

"With two *ns*?"

"What can I do for you, Mr. Shanahan?"

"Does David Holland have an alibi?"

"Lieutenant Rafferty's coming down hard. I can't talk about this case. You know your police department is always willing to cooperate with representatives of the defense. However, I've been instructed to refer all inquiries to Lieutenant Rafferty, who is the official spokesperson on matters dealing with the death of Mrs. David Holland. Or you can rely on the attorneys to sort it out."

He said all this with his usual flat voice, a monotone that made sarcasm, fact, and flattery all sound alike. There was silence.

"However, I feel perfectly able to talk to you about police procedures in general. In the death of a spouse involving possible homicide, the surviving spouse is investigated thoroughly."

"That's what I figured. But if the spouse is a U.S. senator, do our rules and regulations still apply?"

"Of course."

"Did you check the airlines?"

"Assuming the spouse in question was in another city, we would quietly verify the times he or she was in the company of others and cross-check flight times into this city from the city in which he or she was currently residing."

"I'm impressed." Shanahan was amused by Swann's by-the-book answers to his questions. "If the flight was from Washington, D.C., say, would you check out airports in Baltimore?"

"Yes. Shanahan."

"Yeah?"

"Oh, Shanahan," he said with a sigh. "Why do I do this? Listen, David Holland was having dinner with his aide until at least nine the night of the death. He also met with this guy, Barton, at eight or nine the following morning. Senator Holland is not listed on any flights from anywhere in the vicinity of Washington to anywhere within a hundred and fifty miles of Indianapolis. And we can't put together any connections elsewhere that would get him in and out of Indianapolis in a time frame consistent with the events of the murder"—he paused for a moment—"as we see it. There's another matter here. No motive."

"Like I said, I'm impressed. A time frame consistent with the events of the murder? Nice touch."

"Figure it out. Sometime after nine in the evening, he somehow gets from Washington, D.C., to Indianapolis, gets from the westside airport to his home, punches her out, loads her in his car, drives her to a bridge, takes her out, carries her a long way through the dense woods at night...at night, Shanahan...throws her in the water, traipses out, gets in his car, goes to the airport, catches a plane, and is in D.C. for a morning meeting. All this with no planes coming into Indy."

"Private plane?"

"We checked. The only private jet landing that night was carrying The Grateful Dead. You're forgetting what I told you about hair and skin particles. He'd have to bring a baggy of those and toss them around your guy's apartment. Doesn't make sense. Then, as I said, we have this little problem of motive."

"Domestic quarrel?" Shanahan suggested feebly.

"What could the disagreement possibly be that brought him all the way back from Washington in the middle of the night? Won't work, anyway. An unfinished letter to her aunt suggests that Sally Holland had finally agreed to move to Washington if her husband was reelected, I might add, at his urging. She was a happy woman. Happy with her husband. Happy with her life."

"You have the letter?"

"Of course."

"What about Byron Jaegar?"

"What about him? Heart attack. The doctors have a longer name, but I forget what that is. You're not thinking what I think you're thinking, are you? He wanted her body, maybe?"

"I hadn't thought of that. Maybe he was hired?"

"By who? Holland? The CIA? C'mon."

"Is it that preposterous?" Shanahan asked. "It's pretty strange, him dying right after the murder."

"You've been seeing too many movies. If you knew the deputy coroner, you wouldn't even ask. He's a young guy who'd like nothing better than to get into something like that. He had a plot similar to yours. Very excited. He examined every inch of Jaegar's considerable body inside and out. The deputy coroner was very disappointed when he discovered it was something as mundane as a bad heart. And it *was* a bad heart. No question. Oh, Mr. Shanahan? The medicine Mr. Jaegar was on? It's very doubtful he had much of a sex drive."

"Thanks."

"You're really not convinced Ramirez did it?"

"I don't know," Shanahan said. "Are you?"

"I'd like to have an eyewitness. But I'd go to court with it and feel okay about the conviction. The kid is telling us she was never in his apartment. Mr. Shanahan, she *was* there. The evidence is darned near as strong as if we had found her there with him hovering over her. And why would he tell the security guard he was having trouble with his girlfriend?"

"What was he supposed to do? Tell the guy he got a strange phone call in the middle of the night? One more question. Did the coroner have anything to say about those long, odd marks on the outside of her thigh?"

"Why did I start this? Mysterious, yes, but not serious. Not the cause of death, by any means."

"He couldn't figure out what caused them?"

"No. Upset him too. Heat, he said. How we don't know. Maybe it's just something weird in her system."

"You believe that?"

"Doesn't matter."

SWANN HAD TOLD HIM, before he hung up, the marks could have been caused by the sun. Maybe she spent some time under some branches of a tree with only those parts exposed. It was halfhearted speculation. Shanahan didn't buy it.

Street map in hand and in his rented Buick, Shanahan ventured out. The Hotel Willard wasn't far from the center of government. If you discounted the suburbs, D.C. wasn't that large, geographically. And it wasn't that dissimilar from Indianapolis. A preponderance of formal, grayish monuments. The streets were wide, and the buildings were low. It was even laid out like Indianapolis, only easier. Streets were named either after numbers or letters of the alphabet and followed the respective order of each.

Once in the congressional offices, it was a different experience. He couldn't make sense of the hallways. He was surprised by the lack of people bustling about. He eventually found his way to the office of Senator David Holland.

"I'm sorry," the woman said, "he's not in. You didn't have an appointment, did you?" She was desperately searching through a thick, ring-bound book.

"No. Just a Hoosier in town. Thought I might get a chance to shake hands with the man. Give him my condolences."

She smiled warmly. "He'll be sorry he missed you."

"You expect him back soon?"

"Congress is in recess. He kind of comes and goes." She waved her hands as if things were out of control.

"Millie!" came a sharp voice.

Shanahan looked up. It was Eric Barton. He recognized the young man from TV. Barton stood in the doorway of an inner office. Beyond him was an office in disarray. A cardboard box sat on a desk.

"Yes, Mr. Barton." She looked up, giving Shanahan a helpless look, then moved quickly toward Barton.

They conferred in whispers.

Shanahan grabbed a copy of the senator's newsletter from a wire rack by the door as he left. He didn't go far, merely down the hall, where he leaned against the wall by the elevators. He didn't push the button, waiting for young Eric Barton to appear. A slow, small elevator was a great place to start a conversation, especially if the person you wanted to talk to wasn't too keen on the idea.

SHANAHAN HAD second thoughts about waiting. What if the guy was in there for hours?

The fear was unjustified and short-lived. In less than ten minutes a man, barely able to see over the two cardboard cartons he carried, came out of the Holland of-

fices and headed toward Shanahan, who pressed the
down button on the elevator.

"Thanks," Eric said without looking directly at
Shanahan. The young man stared ahead. He looked angry. Perhaps it wasn't Barton's idea to take a leave of ab-
sence, Shanahan thought, remembering the press
explanation. And maybe now wasn't the time to talk to
him.

Outside, Shanahan found it wasn't easy trying to keep
track of where he'd parked his car and follow a convoluted stretch of sidewalk, presumably to the place where
Barton had parked. He stopped about fifty feet from the
white Lexus parked illegally in a fire lane. Barton put
down the boxes on the concrete by the trunk and was
fishing for his keys when Shanahan decided he should
head to his rented set of wheels.

By the time he'd figured out how to get back to the
spot where he'd left Barton, the Lexus was gone. Shanahan drove back to the hotel, asked the doorman not to
park it for him. He'd only be a moment. Inside, he found
the telephones, thumbed quickly through the phone
book. He was saved. Eric Barton's name was listed. So
was his address. Shanahan jotted it down. He handed the
doorman a five and showed him the sip of paper. How
would he get there?

"You know Foggy Bottom?"

"Never heard of her."

The guy laughed. "I always figured it was the last
drink of the night. Anyway, it's over near the Water-
gate."

"Can you help me a little more?" he asked, pulling out
the little, laminated D.C. street map.

SHANAHAN GOT lost twice, got snarled in rush-hour
traffic, which reminded him of the time of day and the
fact that, aside from picking at his high-altitude lunch,

he had not eaten. All of this and there was no assurance that Barton had gone home or, if he had, hadn't left again. Finally Shanahan located the residence of Eric Barton. Parked in front of a small, well-kept apartment building on a quiet side street was the white Lexus. There was, however, no parking space for him.

His rented Buick hovered in the street. He waited, hoping someone would have to make a grocery run. Eventually he began feeling conspicuous. He drove around the block a few times. On his fourth pass, he saw someone leaving Barton's building. A space would open. As he cruised closer, he saw that the space that would open would be the one now taken by the white Lexus.

It was Barton. He'd changed clothes. Instead of his suit, he wore light tan slacks, a white shirt, and a white cardigan sweater. There'd be no time to intercept him before he got to his car, because he was almost at a run. Fortunately the two cars were facing the same direction, so Shanahan hung back. He would simply follow the guy. He had nothing else to do since he didn't know how to find the senator.

The Lexus pulled out with a screech and shot down the quiet, car-lined street like a bullet.

"Damn!" Shanahan said out loud. There is nothing more difficult than a discreet tail when the tailee is going ninety.

TWENTY-TWO

IF ERIC BARTON had any inkling he had been followed during his harrowing drive through the city, he didn't show it. Fortunately Shanahan could make up the lag time at the traffic lights. Barton found a parking spot, and Shanahan waited until he saw the young man go into a bar on Seventeenth before trying to find a space for himself. The guy never looked back.

The long narrow bar was light and sunny. Barton was talking to a few people at the bar. Then he moved on, stopping again to speak to a group of men at a table by a huge picture window, but he paid little attention to what was being said to him. Instead he looked around furtively.

It looked as if he were searching for someone—someone in particular. And it wasn't Shanahan. Whoever it was, Barton wasn't having much success, judging by the look on his face. He went back to the bar, and the bartender brought him a drink without having been asked.

Shanahan, who hadn't ventured very far in, went to the bar as well, ordered a beer. He watched Barton climb the set of stairs at the far end, then come back down, again searching the space. Shanahan turned his attention to the patrons. All were well-dressed, either in business suits or in stylish casual clothes befitting a somewhat monied crowd enjoying Happy Hour on a hot day. Almost all of them were engaged in conversation, and all of them were men.

What he could surmise so far was that Barton was a regular here—that he was not happy, and that even if it had something to do with Senator Holland, it also had something to do with someone he was having trouble locating. The other thing he could be pretty sure of was that Eric Barton was gay.

None of that meant anything to Shanahan. The guy's problems, more than likely, had nothing to do with Shanahan's problems with the murder of Sally Holland. It's easy to get caught up in events and believe that everything happening anywhere is somehow connected. More than likely it was a separate deal.

Barton set his drink down on the bar and headed toward Shanahan. Had he been made? No. Barton passed, eyes not revealing a hint of recognition as he went out the door. Shanahan started to follow, but hesitated a moment. Instead he looked out the window, and Barton appeared outside, putting a quarter in the public telephone. He dialed and waited. And waited.

Shanahan pretended to watch the kids playing soccer in the vacant lot on the opposite corner, but watched as Barton either got a no-answer or was retrieving messages from his answering machine. In moments Barton was back in. He was steamed. Some guy came up to him, smiling, tried to talk to Barton. It was obvious he didn't want to be talked to. He ordered another drink.

Still not the time to talk to him, Shanahan decided.

BARTON HAD two more drinks and used the telephone twice more before leaving. Shanahan followed. Barton didn't go far. Just to the next block on a street with outdoor cafés, bustling with people celebrating the end of the workday.

Eric Barton went into a place called Annie's Paramount Steakhouse. After looking in the dark bar, Holland's former aide went into the glass-enclosed dining room and asked for a seat near the window facing the busy street.

Shanahan, who picked up a copy of the *Washington Post* out of a little box next to the restaurant, settled at the bar, sitting at the end so he could see Barton's table and catch the little bit of light that filtered into that part of the restaurant. The detective ordered a cheeseburger, fries, and coffee. He really wanted a beer, but at this point he had no idea how long the evening would be.

One thing he wanted to do, and maybe it was only idle curiosity, was to see who it was Eric Barton was so impatient to find. The other was to wait for Barton's drinking to soften the anger, reduce the inhibitions, allowing Shanahan to get more from him. Sometimes it worked that way. Sometimes not.

Eric Barton had ordered dinner with his drinks, but only played with the food on the plate. Twice he left to make phone calls and to hit the john. When he left Annie's, Barton didn't head for his car. Instead he walked. He was walking steadily, but perhaps with less purpose.

Shanahan followed Barton across busy Connecticut Avenue. The day's light was finally giving way. And the stores along the avenue were all lit. Barton went into a bar called Rascals. Again, the patrons were all male, but seemed to represent a broader slice of social strata. Shanahan felt more comfortable here. At the other place he had felt as if he stood out among the upwardly mobile patrons. Here he saw a few people his own age and people in his own social milieu.

Barton seemed to know his way around. He talked with a few people. However, it was clear he was asking for information, not engaging in idle, sociable chat. People shook their heads "no." When they did, Barton disengaged abruptly. Finally he wedged himself into the crowded bar and retrieved a drink, one he had to ask for.

Seeing Barton settle back against a wall, sipping his drink, beginning to look more sad than angry, Shanahan took the opportunity to go to the john. Tacked on the inside of the bar door was a flier giving the hours of the upstairs bar, Shooters, an all-male go-go bar. He looked at his watch. It would open in an hour.

Back in the bar, he noticed Barton glancing at his watch and looking in the direction of the stairs that led up to Shooters. During the next hour and a half Barton would look at his watch many times, look at the front door, then scan the crowd. He continued to drink, only more slowly. Shanahan allowed himself one beer, which he nursed.

Despite the fact that many in the bar were moving upstairs, the bar downstairs remained crowded. It was apparent that the object of Barton's search wasn't among them. Barton was growing impatient. A few minutes after downing his drink, he left.

Outside, Barton's pace was slow but surprisingly steady. Shanahan followed him back to the white Lexus. There was only a subtle weaving of Barton's car as he drove. He was driving much more slowly and much more cautiously than he had earlier.

Barton pulled into a space close to the Convention Center and walked the unpopulated downtown streets at midnight. He entered a bar on Ninth Street, a little building standing by itself on the corner of a huge, empty parking lot.

Shanahan found a space easily. He waited outside the bar, standing with a couple of people at the bus stop just around the corner. Barton would have to come back that way to get to his car. The bar wasn't very big. Maybe Barton would only go in, look around, and come out again.

After ten minutes Shanahan decided to go in.

At the door there was a man seated on a stool. He asked for the cover. Shanahan, who had to ask twice what the guy said because of the loud music, could see only a small portion of what was going on inside—a few guys drinking and laughing. The rest of the bar was blocked by a wall. He had no idea what he was paying for, but handed the guy the few bills required for entry.

LYLE BRODY stood on the balcony of his apartment. The day had been hot, but the night had cooled, so much so that he turned off the air conditioning and merely left the balcony doors open.

He looked out at the vast, flat expanse of the city to the north, the twinkling yellow and white lights that seemed closer to each other the farther they went away. He looked up. This close to the city, the sky was never pitch-black. There was almost a phosphorous glow to it that rendered the stars invisible. The stars, it seemed, were all on the ground.

He tugged at the ties of his black silk robe with the Chinese red piping that matched exactly the color of his pajamas. He sipped his Stolichnaya on the rocks.

He remembered he hadn't eaten today. It didn't matter. He still wasn't hungry. In fact, he wasn't much of anything. He didn't want to go out. He didn't want to stay in. He wasn't sleepy, but he wasn't entirely sure he wanted to remain conscious. Even the vodka didn't taste as good as it usually did.

Brody went inside, walked through the darkened living room, and didn't bother turning on the lights in the bedroom. He kept on his slippers and robe. He didn't pull back the bed covering, merely lay down, his head on the down pillow, feeling the hardness of the snub-nosed .38 beneath it.

SHANAHAN SAW Barton right away. He stood, his full weight against the wall, halfway down and opposite the bar, holding a nearly empty glass. He stared blankly at nothing in particular. The adrenaline of anger works only so long, then it takes its toll. Shanahan was pretty sure this was going to be the end of the line.

He glanced toward the bar. On it, dancing, were two naked young men. "Buck-naked" was the term Harry would have used. One was crouched in front of a patron, so close, in fact, that he could easily stir the guy's drink without using his hands. Above and behind the bar was a catwalk, where still another naked dancer was trying to work himself up into a state of excitement.

Shanahan looked back at the subject of his little adventure. A waiter was there, a drink on his tray, waiting as Barton clumsily searched his pockets for some money.

"Here, let me get it," Shanahan said to the waiter, handing him a twenty. "Bring me a beer, wouldya, any kind."

Barton looked up, trying to focus his eyes on Shanahan's face. "Thanks. But I...uh, want to be fair, or honest...or something. I'm not interested in older guys."

"I know what you mean," Shanahan said. Barton turned away. "You look a little lost."

"What?"

"I said you look a little lost."

"Me? No. I'm not the one who is lost, my friend. Did I thank you for the drink?" Shanahan nodded, but Barton hadn't noticed. "Anyway, it is not me who has vanished."

"You thought you'd find this person here?"

"Uh, yes. Yes, I did as a matter of fact. I certainly did." As if it needed further clarification, Barton nodded his head with exaggerated emphasis. "And as a matter of fact, I don't come to these places. He does."

Barton didn't seem too interested in the abundance of flesh on the bar fifteen or twenty feet away. Perhaps, in his condition, he couldn't see that far.

"Maybe I know him," Shanahan said. "What's his name?"

Barton looked at Shanahan, square in the eye. Then his head began to tilt, first to one side, then to the other. His eyes, suddenly heavy, closed and remained closed for several seconds.

The waiter brought Shanahan his beer and was pleased that he was told to keep the change. The detective didn't want to disengage young Barton by having the waiter fiddling with change.

"No," Barton said, his eyes opening slowly. "You don't know him. Nobody knows him, you know what I mean? Here, hold my drink a minute."

Barton, though less in control of the coordination necessary to talk, nevertheless managed to get to the rest room, which fortunately was only a few steps away. Shanahan looked toward the bar. Apparently touching wasn't forbidden. And for the privilege, it was customary to pay. One customer, Shanahan's age, used his free hand to pick up a dollar from a pretty big stack and tuck it in the dancer's sock.

Shanahan was pretty sure the dancer would stay right there until the stack of bills was gone or the customer stopped tucking. He glanced at the door, wondering what the chances were of the place getting raided.

Instead of coming directly back to retrieve his drink, Eric Barton headed for the door, passing Shanahan without uttering a word. Shanahan followed.

Outside Shanahan caught up with Barton, grabbing the unsteady pedestrian's shoulder. Eric Barton turned.

"Thank you for the lovely evening," he said.

"I don't think you ought to be behind the wheel. If you don't kill yourself or someone else, you'll get arrested and spend an embarrassing night in jail."

Barton tugged his arm away from Shanahan, stood tottering as if the sidewalk were moving.

"Well," he said. Then after a long pause, in which he seemed to be contemplating quantum physics, "When you're right you're right." His attempt to nod his agreement turned into a deep bow, which caused him to lurch forward.

Shanahan grabbed his shoulders. "I'll drive you home."

On the way to the car, Barton suddenly stopped. "What if you're an ax murderer?"

"Then I'm in trouble. I forgot my ax."

"So...UH...did you have a nice vacation? You went with the wife and kids?" Letterman asked the star of some movie soon to be released.

The senator, snug under the covers, head propped on a couple of pillows, pushed the button on the remote, catching an ad for a Manhattan escort service. He could hear the water running in the bathroom. Maybe he should have just called one of the Oriental ladies.

"If you're spending the night in there," he shouted in the direction of the bathroom, "I'll just roll over and go to sleep."

"No, David. I'll be out in a minute. Why don't you shut off the TV, put some quiet music on the stereo, then climb back into bed and turn the lights off."

"The dark. With you, my dear, it's the only way," David said as he climbed out of bed.

"What? I can't hear you."

"Nothing." He knelt down to reach the little shelf below the TV. The hotel had provided a small but better than average stereo system. He found an FM station playing some sort of bluesy jazz. It was the saxophone that made it right.

He got up, passed the unopened bottle of Scotch she'd brought with her. He'd been good about not drinking. For a moment, though, he grappled with his resolve. A couple of shots would make what was about to happen a little more fun.

He climbed into bed, a little chilly from the air conditioning, and turned off the light. Soon, the little path of light from the bathroom appeared on the carpet, then disappeared. David Holland smelled her nearness before he felt it. Her body was next to his, her hand running down his body.

"Guess we have to get your motor running," she said.

TWENTY-THREE

ON THE DRIVE to Eric Barton's place, Shanahan turned the rented Buick's air conditioner up as far as it would go, hoping that would help keep the young man from passing out. He also kept up a constant stream of questions to keep him talking.

That's how Shanahan learned that the object of Barton's furtive search was not as interesting as, say, David Holland, but a fellow named Robert, with whom Eric Barton had fallen in love. Robert was older, though older only meant thirty-six, and had a periodic craving, said Eric, for street trade. This was the reason for the tour of male strip bars.

Once back in Barton's apartment, which was filled with what Shanahan thought was expensive overstuffed furniture and Old World paintings and antique bric-a-brac, Barton was plied with several cups of strong black coffee.

"Who are you, anyway?" Barton asked as he seemed to emerge slowly from the thick fog of inebriation.

"I'm a private investigator," Shanahan said, sitting in the wing chair facing Barton, who was on the sofa.

"Why the interest in me, pray tell?"

"I'm looking into the murder of Sally Holland."

"You were following me, then?"

"Yes."

"I still don't understand. Why me?"

"You had dinner with Senator Holland in Washington the night his wife was killed."

"Yes. That is true."

"You're sure."

"Very sure. I left David at maybe nine. I was supposed to meet Robert at J.R.'s for a drink at ten. I remember it clearly. Robert and I were going to discuss our troubled past and whether or not we had a future. I drank too much at dinner. David was pissed. He wanted to talk about the campaign, about whether I could manage it. Needless to say, I wasn't impressing him with my maturity. That was the least of my worries. It showed. That's why he set up the meeting for the next morning."

"Can I ask you a personal question?"

Barton laughed. "After my telling you the perils of Pauline in the car, I don't know what it'd hurt."

"Were you...are you in love with Senator Holland?"

"Oh, Christ." Barton shook his head. "I suppose I was...early on. When I first started to work for him. Who wouldn't have been?" He looked at Shanahan, smiled. "Maybe not everybody, but he had this almost golden glow, you know. Young, ambitious. You forget people like that are human. But if you think I'd play alibi for him, you're mistaken. First, I got to know him better. And to know is not to love him. Second, he tossed me out in the middle of some godforsaken highway in Indiana."

"Does he know you were gay?"

"Yeah, probably. Who knows? We've never talked about it. If he did, I doubt he cared."

"Why wouldn't he? A conservative politician like Senator Holland? Is he?"

"You get right to the point. No. There are plenty of conservative queers, all tightly closeted and all homophobic as hell, but in politics hypocrisy is prerequisite. David wouldn't care if I had sex with a kangaroo as long as I didn't become a liability. Is he gay? No. David's womanizing is genuine, not a cover. No woman is too old, none too young. It would take a pretty big campaign contribution or a long time without women for anything else to happen."

"How was the senator taking his wife's death?"

"Bad. He hung up on the President when the man called to offer his condolences. Bad judgment."

"Were he and the President close?"

"Politically, they shared a lot. David could be counted on to do what the President wanted. But David was a little pissed. He thought he ought to be V.P. He thought he had some angle having to do with saving the President's ass on some drug business in Central America. I think he tried to apply the pressure to get on the ticket."

"Really, blackmail."

"We don't call it that in Washington. We call it a compromise. But the President wasn't buying it, apparently."

"Could Holland have killed his wife?"

"I thought they had someone cold. Some boxer."

"Yeah. Seems like it. Just trying to clear up some details."

"Morally, maybe. Frankly, he wouldn't have had the guts. And of all possible times, it just doesn't fit. He and Sally had worked out an arrangement. She and Elizabeth were moving back to Washington. Sally's interest in saving the planet was going to be part of the senator's reelection campaign. It's real popular now to want to clean up the environment. We all thought it was a real stunner for David. He was going to show his warm, caring side. And Sally was going to set up a foundation, with the help of the senator and his connections. They were going to write a book together—about the environment. It was to be a launching point for his own bid at the presidency later."

"Could she have found out about the senator's womanizing?"

"She knew." Barton got up, went into the kitchen, came out with the coffeepot, poured each of them a cup. "She had already accepted that, gotten busy with her own work. He probably loves . . . loved her in his own way." Barton went back into the kitchen as Shanahan took a sip of coffee. "All this is confidential. I don't want to show up in one of those sleazy supermarket tabloids."

"I don't think you will—at least not from talking with me. You know anything about Sally's brother, Lyle Brody?"

"No, except that David thinks he's a creep. He said he didn't know how the two of them came from the same womb."

"Where's the senator now?"

"New York, probably. Trying to get some money out of Jamie Brothewaite. I went in today to clear out my office. Millie told me Jamie called, and that the next thing she knows, David's asking Millie to get him a flight to La Guardia."

"Does this woman have a place in New York?"

"Probably. She has homes all around the globe. But David likes the trendy hotels."

"What if I wanted to find him?"

"There's a little place, very nice really, called Morgan's on Madison. Hell, even the cabdrivers don't know how to find it. It's where celebrities stay when they don't want to be noticed. Then there's the . . . what the hell's its name . . . something blue. No, no. Royal. The Royalton. It's on Forty-fourth or one of those. Same kind of place. Very 'in.'"

"Thanks," Shanahan said, taking a final swig of the coffee as he got up.

"You can stay here if you want. I have a guest bedroom." Eric smiled.

"I've got a room. Thanks."

"I appreciate your helping me out."

"I had an ulterior motive."

"Doesn't everybody. But thanks anyway. I probably would've gotten mugged. And if I'd made it to the car, that might have been worse."

SHANAHAN FELT his first tinge of anxiety when he tried to make his way through La Guardia. The second came when he saw the Manhattan skyline from a taxi heading for New York. He felt the third, slightly deeper wave when, after traveling bumper to bumper through a tile-lined tunnel, they came to a complete stop somewhere in the middle of it.

The driver, whose picture clipped to the dashboard looked like it belonged on the wall of a post office, and whose name had no vowels, began flailing his arms. He shouted what Shanahan was sure were obscenities, though the detective understood not a word.

It occurred to him that they'd hit the rush hour. It was seven in the morning. He'd had no sleep. All he'd had time to do was rush back to his hotel from Barton's and make a few phone calls. One was to The Royalton Hotel in New York. Senator Holland wasn't registered there. He called Morgan's. The answer was the same. Maybe it wasn't registered in the senator's name, he thought. That would figure. Was there a Jamie Brothewaite registered there? Still no cigar.

He dialed the Royalton back. Bingo. Did he want to ring her? No. It's a surprise. Could he get a room this evening? Yes. Shanahan immediately called Jennifer Bailey's secretary, who promised to make all the arrangements. He took a quick shower and then called Maureen, who, after she shook off the effects of sleep, seemed just a little pissed that he hadn't been in his room the length of an entire evening.

Later, in the brief conversation, she explained that Jennifer Bailey had sent over Xerox copies of some little girl's diary and that Howie Cross had called with some "interesting news." She did add, before letting Shanahan check out and race to get a taxi, that she was surprised she missed him.

"It's different," she said, "when you leave me here from when I leave you. And it's raining here. Cool, wet, and gloomy, thanks to you."

He was sorry he'd worried her. However a little part of him felt glad she was a little jealous.

At the moment he was more concerned about being asphyxiated by the exhaust fumes of what he imagined to be several thousand automobiles stuck in a tunnel under several million gallons of water.

Once the cab inched its way back into the sunlight, the cabbie whirled his car through the streets in a replay of Barton's whirling through Washington early last night.

The cabbie spoke, but the only word Shanahan could understand was "Hilton."

"No, The Royalton," Shanahan said.

The cabbie shook his head.

Shanahan read the address. Still no comprehension. He showed the cabbie the piece of paper he'd scribbled on.

"Hotel? No Royalton hotel there. Algonquin?"

"Go anyway," Shanahan said curtly. But it was definitely anxiety wave number four.

"Okay. Okay."

THERE WAS, in fact, a hotel there, though no one would have ever guessed. There was no marquee. Fortunately, there was another cab there. The people who stood waiting as the cabbie stuffed some expensive-looking luggage in the trunk gave it away.

Shanahan paid his driver and climbed out with his one bag. A young man dressed in black came quickly, took it from him, and headed up a few steps to a glass door.

"How are you today, sir?" the youth said.

"Fine," Shanahan said, following him in. The interior wasn't like that of any hotel he'd ever been in. Then again, he thought, he hadn't been in that many hotels in the last thirty years or so.

Large chairs, wrapped in white cloth. Elegant vases of exotic flowers. Huge, clear-glass bowls of water were lined up across a long shelf, each with a single colorful fish floating in it. All of this was to the left as he followed his luggage. To the right were walls with richly stained paneling.

On their way to check in, presumably, Shanahan passed another youth, dressed in a black turtleneck sweater, black pants, and a black wool blazer.

The woman behind the counter, who looked up and smiled at Shanahan's approach, also wore the same turtleneck and blazer. She was young, beautiful, and surprisingly friendly.

"May I help you?"

"My name is Shanahan. I have a reservation." He turned to tip the youth who carried his bag, but he had disappeared. Shanahan felt underdressed and completely out of his element. Yet he detected no trace of snobbery in the hotel staff.

"Yes, here it is. A single room. For one night only. Is that correct?"

"Yes."

"It's very early for a check-in," the woman said apologetically. "However they are making up a room now, Mr. Shanahan. It might be half an hour. Is that all right?"

"Yes, fine. I'll grab a cup of coffee somewhere." There was a small buffet at the far end of the lobby. But no one was there, and he didn't know how it worked. Was it free? He wouldn't chance it. He thought it might be cheaper in some small coffee shop than in the hotel.

"Your luggage will be in the room when you return."

Outside, the streets were busier. He looked around, to get his bearings, then headed down Forty-fourth Street. Almost immediately he discovered a little hole-in-the-wall deli. The place had no seats, and the coffee came in a paper cup. When he ordered his coffee, the guy asked if he wanted it "regular." Shanahan, thinking regular meant black, said yes and got a healthy shot of cream.

Shanahan bought a *USA Today* and walked back to the hotel. He felt a little silly sitting in this elegant environment, sipping coffee from a paper cup. That's just the way it is, he told himself. With the exception of Harry's bar, he never felt comfortable anywhere anyway. He sipped his coffee, tried reading the paper. Wasn't much to it, he thought. He glanced at the little section labeled "Indiana" and noted that a former lieutenant governor had died at eighty. That was it. That was the news from Indiana. Why did they bother?

He turned to the sports section. From time to time he'd look up. People were gathering to check out. Unusual people, either well-tailored or exotically dressed. If any of them were celebrities, Shanahan probably wouldn't recognize them.

He did recognize Senator Holland, who just stepped out of the elevator with a woman whose garish clothes seemed to precede her into the lobby.

TWENTY-FOUR

SHANAHAN WASN'T PREPARED to confront the senator and the woman he assumed to be Jamie Brothewaite. On the short plane ride from Dulles to La Guardia, he had mulled over Barton's words about Holland's attempted blackmail to get on the presidential ticket. It was possible.

It fit the conspiracy theory. Unable to keep Holland from spilling his guts to the press and terminally embarrassing the President, Sally Holland had been killed. They upped the ante by threatening the life of Elizabeth. Byron Jaegar accomplished the task for these shadowy folks working with or without the President's knowledge. Jaegar, who would have seen Ramirez around and could have easily found out where he lived, killed Sally, called Ramirez to get him out of the house, then placed the body at Ramirez's place.

But what Shanahan should have been doing on the plane, instead of continuing to focus on an unprovable government conspiracy, was figure out how he would get to the senator and what he would do when he got to him. Now the senator was moving toward Shanahan as the woman moved to the group of people checking out. It was now or never.

The senator sat in a chair about fifteen feet away. Shanahan set his coffee cup on the carpet and had started to get up when the woman came rushing over to the senator. Shanahan waited.

Her voice cut through the room like a siren at 3:00 a.m.

"I'm not standing in that goddamn line," she said.

"We can wait," Senator Holland said, standing up.

"Wait is your middle name."

"Let's not start that again," he said wearily. He sat back down. She didn't.

"Just give me a time frame," she said.

"Jamie, let's not talk here, okay?"

"No, it's not okay. It's always 'not here,' or 'not now.'"

"Your voice carries, Jamie."

She took a deep breath, let it out, and sat down beside him. He talked to her patiently, calmly, quietly. Shanahan could no longer hear exactly what he was saying. He picked up, "Maybe in a year." He heard the word "election" and saw her nod unhappily.

The senator continued talking, and she seemed to be relaxing. Finally she patted his hand.

Shanahan heard her say, "I just need a promise." She looked at him.

The senator nodded. She kissed him on the cheek. She got up and walked to the hotel desk.

Shanahan wondered if the senator's nod of agreement was the promise or merely acknowledgment that she needed one. He thought they each might have their own interpretation.

Shanahan got up, went to the senator. Holland stood up, a smile on his face, arm reaching out in reflex.

"Senator Holland." Shanahan shook hands briefly.

"What can I do for you?" His blue eyes sparkled. His voice was friendly, perhaps even sincere.

"My name's Shanahan. I am working with the defense counsel on the Ramirez case as private investigator."

Holland's smile shrank only slightly and only for a moment.

"And a good one, it seems."

"I just have a couple of questions, if you have a minute."

"Shoot," the senator said. He gave Shanahan his full attention.

"Did you know Emilio Ramirez personally?"

"Never met him."

"Did you know of him?"

"If Sally had ever mentioned his name, it didn't register. She tried to help a lot of people. I wasn't as involved in Sally's wonderful efforts, though I should have been. I regret that very much."

"How long have you known Jamie Brothewaite?"

"Whew!" The smile came back. "You're one helluva a P.I. Eight, maybe nine years. She's been very active in my political career. That's why I'm in New York... to meet her for breakfast and discuss my reelection campaign."

"You're running, after all."

"Yes. And there you are, you see? You're among the first to know. Listen, why don't you give me one of your cards? If I ever need someone..."

"I don't have a card, Senator."

"Well, you're good just the same. Listen, I'm sorry. I have an unfinished agenda, Mr. Shanahan. And I have a mission. I want to carry on Sally's environmental work. I've just decided, because of what's happened, to set up a foundation in her name. Sally would have loved the idea. I'm hoping that Miss Brothewaite will help me do that. So if you'll excuse me?" He started to turn.

"Did you know Byron Jaegar?"

"Not well," Holland said with remarkable patience. "He'd worked for the government, one of the security branches, I think. He was from Indianapolis originally and wanted to return there when he retired. I thought it would be great having someone like him around. I was mistaken, apparently."

"The two of you didn't talk every once in a while?"

"No. The only time I ever met him was when I discovered his body."

"Not even when you hired him?"

"It was all résumé and telephone. He came highly recommended by someone in one of the departments I dealt with regularly. I talked to Sally. She said okay. I'm sure she talked with him."

"You're saying that you never talked with the guy who rented your coach house?"

"Yes, that's what I'm saying. He didn't come out much, and I was rarely at home. That's something else I regret. Spending so little time with her. Being so consumed with my career. In fact, Sally was going to move back to Washington, depending on the outcome of the election."

"And your daughter, was she moving with you?"

"Of course," Holland said, eyes finally disengaging. "Of course my daughter. Now I really must run." He held out his hand again.

"I extended our stay for two more nights," Jamie Brothewaite told him as he approached her. "Is that all right?"

The senator's back was to the detective. All Shanahan could see was a stiffening of the shoulders.

BARTON HAD been right. The senator made a great first impression. His ability to think on his feet and stay cool was even more impressive. Shanahan found his answers straightforward on the surface. He had carefully woven into the conversation a scandal-blocking explanation for the early morning meeting with Jamie Brothewaite. And he had done it without being defensive.

Jamie Brothewaite's operatic voice aside, Holland lied very well. He not only lied about what he was doing with Jamie Brothewaite; he was lying about just now deciding to set up a foundation in his dead wife's name. That, according to Barton, had been set up months ago while she was still alive.

Shanahan sat back down, picked up his lukewarm "regular" coffee. What, after all, had he learned from this expensive trip? That Jamie Brothewaite had expectations beyond periodic trysts in a rented room. And it *was* a rented room, no matter how expensive it might be.

Just as he was narrowing in on the grand conspiracy theory, he'd been thrown something else. Some other bizarre possibility with equal though not necessarily any more substantial plausibility. Was Sally Holland to make way for Jamie Brothewaite and her reputed millions? Would Holland have done it for that? With Sally alive, it seemed more likely that Holland could have his cake and eat it too. So why would he kill her? Could Jamie Brothewaite have seen to it that the senator's wife was eliminated so she could eventually become a Washington celebrity or, better yet, an eventual First Lady? Certainly homicide files are full of such plots, with people doing more and having less to gain.

"It'll be just a little while longer," the desk clerk said as Shanahan passed her on the way to the pay phone.

"I might need to cancel," Shanahan said. The airline number was on his ticket. He dialed and was asked to wait by the voice of an obviously female computer.

No point in staying, running up Jennifer Bailey's bill. There was nothing else he could accomplish in New York.

Finally a human voice, also female, asked how she could help. Shanahan explained. They could get him out on a 10:00 p.m. flight and that would be to Cincinnati, she explained, where he'd connect to a late flight to Indianapolis. He wouldn't get in until two in the morning. The other choice was to fly standby. Even first class was booked.

"You might try another airline," she said. "But I don't think it will do any good."

"Why is everybody going to Indianapolis?"

"I don't think it's that," she said. "There's a rush in the morning to get in and a rush in early evening to get out," she explained.

All but Shanahan, it seemed. He decided to stay and go in the morning where he was already safely booked.

ONE OF THE young men in the charcoal blazers carried Shanahan's bag. The detective followed. Once out of the elevator, it was another world still. Dark, dark hallway. The walls were deep blue, the ceiling was deep blue. So was the carpet. Some of the lights were down on the carpet along the wall; others, very dim, hung like little moons over the room numbers on the doors. There was no sound.

Shanahan was disoriented. He had the feeling he was under a vast pool of water.

"Are you all right, sir?" the young man asked as he opened the door to Shanahan's room.

"Fine. I'm tired, that's all."

The bellhop gave Shanahan a quick explanation of the TV, VCR, and stereo. Shanahan wasn't in the mood for a tour. The bellhop opened the thick blue draperies, rolling them back. Below the window was a long bench seat that looked like a church pew. He opened the built-in closet that looked as if it belonged in a ship's cabin and hung Shanahan's bag.

"I think I'm just going to go on to bed," Shanahan said by way of a kind dismissal. He handed the young man a five-dollar bill. He hoped it was somewhere in the ballpark of propriety for such things in such a place.

"Let me fix the bed for you, then."

With great care, the youth took the top covering off the bed that was partially built into a wood-paneled frame.

He carefully folded the spread, setting it on the pew. He removed a few of the pillows, laying them carefully on the wooden pew as well. He pulled back the sheets, fluffed the pillow, then left. Shanahan undressed, climbed in. He didn't feel comfortable having people do things for him.

SHANAHAN WAS on the edge of a cliff, looking down over the breakers. He didn't want to jump, but something was urging him to. He was holding a book. For some reason, he knew that as long as he held that book, he wouldn't jump.

"Dad? Dad?"

Shanahan turned. It was his son, Ty. He was older now, but Shanahan knew who he was.

"Someone needs your help, Dad. You hear them? You hear them knocking?"

Shanahan opened his eyes. He heard the door open to the hotel room. He lurched out of bed only to confront a Asian woman in a gray uniform, carrying a clipboard.

"I'm sorry," she said, backing away. "I did not know you were here."

"No, I'm..."

"I come back later," she said, turning and hurrying out.

The room was darker, but still some light came in through the window. He looked at his watch. Nearly seven. Seven what? In the morning or evening? He looked out of the window, but could tell little from the scurrying on the street.

He picked up the phone, punched zero.

"What time is it?" he asked.

"Six fifty-eight."

"Morning or evening?"

"Evening."

"Thank you."

Shanahan tried to make sense of his dream. It was odd to dream of his son. But it was all quite explainable. The nautical look of the hotel room had set off the sea background. That kid Moogie had reminded him that he'd had a son. And the jumping-off-the-cliff part was merely the strange, out-of-control feeling he had had since he arrived in New York.

The book was the only puzzle. Was it a Bible or something, some religious sign?

He went into the bathroom. The strange sink looked as if it were part of some elegant space station. There was no tub. The shower was a small room with clear-glass double doors. The large gray tile that covered the floor went up the walls. The room had the feel of a mausoleum. Shanahan thought that was nice if you liked that sort of thing. Right now he didn't like the implication.

Once he figured out how the shower worked, the hot, fine spray began to revive him. He realized he had slept for eight hours. Rip Van Shanahan, he thought—in more ways than one.

Afterward he shaved. He felt rested but hungry. He dressed, checked out the room service menu, saw the prices, decided to go out. He needed to go out. He walked down the long blue, slightly curving hallway. There was no sound. No sound at all. He couldn't even hear or feel his feet move, the carpet was so plush. He felt as if he'd stepped into someone else's life, one he felt uncomfortable in.

The lobby was busy. All the chairs, so empty in the morning, were full. Most of the occupants were under thirty, all fashionably dressed, all talking among themselves and looking around while they did. One of the charcoal-clad youths opened the door for him and wished him a good evening as he ushered Shanahan into the Manhattan twilight.

In the fading light he walked west in search of a restaurant where he might not feel so alien. Suddenly, it seemed, he was in a vast sea of people. It was a wide, wide avenue, where legions of yellow cabs swirled and honked. It took him a moment to realize he was in Times Square. He'd been there before, had laid over in New York on his trip back from Europe, after the war.

People of all shapes, sizes, colors, and in all manners of dress moved about under the glow of a zillion kilowatts of neon. Vendors with little folding tables sold books, jewelry, paintings, and food. A strange smell permeated the air and puzzled him until he saw that the dark, bearded man selling religious tracts had a stick of incense burning. A man handed him a flier. It advertised a strip club. A moment later he was handed another: "Are you ready to meet God?"

"Meet your Maker," Shanahan thought. He remembered Harmony's video and the Bible in the dream. He sensed danger, but wasn't sure it was physical. Perhaps his mind was going. He wanted to be home. He wanted that more than anything else.

He'd embarked from the strangely quiet room and halls of an exotic hotel and now found himself in the middle of a modern Moroccan marketplace.

He walked up a few blocks, saw a Howard Johnson's across the wide streets. It looked to be too far.

"Well, Mrs. Schmidt, the world seems to be getting away from us, doesn't it?"

TWENTY-FIVE

IT WAS the thought that he might spend the night in a strange hotel room completely awake that prompted him to call the airline. Space was available on the 10:00 p.m. flight to Cincinnati and if he hurried he could make it.

Because of the time change, he had more than an hour layover at the southern Ohio airport, and it occurred to him that by the time he got to Indianapolis by air, he could have driven home.

Maureen, draped loosely, comfortably, in her terry-cloth robe, had waited up for him. She sat on the sofa. An empty pint container of Häagen-Dazs Vanilla Swiss Almond sat on the end table. Several home design magazines were strewn on the floor at her feet.

"You didn't have to wait up," he said, giving Casey, who'd come over to have a good once-over sniff, a solid ear rubbing.

"I just wanted to make sure you passed customs," she said, smiling.

Einstein, curled up at the other end of the sofa, opened his eyes, blinked once, then closed them.

"I'll bet you're tired."

"No." He wanted to tell her about how strange all of it had been, how, like a little boy, he'd been frightened at the world out there. "But I am glad to be home."

"Something's wrong, isn't it?" she said, getting up, coming to him. They hugged. Casey barked.

"Everything's fine, really."

"Then I've got something to show you," she said, grabbing his hand and leading him into the bedroom. "What do you think?"

The room had been painted. The walls were a light clay color, the carpet was a deeper shade of clay. There was a new bedspread and the chair had been draped in cloth.

He didn't dare tell her how he felt—that at this moment what he wanted most was to see the faded, ugly, flowered wallpaper his wife Elaine had put up more than thirty years ago.

"Speechless, huh?" she said, smiling.

"Absolutely."

CHARLEY BAKER didn't seem the same, dressed in a suit and tie, sitting in front of Jennifer Bailey's huge glass-topped desk. He looked smaller, certainly less of a threat than he had been wielding a two-by-four.

The defense attorney had called Shanahan at eight in the morning, asked him to be there if he could.

"This is purely exploratory, Mr. Baker," she said, looking up as Shanahan came in. "I'm sorry I had to serve papers to get you here, but I appreciate it nevertheless."

Baker looked at Shanahan like it was all his doing. But only for a moment. He looked away, then down at his knees. Shanahan understood. There was something intimidating about Bailey's office. And the poor man was out of his element. Completely. And surely to God, Baker would rather be pushing around a two-hundred-.pound, iron-muscled boxer than the no-nonsense Jennifer Bailey, with those cold, piercing eyes magnified by the thick glasses.

Shanahan sat down beside Baker.

"Maybe I should have me a lawyer," Baker said.

"If you wish. But you're not being charged with anything. What we are trying to determine is if you are an appropriate witness for the defense. This is all informal. Nothing you say is binding.''

"What's he doin' here?" Baker said, nodding, but not looking at Shanahan.

"I thought he might have some questions as well.''

"He already asked me a bunch of questions. I got no more to say to you than I did to him.'' He shifted uneasily in his seat.

"Mr. Baker,'' she said, unshaken, "Emilio Ramirez has no one else in the world to vouch for his character. No one.'' She waited for a response, got nothing. "You know him. You work with him. Please, just tell me, in your own words, what kind of person he is.''

"Papers say I gotta come down here. They don't say I gotta talk to you.''

"No, Mr. Baker. You're absolutely right. But during the trial I can call you as a witness anyway. I can declare you a hostile witness. I can ask you these questions while you are under oath. And if you refuse to answer them, you will be put in jail. Do we understand each other, Mr. Baker?''

Baker looked up. "Ma'am, if you his lawyer and you make me tell the truth, so help me God, you be makin' a big mistake.'' He stood, started to leave.

"Why is that, Mr. Baker?''

Charley Baker didn't answer, merely headed toward the door.

"Tell me why that's so?" Jennifer asked again.

"Because Charley Baker believes Emilio Ramirez killed Sally Holland," Shanahan said.

Charley stopped, turned around. "Listen to the man,'' he said to Jennifer Bailey.

"Charley?" Shanahan called to him.

"Whatchou want now?''

"You know those back trails by the canal and White River like the back of your hand, don't you?''

"'Bout as well as anybody."

"You could walk them blindfolded."

He nodded.

"You went by to pick up Emilio for his morning run. He wasn't there, but Sally Holland was."

"All I could think of was I gotta get that poor dead baby outta his house."

ON THE DRIVE from the attorney's downtown office to Howie Cross's house five miles north, all Shanahan could think about was her cold, silent, expressionless face as Jennifer Bailey realized she'd found an excellent witness for the prosecution.

Shanahan also understood why Sally Holland's body hadn't been tossed off the bridge. A guy like Charley Baker couldn't have been so callous. He had taken the time to lay her gently at the water's edge.

At Howie's front door the bleary-eyed former cop just shook his head as he buttoned his jeans.

"Am I interrupting anything?" Shanahan asked.

"Unfortunately just sleep." He sat on the sofa, leaned down, and put his head in his hands. "I'm usually up at the crack of noon. Tell you what you do. You go in the kitchen, find two cups, put water in them, then put them in the microwave. There's a jar of instant coffee out there somewhere."

Shanahan went into the kitchen. It was no better than the living room. The countertop was littered with dirty dishes. The petrified remains of half a pizza were still in the box. There were three unopened boxes of Kraft macaroni and cheese, two cans of tuna, a jar of peanut butter with the lid off, and half a loaf of bread, opened at the end and showing the promise of a new medical discovery.

Shanahan washed out two cups, put them under the tap, and finally figured out how to open the little door on the little black box with a window.

"Now what do I do? I'm supposed to push a button, right?"

"You don't know how to use a microwave?" Howie said, coming into the kitchen.

"No, but I know how to wash dishes."

"I failed home economics." He pushed some numbers on the face of the oven. "You're not wearing a pacemaker, are you?" Shanahan shook his head, and Howie pushed another button. There was a slight whir. "Now that it's about over, welcome to the twentieth century."

"I've been getting a healthy dose of it lately. I'm not sure I like it."

"Phone sex," Howie said, watching Shanahan for a reaction. Then, not getting one, "Another twentieth-century phenomenon."

"Where is this leading, Howie?"

"It is leading to Lyle Brody. More than seven hundred dollars on last month's phone bill. All to 900 numbers. Mostly to one 900 number."

"So? He is a lonely guy."

The little box with a window sent out an electronic beep. Howie pulled out two steaming cups of water. "*Voilà,*" he said, setting them down and putting a tea-spoon of freeze-dried coffee in each.

"So," Howie said, heading back toward the living room, throwing a jacket off a chair, indicating it was where Shanahan should sit. "So to try out my newly re-instated telephone service, I called the number he dialed most frequently." He sat on the clean spot on the sofa.

"Was it memorable?"

"Mmmmnnnn," he said, sipping his coffee. "It might surprise you to know that I'm a romantic at heart. Music, candlelight..."

"Kraft macaroni and cheese."

"A garter belt, maybe on a long, smooth thigh..."

"I'm glad you feel you could share that with me," Shanahan said.

"Well, then, let me share Mr. Brody's idea of romance with you."

"Do I care?"

"I think so. Verbal abuse. The number he called most frequently has a lot to do with groveling. Now, the problem is that once you place the call, you get to choose whether you want someone to humiliate you or whether you want to humiliate them. I chose to be humiliated for a few minutes. But I don't know about Brody."

"Did you have a good time?"

"I thought I'd been called some pretty rotten names while I was carrying a badge. She came up with some new ones." He paused for a moment to let it sink in.

"Violent?"

"Sure," Howie said. "Verbal, but yeah, some pretty violent suggestions. I was amused at first. But I can't think of anything more likely to still the stirring of a healthy young man than what she was suggesting."

"Any other calls?"

"Whatever gets you through the night," Howie said, still lost in the memory of the conversation, "Oh, uh, there were several calls to Europe too. A few different numbers, but the same company. I wrote it down somewhere. What next?"

"Go see him, I guess."

"You want some company? Could get dicey."

"HOW DID YOU hurt your hand?" Jennifer Bailey asked Emilio Ramirez. He sat directly across from her at a large table in the stark attorney room at the jail.

"It's nothing. Little accident, that's all. How's Elizabeth, do you know?"

"No, I think I heard she was with the grandparents up north somewhere. Are you all right? Getting enough to eat?"

"Everything is fine. I'm doing okay."

"Can I bring you something?"

He smiled. "No. I'm glad you came down. It's good to have somebody to talk to."

"Emilio, I don't have good news, exactly."

"Couldn't get a whole lot worse, could it?" he said, smiling, trying to make a joke of it.

"It's about Charley Baker."

"Is he all right?"

"He's healthy," she said, noticing him relax. "You've got to absolutely level with me, Emilio. I can't tell you how important this is."

"I've told you the truth so far. So far as I know it myself." He looked hurt.

She wasn't sure how to say it. "Charley Baker has corroborated the lab findings that indicate the whereabouts of the body of Sally Holland before it was placed in the water."

"Can you say it plainly, Mrs. Bailey?"

"He saw the body in your apartment, Emilio. In fact he removed it to protect you. He didn't tell you that?"

Emilio put his hands to his mouth in a gesture that almost looked like a prayer. His eyes locked onto some space high up on the empty wall behind her.

TWENTY-SIX

SHANAHAN DIDN'T WANT to use the intercom. Lyle Brody's previous good-bye hadn't been altogether hospitable. However, there was no need to wait outside the apartment towers in the stifling heat for a woman with a bag of groceries to let them in. Howie Cross had the lobby door open in sixty seconds.

He simply pushed the buttons until he got the right female voice. "Honey, it's me," he said. And they were buzzed right in.

"I didn't lie," he said as the elevator jerked for a moment, then moved up steadily, making no stops until the seventeenth floor.

Shanahan knocked on the door. No answer. He knocked again. Howie Cross peered in the little peephole. "I see light. At least he's not standing by the door."

"Not home," Shanahan said.

"Good," Howie said. "You good with locks?"

"Fair, but I didn't bring..."

"Never fear." From his jacket pocket Howie Cross pulled out what looked to be a small pistol.

"You going to shoot the lock off, Wyatt?"

"It's a pick gun. You've never seen one of these?"

"I'm not in the twentieth century yet, remember?"

Howie put the nose of the gun to the keyhole. "What this does is send a little rod out that lifts the little pins in the lock." It didn't take long. "There. Now for the dead bolt. Okay," he said, opening the door.

The balcony door was open and the air conditioning off, apparently. It was hotter inside than out. The apartment was as Shanahan remembered it. Very tidy. Shanahan moved toward the kitchen. Spotless.

Howie headed in the other direction. "Shit," Shanahan heard him say. When Shanahan got there, Cross was standing in the hall, his hand on the knob of a closed door.

"Brody. A chubby, bald-headed guy?"

"Yeah."

Cross opened the door. A sickeningly sweet smell hit Shanahan. He caught a glimpse of Lyle Brody, decked out in his finest go-to-bed clothes, his face a pale blue, a small pool of blood on the pillow. The nickel-plated .38 was still in Brody's hand. The detective stepped back out of the room, shutting the door.

"Shanahan, you sure know how to show a guy a good time."

"SHANAHAN, what're you doin' hangin' around with this sleaze?" Lieutenant Rafferty said, nodding toward Cross.

Lieutenant Swann stood by the door to the balcony, not saying a word, while three uniformed cops huddled in conversation at the entrance to the kitchen. The coroner, his assistant, and a photographer were in the bedroom. Two white-coated ambulance attendants waited in the hall with a collapsible gurney, which doubled as a barrier to keep out a small gathering of curious apartment residents.

"Hey!" Rafferty shouted at the uniforms. "You wanna break up your little hen party and come over here? Have these two empty their pockets, then pat 'em down. You remember how to do that?"

"We called *you*, remember?" Shanahan said to Rafferty as the three policemen stumbled over one another.

"Hey, Shanahan, nothin' personal. You're hangin' with the wrong crowd, that's all."

Cross emptied his pockets onto the cocktail table, saying nothing.

"And what's this here?" Rafferty said, picking up the small lock-picking device.

"I believe that's to open locks, officer."

"I believe it is too. And why might you be carrying it?"

"So I can open locks, officer."

Rafferty tossed the pick gun down on the table and headed toward the bedroom.

"Moody, isn't he?" Cross asked of no one in particular.

One of the cops started to pat Howie down.

"Forget it," Swann said to the cops. "Rafferty's just having a little fun, boys. Go see if any of Mr. Brody's neighbors know anything, okay?" As they left, he walked over to Shanahan and Cross.

"How are you doing these days, Howie?"

"Oh, you know me. A real gypsy. It's a shame seeing Rafferty taking life so seriously."

"He's under a lot of pressure."

"Yeah, but now he's beginning to think he's a real cop," Cross said.

"What brought you guys up here?"

"Wanted to ask Brody a couple of questions," Shanahan said.

"You find him that interesting? Tell me about it."

"He's got a curious taste in videos," Howie said.

"A couple of days after the funeral," Shanahan said, afraid Howie would begin discussing the 900 numbers, "he gets tied and tossed off a balcony. Some other things don't sit well, either."

"What happened to the CIA? Wasn't that your last theory?"

"You didn't tell me that," Howie said, looking worried.

"I just said there were some things that needed some checking, that's all."

There might have been a smile on Swann's thin lips, but he had it under control.

"A guy came in yesterday," Swann said, straight-faced as usual. "Said he saw everything. This big round thing came down from the sky and a couple of yellow, one-eyed characters took her away."

"Oliver Hogsmith was right," Howie said, grinning. "Did she have any strange marks on her body?"

"Yeah, she did, Howie," Shanahan said. He looked at Swann.

"She did, Howie," Swann said in his normal, unexcitable, monotone voice. "She certainly did."

"What?" Howie asked. "What?"

"WHAT MARKS?" Howie asked, once they were out of the apartment, heading toward the car.

"Not the marks of Mr. Hogsmith's aliens," Shanahan said.

"I know, I know, I know," Howie said impatiently. "Describe them. Scrapes, cuts, holes, what?"

"They were like little stripes where decomposition occurred at a slightly faster rate. They ran along her outer thigh and on the outer portion of one buttock."

"And that was her brother upstairs?"

"Yeah."

Shanahan unlocked his car, slid in, and reached across and unlocked the passenger side for Howie. He slid in.

"Heat," he said.

"Yeah, open some windows."

"No. Heat causes decomposition. After she died, that part of her body was in contact with something emanating heat."

"That's true. It could have been the sun coming through something, only it was dark out." Shanahan tried to remember if Emilio Ramirez had a radiator. But then it wouldn't make any difference. There'd be no steaming radiator in August.

"Maybe some form of torture or necrophilic ritual," Howie suggested. "Some very private kink in Brody, maybe. You get a load of those videos in the bedroom? If Silvers were still prosecutor, he'd haul Brody's dead ass to court."

"Brody?" Shanahan asked.

"First thing I thought of when I realized you weren't kidding about the marks on her body. You see a lot of weird shit working vice. Maybe some final vengeance on a woman, his sister as surrogate for his mother, maybe. Son of Norman Bates. Then afterward, he can't live with himself. Boom!"

"If so, he took his dirty little secret with him," Shanahan said. It was plausible, he thought as he turned the key in the ignition.

But Lyle Brody had seen to it there was no deathbed confession. There was no suicide note to ease his conscience or to cancel the reservation being made for Ramirez's seat in the electric chair. And the weapon used to kill Sally Holland was at the end of someone's arm. If it were Brody's, it would be buried with him. Shanahan might as well try to convince the police it was a little one-eyed yellow being from another galaxy.

"Where's Alfred Hitchcock when you need him?" Howie said. "You suppose we should call in Dr. Freudenstein?"

SHANAHAN DROPPED Howie off at his place, stopped at Harry's, called Maureen, and asked her to meet him there for a late lunch. He wasn't hungry. That was always a good time to eat at Harry's. Then he dialed Jennifer Bailey.

He filled her in about Brody, but avoided discussing the unsubstantiated theory that he had killed his sister, wondering if she'd connect the details herself. She didn't. Her concern was for Emilio. He looked terrible, she said. He had a strange look in his eyes.

"I have nothing to tell him to give him hope," she said.

"Have they set a date for the trial?" he asked her.

"If I don't find something soon, there may not be a trial." He knew what she meant. "I told him about Charley Baker. I shouldn't have."

"He didn't change his story about Sally's being there?"

"No. After I told him about Mr. Baker, it was like he wasn't there anymore. His eyes glazed over."

There was a game on. The Reds versus the Mets, but Shanahan's mild interest in the Mets had diminished after Strawberry was traded to the Dodgers.

Harry, disgruntled that neither Shanahan nor Maureen wanted the stew, brought the two chicken salad sandwiches they ordered, tossing the plates carelessly in front of them.

"You know you're beautiful when you pout, Harry," Shanahan said.

"What I don't get," Harry said, standing there with his hands on his hips, "is why all of a sudden nobody wants stew around here. When Delaney had this place, all you'd ever hear was 'Hey, Delaney, great stew,' or 'Delaney, you ought to can this stuff and put it in the supermarket.' It's Delaney's goddamn recipe, Deets, the one everybody was clamoring to get."

"And he'd never give it to anybody, would he?"

"He gave it to me."

"Harry," Maureen said, "maybe he left some things out."

"Now, Maureen, why in the hell would he do that?"

"Maybe it was special to him, Harry."

"So he could be the only one can make it?" Harry softened a bit, shook his head. "I'll be damned. It never tasted like Delaney's." He left, still shaking his head.

"This isn't Delaney's chicken salad, either," Shanahan said.

"Shhhhh," Maureen said, grinning. "What'd you do today?"

"Went out with Howie, nosing around," Shanahan said. It wasn't the kind of conversation to have over lunch. "How about you?"

"Made some calls," she said, but she had that funny look on her face, the one she always had when she was hiding something.

He wasn't sure what it was he caught in her face. But it was an expression he'd see on the faces of poker players who couldn't finish the straight but had too much in the pot to back out. Maybe they tried too hard not to show any expression.

"Just sat around and made some calls, huh?"

"Yes," she said, nodding with emphasis. "Is that all right with you?"

"Sure. I don't have any problem with you making phone calls."

"Well, you're acting like you don't believe me."

"I do. I do, Maureen. I believe you made phone calls."

"Why are you smiling? You never smile."

"I don't know. Sometimes when I least expect it, it just happens." He took a bite of his sandwich and looked up to see a Cincinnati player try to steal second base. The Mets' catcher caught the ball, was up on his feet, firing a bullet. The umpire called the runner out.

Shanahan was glad. He'd started disliking the Reds when the team's owner said that Indianapolis would get a major league team over her dead body. A shrewd businesswoman. She didn't want to lose all the ticket sales to Indiana folks who attended Reds' games. The ballpark was only a two-hour drive from Indianapolis. Less if you were in a hurry.

His mind drifted back to Emilio Ramirez. As far as Shanahan could see, there were only three people who meant anything to Emilio. One was Sally Holland. One was Elizabeth. The other was Charley Baker. One was murdered and the other believes he did it. A pretty dark picture emotionally and legally. Emilio is a bright kid, and he's not seeing any light at the end of the tunnel.

"All right, all right," Maureen said.

"What?" Shanahan said, suddenly jolted from his thoughts.

"You don't believe all I did this morning was make phone calls."

"Maureen, it's none of my business, anyway. I'm sorry I asked."

"Actually, it is your business. You know the copy of the daughter's diary the attorney sent over? I read it."

"It's not a capital offense. What did you think?..."

"It's wrong. I mean, number one, it's your business, not mine. Number two, it's someone's personal diary. I feel terrible. I was curious, you know. I just looked at the first page, then I got caught up in it. I read the whole thing."

"Maureen, it'll probably be put into evidence anyway. It will be open to the public. You are the public."

She looked a little relieved.

"You feel better?" he asked her.

"About that, a little."

"Something else bothering you?"

She nodded her head "yes," and took a bite of her sandwich.

TWENTY-SEVEN

"TONIGHT," Maureen had said when Shanahan asked her if she wanted to talk about what was still troubling her. "We'll talk after dinner, tonight, when it's quiet."

The discussion was further postponed until Maureen could get back from a late showing of a house on Fall Creek Parkway, near Washington Street—one of the prettier neighborhoods on the eastside.

The showing was at seven. At ten thirty Shanahan went to the now unfamiliar bedroom and climbed into bed alone. The house was cool. He thought about turning on the heat, but got under the blankets instead. It took less than half an hour to reread Elizabeth's diary. By eleven Shanahan was convinced Maureen must have had an accident, was mugged, or worse, he thought shamefully, she was having an affair.

He flicked on the remote. There was an inane beer commercial, followed by some black sedan cruising through a curving country road. The price tag: $29,995*. Shanahan wondered what the asterisk was for. He remembered paying $1500 for his first new car.

Next was the tease for the news. Something about the mayor and the downtown mall. Something about a narcotics bust. There was the final installment on prostitution and an update on Edward Carem taking off the gloves in his bid for David Holland's senate seat. Then more commercials.

Shanahan punched the mute button, hoping to hear a car door slam or a front door opening. Casey paced around the bed, refusing to settle in until Maureen was home and everything was normal. Einstein was probably still on kitchen patrol, standing in some dark corner, scanning the linoleum, waiting for a field mouse to penetrate the perimeter.

He glanced back at the screen. Some grinning buffoon was trying to push a warehouse full of ugly furniture. Enough was enough, he thought. He got out of bed, put on his clothes. He knew the neighborhood. He'd just drive over and see if he could spot her car.

As he sat on the edge of the bed, putting on his socks, the news came on. Shanahan punched up the sound. Carem was the lead story. He was challenging Holland's ability to function "in light of the senator's deep personal crisis" and criticizing the hospital for refusing to explain why the senator had been hospitalized after the funeral. The moratorium given Holland to recover from his grief had apparently passed.

"From the Holland camp," said the anchor, "former aide and recently appointed campaign manager Eric Barton said the senator will return to Indianapolis tomorrow to hold a midafternoon press conference on the front lawn of the family home."

"Will he be bowing out of the race, or will he come out fighting?" asked the male anchor.

"We'll be there and you'll have the complete story tomorrow at six," said the female anchor.

Shanahan knew the answer to that one. The senator had told him he was "the first to know" during their brief exchange in the Royalton Hotel lobby. And as far as Carem was concerned, he'd given Holland credit for more grief than he seemed capable of. One other oddity: Eric Barton was not only back in the senator's good graces, but was now campaign manager.

Shanahan flicked off the TV, grabbed his wallet, and went into the living room for the car keys. When he opened the front door, Maureen was on the other side, sorting through her keys for the one to the house.

"Where are you going?" she asked, stepping in.

"To open the door for you," he said.

"With your car keys?"

"Well...they just happened to be in my hand." He put the keys in his pocket. "Pretty feeble, huh?"

She smiled. "I'm sorry I'm late. But I've got to tell you it was worth it." She flung her briefcase, then her purse, onto the chair. "First," she said with great drama, "this couple walks through the house, then they walk through it again. And a third time and a fourth time. And they'd go into a little corner and talk, then they'd go through the house again."

"They must've liked it," Shanahan said, glad the subject had changed.

"Liked it? The people who own the house came home—a sweet retired couple who bought a condo in Fort Myers. Anyway, I'm not supposed to let the buyers and sellers get together. That's one of the rules. But I couldn't help it. Then everybody started talking to each other, and we ended up sitting around the kitchen table. And they talked and talked about heating bills, how old the furnace was, whether the appliances were included, things like that. Meanwhile, this old, old refrigerator, that must've been as old as the house, kept making these dying sounds, and I wanted to go over and unplug it. Then when we leave this couple calls me over to the car. They want to make an offer."

"That's great!"

"That's not the great part. The great part is they sat in the back seat of my little jalopy as I wrote out a cash offer—I've got to get a new car, a bigger one. Anyway, I went back to the house, sat around the kitchen table, and the owners accepted the offer, worked out the points and

everything. They accepted the offer! Right then and
there!''

"That's wonderful. Your first house."

She hugged him.

"Congratulations."

"Let's have some wine." She went into the kitchen.
"That godawful refrigerator was worse than this one."
Shanahan came in as she pulled the bottle of white wine
from the shelf, kicking the door shut. The little vent below the door rattled. "See?" she said.

"I see," Shanahan said.

SHANAHAN GOT OUT of bed at 6:00 a.m. Long, horizon-
tal slices of sun squeezed through the slits in the blinds.
He hadn't slept. The two of them had talked until three.
She was so wound up over the sale that she couldn't sleep.
The conversation eventually turned to Elizabeth's diary,
and finally to the sealed envelope addressed to Maureen,
the one she'd found among her father's belongings after
his death. She hadn't opened it, she said. She told him
why. When she ran out of words, she slept, her head in
the crook of his arm.

Then it was Shanahan who couldn't sleep. The pieces
of two puzzles began slipping into place. The first puzzle was Maureen. He began to understand why she
wanted to deal with her father's death alone, why she'd
kept him at a distance for those many years. The second
puzzle was the terribly sad circumstances of Sally Holland's death. And the two puzzles oddly connected.

Shanahan fixed a pot of coffee. While it brewed, he
went out into the backyard and tossed the ball for Casey.
It wasn't raining, but it was almost cold outside. He
thought he should have worn a sweater.

The dog didn't seem to mind that, distracted, Shanahan tossed the ball automatically, without the usual

taunts and challenges. There were no congratulations for a difficult catch.

Shanahan had two phone calls to make, but it was still too early. He went to the kitchen for more coffee, this time to warm up. Einstein was lying by the front door of the refrigerator.

"You standing guard, kid?"

Einstein looked up. Blinked.

"Jesus!" Shanahan said out loud. "You're getting warm, aren't you? So am I. Thank you, Mr. Einstein. You get something special for dinner tonight. I guarantee it."

Shanahan knelt down in front of the refrigerator, ran his palm over Einstein's fur, then ran his hand along the vents at the base of the refrigerator.

With his second cup of coffee, he sat at his desk, cleared a space, and began to piece together the expenses, trying to hold back a mind that seemed to be racing. Mentally, he was revisiting, tracing every step of Emilio Ramirez's apartment.

"Concentrate on something else for a while," he told himself. He looked down at the blank sheet of paper, picked up a pencil. There was Howie Cross and the trip East, the taxi receipts, what little food he'd consumed, and the drinks he bought for Eric Barton. He started to write down the car rental in Washington but realized he hadn't paid for that.

It had been Jennifer Bailey's secretary who had taken care of it over the phone with the law firm's American Express. And another piece of the puzzle fell into place.

At eight o'clock he figured Jennifer Bailey would be in her office. She was the kind of professional who started early and ended late. She was there. He was glad he waited. He had something else to tell her now.

"I believe I can prove," Shanahan said to her, "that Sally Holland was not killed in Emilio Ramirez's apartment."

"What? She was there, Mr. Shanahan. The police have evidence, and Charley Baker will corroborate it."

"Yes. Charley found the body there, and that's why he believes that Emilio did it. But she wasn't killed there."

"You want to tell me more? For example, where she was killed and by whom?"

"Not yet," he said. He wanted to make sure what he thought he remembered seeing a few days ago was what he actually saw. "I just wanted you to let Emilio know that we believe him and that he should hold on."

"I'm on my way."

Shanahan poured another cup of coffee, went into the bedroom. Maureen was sound asleep. Last night had brought them closer than ever. He'd never been that close to anyone before in his life. He thought that maybe it *was* time for *all* the drab wallpaper to come down, for *all* the rooms to be brightened and changed.

He'd never wanted to live in the past, yet he had, hadn't he? He thought of Mrs. Schmidt. He didn't want to end up living in a house with more memories than life. At least not yet.

At nine he called Lieutenant Swann.

"Charley Baker came in to see us," Swann said before Shanahan had a chance to say anything.

"I know."

"I know you know. Rafferty's pissed. He says you were withholding evidence. I told him you were giving the guy a chance to tell us himself."

"Thanks."

"That just about puts you out of business, doesn't it?"

"No, what Charley Baker did was a separate act. Your evidence already put the body there. It's incidental. None of it makes any real difference."

"What does it take, Mr. Shanahan?" Swann asked, his voice, as always, without inflection.

"I'm going up to the senator's house about noon, you mind?"

"I doubt if they'd let you in. But it's not against the law to try."

"I need a favor," Shanahan said, "and in a hurry."

WITH THE sketchy nature of the details he was provided and the sensitivity surrounding a person with the status of Senator Holland, Swann wouldn't or couldn't promise he'd deliver.

Shanahan would proceed anyway. He'd go to the senator's house about noon. He figured Eric Barton would be there. Perhaps Elizabeth, as a show of family strength. Maybe get some voter sympathy. He would also bet that somewhere, probably behind the scenes, Jamie Brothewaite would be there to protect her investment.

Maureen was up a little before ten, very late for her. They fixed breakfast and ate in the backyard, taking advantage of a pleasant dip in temperature and humidity. The sky was clear. What few clouds there were sailed effortlessly across the blue. Shanahan felt surprisingly at ease with himself. He listened with amusement as Maureen spent her expected commission check several times over.

At eleven he showered and shaved and put on his one dark suit. It was ten minutes before twelve when he was stopped as he pulled into the driveway of Senator Holland's home. Fortunately, it wasn't one of the troopers he and Harry had talked to the day they came out to take "care" of the lawn. Though Shanahan was sure that in his suit and in a different car he wouldn't have been remembered anyway.

"Can I help you, sir?"

"I've come to talk with the senator." Shanahan noticed an older man and a young girl playing Frisbee in the yard. The girl, dressed as if she'd just come back from church, he assumed was Elizabeth. The guy, also dressed in his Sunday best, he didn't know. But the whole picture—the pretty All-American home, the green grass—looked like something developed by Kodak, or the front of a Hallmark greeting card.

"You have an appointment?"

"No, but I think he'll want to talk with me. My name is Shanahan. I'm an investigator working with the defense attorney's office in the matter of Mrs. Holland's death."

The older man had stopped tossing the Frisbee and was heading for the car.

"This is a really busy day for the senator, Mr. Shanahan," the trooper said. "If he's not expecting you . . ."

"Anything the matter?" the older man asked, coming to the officer's side and peering into the window.

"No, sir," the trooper said. "This gentleman wants to talk with your son about the trial. He's with the defense attorney's office—is that right?"

"That's right," Shanahan said.

"I do suggest," the trooper said, "that you try to make an appointment."

"Hell," the senior Holland said, "all they're doing in there is jawing around the kitchen table. The man's got a job to do." He leaned in, looked at Shanahan. "Why don't you pull on in, up there by the garage, and free up the driveway. The back door's there, and that's where they are anyway. I'll go in and tell 'em you're coming. What did you say your name was?"

"Shanahan. Thanks."

"Don't mention it."

Shanahan hoped his luck continued inside.

TWENTY-EIGHT

SHANAHAN DROVE slowly up the drive. He wanted to give the senator's father a few minutes to let them know he was coming. He didn't recognize any of the cars. But there was a black stretch Lincoln, an old bathtub Porsche that looked like new, and a black '87 or '88 Buick, its nose sticking out of one of the garage bays. The other two garage doors were closed.

The elder Holland was at the back door when Shanahan got there.

"Come on in. The gang's all here," he said.

The gang consisted of David Holland and Eric Barton at the round table in the kitchen; Jamie Brothewaite leaning against the old refrigerator, smoking a cigarette; a state trooper leaning against the kitchen doorway; and an older woman, probably the senator's mother, pouring coffee.

"Would you like some coffee, Mr. Shanahan?"

"No, thanks," he said, thinking that he had been announced sufficiently.

"If you change your mind, let me know. There's plenty here."

The senator got up, extended his hand. "Yes, now I remember you. New York, right?"

Eric Barton had looked up, but now he was looking away.

"You know Eric, my campaign manager?"

"Hello, Eric."

The young man looked up, giving him the merest of acknowledgments, then turned away.

"And this is Jamie Brothewaite, my real campaign manager," the senator said, smiling. "You've obviously met my father, and this is my mother."

"There's plenty of coffee," she said, showing him the pot. "Really. And it's fresh."

"I'm afraid you've caught me at a bad time," the senator said, sitting down. "We've got some more folks coming over here in a little while to discuss strategy. Then some of my staff. The media. All very soon now. I've got to give the speech of my life in a few hours."

"It's important," Shanahan said.

"I'm sure it is. Sit down. I just don't want it to take long, okay?"

Shanahan pulled out one of the vacant chairs and sat down. He watched as the young girl came in and tugged on the older Holland's arm. Her grandfather turned and left with her.

"Mr. Barton, did you fly from Washington, D.C., to Cincinnati the night Mrs. Holland died?"

Eric Barton's head jerked toward Shanahan. His mouth dropped open.

"No, Mr. Shanahan. I did not."

"Cincinnati is about an hour and a half from Indianapolis by car, if you hurry."

Eric looked away, toward the window. then, obviously discovering the full implication of the question, he turned slowly back to Shanahan.

"No. I did not, Mr. Shanahan."

"We have a copy of a fax sent to us…" All eyes turned to Lieutenant Rafferty, who seemed to manifest himself suddenly in the doorway. Lieutenant Swann was behind him. "I'm sorry, Senator. I'm Lieutenant Rafferty, and this is Lieutenant Swann. IPD. We have a fax here from the rental agency that says an Eric Barton rented a car at the Cincinnati airport."

"It must be another Eric Barton, officer."

"I'm afraid not. We checked with American Express. Your address matches..."

"What is this? Let me see that," Senator Holland said.

Rafferty handed him the paper. After he studied it for a few minutes, he handed it to Eric.

"It's got to be a forgery, Eric," Holland said.

Eric didn't even look at it. He handed it back to Rafferty as if the paper had some excrement on it.

"It was on your American Express, Eric," Holland said. "Didn't you report that card stolen?"

"Yes, he did," Rafferty said, "several days after the crime."

"This is silly. Even if he made the trip, being in Cincinnati is not a felony. A misdemeanor, maybe." Holland laughed awkwardly.

Only Rafferty joined him. "Yes, I'm sure it's explainable," Rafferty said. "Mr. Barton, just tell us why you were there. Or better yet, give us someone we can call to verify..."

"I wasn't there, dammit. I don't have a fucking alibi in Cincinnati." He stood up. Mrs. Holland got out of the room quickly. "Or anywhere else, for that matter," he said with sudden recognition. He sat back down slowly. "I have never been in Cincinnati."

"Not even to change planes?" Rafferty asked.

"Not even to change planes."

"You weren't there, Eric," Shanahan said.

"Then what's going on here?" Holland asked.

"That's what I'd like to know," Rafferty said, staring at the detective. "Shanahan, you're the one who asked Swann to bust his butt for this information."

"Look, this is ridiculous. You already have the murderer," Holland said.

"Sally Holland wasn't killed in Emilio Ramirez's apartment," Shanahan said.

"She was there, Shanahan, for God's sake." Rafferty was embarrassed and so mad he was turning red. "We've got hair and skin particle samples, and Charley Baker saw her there. I'm sorry, Senator, I had no idea this would happen. Draggin' you through all this. Jesus."

"She was there, Rafferty. She wasn't killed there. She was killed here." Shanahan got up, moved to the refrigerator. "Her body lay here," he said, pointing to the floor in front of the refrigerator. Jamie Brothewaite moved out of the way as if she'd been stuck with a cattle prod. "Here. Her naked body lay here for maybe two hours, her buttocks and part of her leg leaning up against the vent. These old motors generate a lot of heat. But only the old ones. I think we can match the marks."

Lieutenant Swann moved into the room. He looked down at the grate, kneeled, ran his hand along the edge.

He got up, looked at Rafferty. "It doesn't make a lot of sense for Emilio to have come over here, killed her, let her lie here, then take her back to his apartment. But it could happen. What kind of refrigerator does Ramirez have?" He looked at Shanahan.

"A small one, sits up on a counter. No grillwork."

"Christ," Rafferty said, unconvinced. "Who knows what sick minds will do?"

"Well, Mr. Shanahan's going someplace with this," Swann said. "Aren't you?" There was the slightest hint of worry in Swann's usually calm voice.

"Eric and the senator had dinner near the airport. They separated at nine or maybe slightly after. Barton left in a hurry to take care of some important personal problems. Senator Holland got on a plane..."

'Oh, so this is where this is leading?" Holland said, smiling, shaking his head.

"Shanahan, let's call this off," Rafferty said. "Right now!"

"No, let's not," Shanahan said.

"Let him finish," Holland said. "Let him explain how I could have done all this without Superman's cape."

"Shanahan, it's Barton's credit card, remember?" Rafferty said. "And we checked on Senator Holland on the passenger manifest a long time ago."

"You didn't find it. You won't find Eric Barton there either. You can pay cash for an airline ticket. You present no I.D. But you can't pay cash for a rental car. I learned that the hard way."

"I ripped off Eric's card, you're saying?" the senator said with disgust in his voice.

"Yes. It wasn't so hard. Eric was upset. A romance on the rocks, and a two-hour dinner leaves plenty of time to get a little tipsy. He pays the bill with his American Express. You pick up the card."

"While I'm making a phone call," Eric said almost involuntarily.

"Oh, Eric, don't get pulled into this nonsense," Holland said. "I did no such thing."

"I figure," Shanahan said to Rafferty, "the senator is in Cincinnati by eleven thirty. In Indianapolis by one thirty. That gives Senator Holland two hours to figure out where to dump the body. That's three thirty. Less than an hour to dump it at Emilio's place and two hours back to Cincinnati. That's six in the morning. Plenty of time to catch an early-bird flight to D.C. and meet Eric again for breakfast."

"Whew!" Holland said, laughing. "I don't know about you guys, but I'm exhausted just thinking about it. I'm impressed with how your mind works, Mr. Shanahan. But tell me why. Why would I do such a thing? We were happy. For the first time in years. We were beginning to work things out."

Shanahan looked at the two cops. As always, nothing could be read in Swann's face. Rafferty, on the other hand, was still angry.

"I don't buy it for a minute," Rafferty said. "Just the ramblings of a tired old gumshoe who don't know when to quit. Again, please accept my apologies and the apologies of the police department. We had no idea..."

"How in the hell would I know where this Latino character lives?"

"It's in the back of Elizabeth's diary. His address is there. His phone number is there too. She wrote to him."

"Now you're saying I go around looking in my child's diary."

"You had to look in the diary, didn't you?"

"This is silly. The whole thing is just..."

Shanahan saw Holland's confidence begin to crumble. Now, for the first time, he knew he was right. He could continue.

"You want to know why you had to look in Elizabeth's diary, Senator Holland?" Shanahan looked at Holland, square in the senator's sad eyes.

"I'm not engaging in any kind of ridiculous speculation. I won't have my daughter brought into this. This is where the game ends, folks."

"Why did he have to look in the diary?" Swann asked. Judging by the look he got from Rafferty, Swann had just joined Shanahan on the big cop's shit list.

"I'm not putting up with this foolishness," Holland said.

"You had to be sure that Elizabeth hadn't written anything about what your wife had told you." Shanahan looked at the senator. "And you saw that address, didn't you? Isn't that right, Senator Holland?"

"This man is accusing me of cold-blooded, premeditated murder," he said, turning to the police officers.

"Sounds that way, Senator Holland," Rafferty said, with sudden indifference to the senator's position in the world.

"What motive could I possibly have had? She was part of my plans. I'm ahead in the polls. Life was good. Why would I do that?"

"Fear," Shanahan said. "It's a pretty strong motive. Your wife called you earlier in the day. I suspect a telephone record will tell us that. She told you something that scared you to death."

"And what might that be, old diviner of other men's thoughts, and knower of the secrets of the dead?" Holland had the look of a man so desperate he'd forgotten how to bluff.

Shanahan took a deep breath. He could almost hear Maureen's tiny, sad voice of last night, when she'd told him about what her father had done. How he'd come into her room in the middle of the night when her mother was asleep. The rough hand covering her mouth. She'd told him before she drifted off to sleep how, like Elizabeth in her diary Maureen would pretend her father didn't exist. And the reason Maureen still hadn't opened the letter from him was that she did not want to forgive him.

"You. And your daughter..." Shanahan began.

"What?" the senator managed to say, but his silly, confused expression probably didn't fool anyone. "Elizabeth, me, what? I'm not mentioned in her diary. Not once!" He was standing, flailing his arms.

"How do you know that, Senator?" Rafferty asked. "Unless you read the diary?"

"Get them out of here, Dad."

"I'm sorry, son," the elder Mr. Holland said. Shanahan hadn't seen Holland's father come in and didn't know how long he'd been there. The older man's lips quivered. "Elizabeth told your mom and me. We wanted to tell Sally, but it was so hard. Lizzie, the poor kid, was terrified of moving to Washington, living in the same house with you. We weren't going to let her, you know."

David Holland stared at his dad, unbelieving. In shock.

"I guess Elizabeth must've finally told her mom," David's dad said. "After her death, we, your mom and me, talked about it. She was going to live with us. We were going to get her some help. Just ignore what you did. That's terrible, huh?"

"Dad, what are you saying?" David Holland's look was of incomprehension.

Shanahan thought it was a look not too dissimilar to a young and helpless little girl in the dark. Elizabeth. Maureen.

"We never dreamed you'd...do that to Sally. Oh, God," the senator's father said. He was sobbing. "If I'd been a good father, I'd have gotten help a long time ago."

"Daddy," Holland said, beginning to cry, "this is all crazy."

The elder Holland put his arms around his terrified son. "I know."

SHANAHAN LEFT as Lieutenant Swann read the senator his rights and Eric Barton tried to figure out what to say to the press. Outside, it was apparent the day had taken no notice of how sad things were inside. Shanahan glanced at the blue sky, took a deep breath, and headed toward his car.

Jamie Brothewaite, stood beside her little red sports car, smoking a cigarette and staring at him. He noticed that his Chevy had trapped her Porsche.

"I wanted to make a fast exit," she said to Shanahan, "but you're in the way."

"Sorry."

"Second time today you got in my way."

"That's the way it goes sometimes."

"You can say that again." She flicked her cigarette carelessly toward the garage. "You've absolutely no idea what a bad investment this little family turned out to be."

TWENTY-NINE

SHANAHAN WAS EXHAUSTED. He reminded himself that he hadn't slept, that the events surrounding the breakfast table conversation had taken more out of him than he would have imagined. More than anything else, he wanted to go home. But he'd neglected Mrs. Schmidt.

He wasn't exactly sure what he'd tell her—perhaps that he'd checked Moogie out with the police, had observed him for a few hours, even had a talk with the boy. Moogie was a little wild, he'd say, but not a bad kid. What more could Shanahan do?

Mrs. Schmidt met him at the door. She was excited about something, about to burst.

"Oh, Mr. Shanahan, I'm so glad you stopped by," she said, opening the door.

"Is everything okay?"

"Yes, it's just fine. Please have a seat. Would you like some iced tea?"

"No, thank you, it's been a long day. I just wanted…"

"You won't believe it," she said, sitting in the chair, taking a moment to straighten the little lace doily on the upholstered arm. "That young man I asked you to—well, you know—he stopped by yesterday and we had a very nice chat. He said he'd talk with Francine about being more responsible. I couldn't believe my ears."

"That's nice, Mrs. Schmidt."

"That's what I wanted to tell you. You don't have to do anything, after all. I think Michael's a nice young man."

"Michael, huh? Well…"

"He even brought me flowers. Can you imagine that?"

"Well, that's something," Shanahan said, feeling that what was left of his fee—forty dollars if you didn't count the gas—had just evaporated.

"I'd like to find something for him."

"You would?" Shanahan went to the door. "Tell you what, there's a brand-new T-shirt out in my car. I think he'd like it. Why don't I bring it in for you?"

"That's very sweet of you, Mr. Shanahan. You've been so nice to me."

MAUREEN HAD LEFT a note. Some details she had to take care of concerning the house she'd sold. Shanahan went out in the backyard, moved one of the Adirondack chairs under a tree. Casey brought the ball over.

"A little later, okay?"

The dog dropped the ball, settled in at Shanahan's feet.

The sound of Casey's barking woke him later. The sun was setting. Casey was at the gate that opened to the side of the house, growling now at Lieutenant Rafferty.

"Quiet, Casey," Shanahan said, approaching the policeman. "What are you doing here?"

Rafferty handed Shanahan a black box. "It's the video of the Ramirez fight. I thought maybe you'd give it to him. Maybe he'd like to see how he looks in the ring." Rafferty looked defeated, but not apologetic.

"Maybe he would, thanks."

"Swann's working on getting him released yet tonight. I called Mrs. Bailey right after. I think she's down there with Swann. She's one tough broad, that girl."

"Yes, she is." There was a long silence.

"What about Charley Baker?"

"I think we can work something out so he won't have to do any time."

"That's good," Shanahan said. There was a long silence.

"Hey, I was doing my job. That's how it works."

"Yeah."

"Well, glad you got lucky, Shanahan."

"The luck of the Irish, Rafferty."

"Yeah, I guess. Hey, you know any place around here I can get a decent bite to eat?"

"I do, Rafferty. Over at Harry's bar. You've been there, right? Delaney's old place?"

"Yeah, the stew. Hell, I forgot all about that."

"Well, Harry follows the recipe Delaney gave him to the letter."

THERE WERE two messages on Shanahan's answering machine when he went back inside. The first was from Harmony.

"Mary and I have set the date. We're going to be married on September sixteenth. The wedding's going to be very small. Mostly family. Some friends. But we would be very honored if you and Maureen could come." Shanahan jotted down the phone number. "Oh, I almost forgot," the tape continued, "the music video is done. It looks great. Thanks for everything."

Then came the next message, one Shanahan wasn't prepared for.

"Hi, Dad, this is Ty. Don't worry. Everything is okay. I decided to call while I still had the nerve...uh...I've tried several times, but when the machine answered, I just hung up. So, listen, I never had a chance to tell you...ummmm...and this is a helluva way to do it, but you, uh...have a grandson. He's eighteen. Before she died, Mom said he looks like you. Anyway, he wants to meet you. I thought maybe we could try to work some things out somehow. I'm in and out a lot. I don't want to miss your call. So I'll call you on Sunday, three in the afternoon, your time...I guess...I don't know. I'll talk to you then."

"Is anything wrong?" Maureen asked.

"I didn't see you come in."

"You're shaking."

"It's been a helluva afternoon," Shanahan managed to say as he headed for the kitchen. "I've got to feed Einstein. He helped solve a crime today."

"You wanna talk?" she asked from the doorway.

"Maybe later," Shanahan said.

"You know it's okay for a guy to talk about his feelings."

"Yeah, I heard about that. Donahue and Geraldo and the guys say it's okay," Shanahan said, stopping just before his voice started to break.